T0163220

A

SMALL

EARNEST

QUESTION

A Novel

J.F. RIORDAN

Yeats, William Butler. "The Countess Cathleen." The Project Gutenberg,
last modified March 26, 2009. https://www.gutenberg.org/files/5167/5167-
h/5167-h.htm.

Yeats, William Butler. "The Second Coming." Poetry Foundation. Accessed
March 25, 2020. https://www.poetryfoundation.org/poems/43290/the-second-
coming.

Yeats, William Butler. "The Rose of the World." The Project Gutenberg, last
modified February 14, 2012. https://www.gutenberg.org/files/38877/38877-
h/38877-h.htm#THE_ROSE_OF_THE_WORLD.

Library of Congress Cataloging-in-Publication Data on File

Hardcover: 9780825308925
Paperback: 9780825309755
ebook: 9780825308024

For inquiries about volume orders, please contact:

Beaufort Books
27 West 20th Street, Suite 1102
New York, NY 10011
sales@beaufortbooks.com

Published in the United States by Beaufort Books
www.beaufortbooks.com

Distributed by Midpoint Trade Books,
a division of Independent Publishers Group
www.midpointtrade.com
www.ipgbook.com

Printed in the United States of America

Cover Design by Michael Short
Interior by Thunder Mountain Design, and Mark Karis

For Moses

Prologue ✤

The telephone rang in the sleek, city office of Victor Eldridge. As he reached to answer the pain came again with a deep, resounding blow that made it difficult to breathe. He braced his hands against his desk, waiting for it to pass as it always did. The ringing phone, mixed in the wake of his agony, was almost beyond bearing.

Victor Eldridge was not a religious man, but what he experienced now was as much of a prayer as he would ever utter. Please, let this be the end of it. Please let the pain stop.

He did not care how.

The ringing and the pain faded at the same moment, and it seemed as if the room echoed with both. He stayed frozen in position, his breathing shallow.

He straightened slowly and leaned back in his chair. There. His breath became deeper, and he could feel his heartbeat slowing to its normal pace. His reason returning from the chaos of suffering, he began to think. He had much to do but very little time. The pain was gone. For now. But he knew it would come again.

And again.

Chapter 1 ❖

It was early spring on Washington Island, which, as any Islander could attest, is frequently an exercise in disappointment. The grass had turned a vivid green, but there were still piles of snow in the parking lots, mountainous ice shoves along the shoreline, and the lake still resonated with the clunking sounds of breaking ice on the waves. The trees were tinged with the lavender of their buds, and the air had an extra sharpness from the melting snow. But the sun shone, and the warming fields gave off a rising mist that carried the scent of earth and moss and leaves.

Fiona Campbell was sitting with her friend, Elisabeth, on the hotel porch, drinking coffee and watching a noisy group of gulls fighting over something on the pier across the road. Elisabeth's big dog, Rocco, lay nearby, mostly dozing, but with one eye open to keep watch on things. Fiona wrapped her sweater more tightly around herself in the chilly spring air and held her mug in both hands for warmth.

Elisabeth's and Roger's plans to re-open the hotel had not gone precisely as intended. News of the long vacant property's purchase and subsequent renovations were quickly the buzz of the Island. Even after the construction and decorating work had been completed, Elisabeth had wanted to wait for the right moment—just in time for the beginning of the new tourist season—to celebrate with a grand opening.

But news spread quickly beyond the Island, and months before the building was ready, the calls had begun, asking to reserve the space for a wedding, an anniversary, or a reunion of a group of friends. Before long, Elisabeth had had to concede to demand. Without advertising of any kind, the hotel already had bookings far in advance, and rather than the fanfare of a grand occasion, it had opened with Elisabeth quietly unlocking the front door to admit a group of well-heeled car enthusiasts.

"It doesn't feel right," she said to Fiona, as one of the bigger gulls attempted to fly off with the object of the flock's attentions. "A place like this needs a celebration, and an invitation to the Islanders, and…a party."

Fiona smiled into her coffee. They had had this conversation before.

"So, have a party. It's your hotel. Do what you like."

"I'm afraid it will be disruptive to the guests."

"The guests will love it. It will be part of their experience."

Elisabeth played with a strand of wavy hair as she stared at the screaming birds. After a long silence she spoke. "Roger wants to bartend."

Fiona, whose thoughts had already drifted elsewhere, shifted her gaze to Elisabeth. Suddenly the obstacle was clear.

"Ah," she said.

Roger's personal skills were barely acceptable at his coffee shop—though very much at the ragged edge—but people expected a bartender to be chatty, a good listener, and, at minimum, civil. These kinds of things were not among Roger's strengths.

"But Roger doesn't like contact with the public," said Fiona, somewhat unnecessarily.

"I know. But he likes to mix things." Elisabeth continued looking out at the water, as if she expected to find a solution there. "All those years in the lab, I suppose."

Fiona stopped herself from pointing out that physicists probably didn't do much mixing in the laboratory. She merely pressed her lips together and nodded. She certainly understood Elisabeth's problem. Leave it to Roger to come at life from precisely the wrong angle.

"Listen," she said, "you can't let something like this stop you from celebrating. I think you should go ahead and start making the arrangements. Roger's bartending isn't going to make or break the experience. Things have worked out fine at Ground Zero. Besides," she added, somewhat hesitantly, "if he wants to bartend, he'll do it with or without an official opening."

Elisabeth frowned and nodded. "You're right. I've been wavering on this for too long. It's what I want to do, and it's the right thing for the hotel."

Rocco, sensing emotion in the air, stood and leaned his big head against Elisabeth. Providing comfort was a key element of his work as he saw it.

She stroked his big ears fondly and turned, smiling, to her friend. "I mean, how bad can it be?"

As Elisabeth and Fiona sat drinking coffee, a small red sports car went past on the road. Fiona recognized it immediately as belonging to Marcie Landmeier, the realtor who had sold her her house. There weren't many sports cars on the Island; four-wheel drive trucks were the usual choice.

Marcie and Fiona were not particular friends, but when they encountered one another on various occasions, they exchanged pleasantries which were entirely well-meant on both sides. They were both, after all, nice enough human beings, and the mores of small-town living forbade them from being anything other than scrupulously polite—a rule occasionally honored in the breach, as anyone who knew Stella DesRosiers might attest.

Had Fiona thought about it at all, however, she might have described Marcie as flashy and possibly trying a bit too hard to seem twenty years younger. Marcie, without any compunction whatever, would have described Fiona as stuck-up.

Now Fiona noticed the car and without actually being aware of it, subconsciously added it to Marcie's list of venial sins, at the same time adding her disapproval to another list comprised of her own failings—in this case, being judgmental. Not that sports cars were bad in Fiona's private, and mostly unexpressed world view. But sports cars driven by people who weren't interested in driving, speed, or handling—merely in impressing others—well, that was pretentious, and Fiona tried to avoid pretentious people. She put the non-driving sports car people in the same category as people who asked interior decorators to buy them books for their bookshelves: unserious and uninteresting. With effort and a certain amount of self-censure, Fiona turned her attention back to Elisabeth.

For her part, Marcie Landmeier barely thought about Fiona at all, except, perhaps, to remind herself of the perils of envy. "After all," she told herself, "age will claim the beauty of us all." This, as it happens, is not always true, but Marcie found it consoling nevertheless.

Marcie's somewhat cynical approach to life had as much to do with her work as with her several divorces. Real Estate was a difficult business on the Island, since lack of demand meant that properties moved slowly and sold for prices that almost always disappointed. Most of Marcie's sales here were of ordinary homes, but there were some extraordinary properties, and a million-dollar place here would be ten million almost anywhere else. Marcie had often fantasized about a billionaire or movie star seeking privacy and quiet purchasing one of the spectacular houses along the lakeshore and drawing a new, discreet—but very expensive— clientele to the Island.

Marcie and Fiona would surely have agreed on one thing: for anyone seeking privacy, the Island surely was the place. Islanders had their own fierce defense against the outside world that impelled them to build a wall of silence against tourists or reportorial enquiries, instinctively protecting even a relative newcomer to the Island and respecting anyone's need for privacy. At the same time, as Marcie admitted to herself, no one could ever hope to be excluded from gossip among the Islanders themselves.

Of course, there would be no way anyone could know any of that without being on the Island already and exposed to its culture. This was the sad confluence of Marcie Landmeier's dreams with reality.

When Marcie got to her office, it was later than usual, but then, there wasn't that much to do. She made a pot of coffee, then sat down to go through her e-mail. Mostly junk. She checked her on-line listings and found an unusual number of page views for her shoreline properties over the past week. She was not particularly concerned or excited. She knew from sad experience that internet activity was not an indicator of serious interest. She popped some nicotine gum in her mouth and switched over to her favorite celebrity gossip site. The real estate business had its high stress moments, but most days in Marcie's office were an exercise in passing the time.

Roger Mason had started his original business, a coffee shop called Ground Zero, in the small postcard-pretty town of Ephraim on the mainland of the Door Peninsula. Now that he was busy with the hotel on Washington Island, Roger's participation in the daily activities at the shop had become sporadic.

Even without his presence, the daily yoga practice continued, led by Roger's beatific shop manager, known in whispers behind his back as The Angel Joshua. Terry, the Lutheran Men's Prayer group, and a few intrepid locals continued to

meet before dawn, often passing crowds of would-be participants gathered in the parking lot like groupies at the stage
door. These tourists had been inspired by a series of articles in
national magazines proclaiming the unique qualities of Roger's
sullen approach to the practice of yoga.

On those occasions when Roger did show up in his battered truck, his arrival was greeted like the appearance of a
rock star. Strangers gathered around him, wanting to speak
with him, to ask him questions, and even to get his autograph.

Roger handled these occasions with his usual grace, which
is to say with complete indifference and a probably unintentional rudeness to which his regulars were well accustomed. As
his fame had grown, the rudeness became part of the legend,
and the visitors accepted it with an enthusiasm that the regulars regarded with much amusement.

Despite their zeal, strangers were not permitted to participate in what Roger still insisted was a private meeting
of friends. The fact that he had never intended nor wanted
anyone to join him had now been lost in the mists of time.

"It's almost a form of cruelty," commented Mike, as he
watched the crowd surrounding Roger.

"Seems more like Roger as usual," said one of the Lutherans.

"Better close the blinds before he gets in," said The Angel
Joshua. He proceeded to do so.

Roger wasn't the only one with fans. The gathering of
yoga pilgrims each morning gave the shop's regulars the secret
feeling that they had somehow attained the kind of adora-
tion normally reserved for celebrities. It was so unexpected at
this time of life, and so enjoyable, that some members of the

Lutheran Men's Prayer Group began private meditations on the subject of vanity.

Terry, a local carpenter who had also been enjoying fame since the videos of his ineffectual yoga poses went viral, sometimes scratched his head about the vagaries of fate and fortune, but good-naturedly signed autographs and offered encouragement to other struggling yoga students. He and Joshua continued to publish their videos regularly online, and the viewership was in the millions.

Joshua, by default, was the interpreter of modern culture to the shop's middle-aged clientele. Patiently, he explained that these were not fans, but 'stans' in popular parlance. Everyone had been delighted by this insight into what the young people were doing and enthusiastically adopted the word. That its origins were a mixture of "stalker" and "fan" turned out to be strangely appropriate.

It was not a term used in the presence of Roger.

Chapter 2 ❖

By the end of their conversation, Elisabeth was her usual tranquil self, filled with plans for the hotel's grand opening, and Fiona drove off with a small sense of satisfaction. Elisabeth was someone whose inner serenity was difficult to shake, and Fiona, being a person of intense emotion, admired this quality in her friend. It was, to her, something of a mystery but, like so many things on the Island, a phenomenon to be admired. She was smiling to herself, imagining Roger as bartender as she drove the short distance from the hotel to the community hall.

Fiona's elected position as Town Chairman was not full-time, but she liked to stop in at her office most mornings just, as she liked to say, "to keep an eye on things." By "things," she meant her eccentric assistant, Oliver Robert.

Oliver had a way of embarking upon projects and taking on responsibilities of which Fiona had not fully approved, or whose existence, in at least one notable instance, she hadn't even known about. Even though he had, so far, proven himself a valuable ally, Fiona still often sensed that he had his own agenda, and she was not entirely convinced that it aligned with her own. His natural secrecy, combined with Fiona's general indifference to numbers, made it difficult to know what he was up to even when they were in the same room.

She walked in to find him already at his desk, engrossed in some kind of accounting software, sheaves of papers on the desk beside him, his quart-sized bottle of hand sanitizer prominently displayed nearby.

"Good morning, Oliver."

Oliver did not look up. "Not necessarily."

Fiona had reached the point at which she was generally unfazed by Oliver, noting, instead, that it was lavender day on Oliver's sartorial calendar. Among Oliver's several idiosyncracies was his habit of choosing the color of his clothing according to the day of the week. Today he wore a starched shirt in the designated color with an expensive-looking orange silk tie. Fiona found the combination very fresh and spring-like. Local dress tended to be casual in the extreme, and while she rather enjoyed the quality of defiance in Oliver's fashion choices, it occurred to her that he was likely the only man on the entire Island wearing a tie this morning. It took a moment for her to break her reverie and respond.

"Is that a new tie?

"No. Are you listening to me?"

"It's very nice."

Oliver sighed peevishly. "Please pay attention. Emily Martin called this morning. She's coming in."

This caught Fiona's attention. "Why?"

"She wanted to 'catch you before you disappear for the day.'"

Oliver smirked, feeling a certain smug satisfaction. He didn't like Emily Martin, but he was content to have her restless quest for improvements directed toward someone else for the moment.

"After all," he added, "the algae across the sea is noticed, but the elephant on the eyelid is not."

Fiona ignored this.

"And if I don't want to be caught?"

"Too late."

They could both hear the door slam and the brisk, unmistakable steps of Emily Martin, striding toward the Town Chairman's office.

"I'm going down the hall." With surprising speed Oliver rose and slipped out the side door before Emily could appear.

Fiona retreated to her desk and prepared for the onslaught.

It would not be accurate to say that Emily Martin burst into the room, but that was the effect when she opened the door. She carried with her a whirlwind of purpose and the self-conscious hauteur of someone who uses principle to hide her own failings.

Emily had been deeply humiliated by the behavior of her son, Caleb, last fall. But she did not use this awareness for deep self reflection. Instead, it drove her need to emphasize her family's superiority to the Islanders and, in a sort of social sleight of hand, compelled her to meddle even more energetically in community life. It was as if her frantic participation in all things could distract her neighbors from what had happened, even though, deep down, she knew that if she had been paying attention, the situation with her son might have been very different.

Had she been more humble, forthcoming, and apologetic,

the Islanders might have opened their hearts to her with sympathy and comfort. Parents, after all, cannot always account for the behavior of their children. Instead, her stance pushed the community away and made her an object of, if not ridicule, then, at least amusement mixed with a great deal of skepticism. If Emily Martin wanted to make herself beloved, she had succeeded only in making herself a nuisance. "Damned nuisance," was the expression most in use.

"Good morning, Fiona," said Emily beginning her usual blitz of meaningless remarks which, Fiona supposed, were meant to cushion whatever bald assertions she was about to make.

"My goodness it's chilly this morning. Seems like spring comes later every year. Or, maybe I'm just feeling it more. We're all getting older, I suppose. Oh, well. Time flies."

Fiona adopted the false smile—tinged diplomatically with the faintest bit of regret—that elected office had trained in her. It was a smile she hated with increasing fervor, but she found smiling easier than making a careless remark that would be repeated all over the Island before day's end.

"What can I do for you, Emily?"

Small talk dispensed with, Emily moved on briskly.

"Well," she said. "I think it's more a question of what I can do for you."

Fiona waited politely. Very little response was necessary in conversation with Emily.

"Mind if I sit down?" asked Emily as she did so.

Fiona's smile seemed to stretch rather than broaden.

"I want to say how pleased I am to see that after everything that's happened…I mean…well, you know…that you have learned to take your public duties more seriously."

One of Fiona's eyebrows twitched.

"Coming in early and getting a good start to the day! Such a wonderful example for the townspeople, I always think."

"A good start would be nice," murmured Fiona, almost to herself.

"I have come," said Emily, "to invite you to join my new committee. I think you'll find that it will be of great use to you as a public servant."

Fiona pondered Emily's habit of telling people what they would think of things. It was hard to know whether she believed she knew others' views, or whether it was her plan to overwhelm all opposition, replacing other people's thoughts with her own. Fiona was inclined to suspect the latter.

"And what is this committee?"

The question came out sounding more rude than Fiona had intended. She was reminded of her father's oft-cited quip that a gentleman never insults anyone accidentally. She needed to work, she realized, on accidental insults.

Fortunately, Emily rarely noticed what other people were saying, so insults—whether intended or not— generally went right past her. With difficulty, Fiona focused her attention back to the matter at hand.

"Oh," said Emily. "I thought for sure you would have heard about it by now, but then, I suppose not everyone has the instinct for community that I have. People just naturally gravitate to me to share their troubles and their news, and I'm always so happy to help."

Fiona's smile felt achy and tight.

"Anyway," Emily leaned in. "I'd like for you to join."

"What is the purpose of the committee?" asked Fiona, with more patience than she felt.

"It's…" Emily paused, as for an unveiling, and spoke with emphasis. "*The Committee for the Concerned.*"

A light came into Fiona's eyes, and she touched her face with her hand, covering her lips as if restraining herself from speech. "And what is it," she asked, carefully, "that you are concerned about?"

Emily paused, as if this should be self-evident. "But, aren't you concerned?"

"Well," said Fiona slowly, "yes, I suppose I am."

To herself she thought, "Perhaps most particularly about your committee."

Emily leaned back in her chair and looked smug.

"I knew it. I just knew you would be." She stopped and looked around brightly. "Were you going to offer me coffee? I'm sure it will be fine. Maybe not as good as mine at home—I mean, I've just gotten the most marvelous new machine—but, really, I could use a cup."

Resignedly, Fiona rose to pour coffee for Emily. She chose the mug with care. It looked clean, and she was fairly sure there was some soap residue at the bottom.

Chapter 3 ❖

When at long last Emily left Fiona's office, she pointedly left her nearly full cup of coffee on the front edge of Fiona's desk. Fiona listened to the sound of her footsteps going down the hall and breathed more freely when she heard the outside door slam.

Oliver, who had avoided the entirety of Emily's visit, slipped back into the office and promptly refilled his own coffee cup.

"Where have you been?" asked Fiona with genuine curiosity.

Oliver looked slightly defensive. "At the library. I had something I needed to look up."

Fiona looked at him with acid skepticism. "Oh? And what was that?"

Oliver's face shifted from guilt to defiance.

"A tax thing. You wouldn't understand." He sat down at his desk and began to move papers fussily.

Having just endured a half hour of Emily, Fiona was in no mood to pursue the prosecution. Her general philosophy these days was to let Oliver be Oliver.

"Emily, it would seem, is concerned," she said, watching as Oliver relaxed his camouflaging busyness and picked up his coffee cup.

He paused and looked up. "Well, now we all are."

"Exactly. The thing is, after speaking to her for what seemed like hours, I still have no idea what she's concerned about."

"A mischievous dog must be tied short."

It took Fiona a moment to digest this, but she was accustomed to Oliver's little rules. Mostly.

"That actually makes sense. But how? How do I rein her in? Emily Martin, as you well know, does not take no for an answer, and she has opinions about everything."

Oliver seemed flustered by this mild compliment, and having revealed his true self for a moment, he now retreated behind the cover of his favorite aphorisms. "A fool finds no pleasure in understanding but delights in telling his opinion."

"That," said Fiona with a certain wistfulness, "is certainly true."

She smiled suddenly. "Thank you, Oliver. That was surprisingly helpful."

Oliver preened slightly, but his face remained blank as he idly shuffled the papers before him.

He was a difficult person to talk to. Fiona could never be sure whether his rules were deeply insightful responses or just random quotations stretched to fit the situation at hand. "I think we'd better get back to work. I've got to get through all these contracts."

Oliver's back was to her as he began preparations to continue with his spreadsheets. "After all, dogs bark, but the caravan goes on."

Fiona closed her eyes for a moment, still smiling. "Indeed."

The influx of yoga fans was a growing problem at Ground Zero.

None of the original morning practitioners shared Roger's imperviousness to human feeling, so it became increasingly difficult for them to resist the pleas of so many onlookers to allow them to participate. With Roger spending more and more time on the Island at the new hotel, the only real check on growth was the size limitation of the shop itself. There was really no room for more than ten—a dozen at best. There were many politely apologetic conversations in the parking lot before the practice, and the regulars frequently complained that they couldn't find a place to park.

This led to some whispered conversations about the need for Roger to expand the shop. No one, so far, had had the temerity to suggest such a thing to Roger himself, but when he was away on the Island, the topic was openly debated. Terry, whose desire for self-improvement had inadvertently drawn so much attention to Roger's private yoga practice, was not among those in favor.

"I like the place fine the way it is," he told the group one morning as he sat on the floor after practice, putting on his white tube socks. "If Roger expands, it will change the character of the whole place. Too many people wandering around in a muddle as it is. Besides, the whole point of the hotel is to take the pressure off us here."

There were nods of agreement.

One of the others spoke up. "I almost hit one of them the other day," he said. "He was just sitting in the middle of the parking lot. I asked him what the hell he thought he was doing, and he just smiled and told me to 'peace out.'"

"Did he actually say it unironically?" asked The Angel Joshua. He was the only one among the group whose view of the world merged in any way with contemporary culture. "I didn't know 'peace out' was still a thing."

Joshua, who managed Ground Zero during Roger's absence, was the unconscious possessor of such astonishing good looks that it sometimes appeared there was a light shining on his face. His whole nature had a divine quality that matched his beauty, and the Lutherans had discussed more than once whether he was, by himself, a manifestation of pure grace.

Joshua set mugs on the counter and poured coffee with a practiced hand.

"Might not have noticed if you ran him over," commented one of the Lutherans, taking his coffee.

Terry shook his head. "Don't know how most of them find their way home at night."

At this moment Mike appeared at the door. Though a yogic non-practitioner, he had special status in the group as local stalwart and a core member of Ground Zero's constituency. Mike was an artist of some note, and his mostly solitary workdays always began with a bit of coffee shop society. He was hastily let in, and the door was locked again behind him. The shop officially opened for business at six a.m., and there was still time for private conversation before the yoga hoards were permitted entrance.

"We were just discussing expansion," said Terry, making room for him at the counter.

Mike smiled his benign smile and accepted the mug Joshua handed him, nodding. There was some blue paint under his nails that defied scrubbing, and the faintest scent of oil paints and turpenoid that lingered on his clean work clothes. "Can't see Roger going for that."

"No," said Terry. "That's what we were saying."

❖ Chapter 4

I t didn't take long for Fiona to put Emily and the
Committee out of her head, and she spent more time at
the office than she had planned. A number of major projects requiring grants and state aid had added considerably
to her burden of paperwork, and she was too conscientious to
sign anything without reading.

Oliver continued his work on the tax rolls with deep concentration, but her compliment had so pleased him that they
spent the morning in an almost collegial silence.

When she was finished, Fiona went out to her car feeling
energized but a bit aimless and dissatisfied. There were plenty
of chores, and a research project she had been hired to do that
waited at home, but these things had no appeal on a beautiful
spring day. She thought, perhaps, they could wait.

Feeling somewhat at a loss, Fiona decided to stop in at the
Mercantile. Aside from the grocery store, it was just about the
only retail establishment on the Island, and Fiona was in the
mood to be out somewhere.

Sometimes she missed the stimulation of the city: the
stores, the restaurants, the theater, the bustle. City life could
be comforting, and distracting, and fun. On the Island there
was very little in the way of commerce beyond the essentials,

and the nightlife's appeal lay chiefly in the companionship of other restless souls.

Fiona was musing on the eccentricities of the Island economy as she walked in to the Mercantile from her car. Mark, whom she had known from her early days on the Island, was just leaving. They stopped to chat in the parking lot. Informal meetings such as this were a feature of Island life, and neither of them was in a hurry. The conversation turned to plans for the weekend.

"Getting ready to go do a little turkey hunting," he said. "You know, hang out with the guys for a few days. It's a good time. Always look forward to it."

Fiona murmured something noncommittal. She didn't understand the hunting impulse, but she knew that to say so here bordered on blasphemy. She was also aware that in the Island's tight economy, hunting put food on many families' tables.

"Pete do any hunting?"

"No, it's not really his thing." As she said this it occurred to Fiona that this was another in the category of things she didn't actually know about Pete. Did he hunt? She doubted it.

Mark accepted this answer with a casual shrug but seemed to hear her unspoken thoughts. "I think hunting is the reason we have so little crime up here. Guys are beasts, too, you know, and getting out and killing something every once in a while just takes the edge off."

Fiona gazed at him round-eyed. She had never had such a need and couldn't imagine it. She thought of her father, of Pete, of Pali—just for a start. Killing things did not at all appear to be in their instincts.

With a jolt she thought of Pete's remarkable skills and his mysterious trips. Did he have that instinct after all, just carefully hidden away? Frowning, she tried to imagine him hunting. He was unreasonably good at everything he attempted, but she couldn't quite imagine it.

But what, she thought suddenly, about other kinds of killing? What did he do when he left the Island? She shivered a little and told herself she was being stupid.

"Are you cold? Sorry. I shouldn't be keeping you out here. Still pretty nippy for spring. I'll let you go."

They said their goodbyes and Fiona went into the store, pensive.

Marcie had two showings that day, but her instincts told her they would both be a waste of time. The first was a young couple whose car seemed to indicate that they couldn't afford the half-million dollar place they were interested in. The second was a young single woman who seemed utterly daunted at the prospect of changing the color of a guest bedroom. Privately, Marcie pegged her as better suited to a condo in Sturgeon Bay down the peninsula, where there was better shopping—or at least more stores— and fast food.

Returning to her office afterward, Marcie could see the distinctive colors of two express envelopes tucked inside the storm door of her office as she pulled into the drive.

She got out of the car, slung her big bag over her shoulder, and tugged at her slightly too tight jeans. Bending to pick up the envelopes, she used her body to hold the storm door open as she fiddled with the lock. The handle caught on her bag, and she struggled to free it without ripping. If she didn't have some more coffee, she wouldn't make it through the rest of the day.

Dropping everything on the chair, she went straight to the office kitchen and the coffee maker, pouring the syrupy dregs down the sink and rinsing the pot, all while desperately craving a cigarette. She fidgeted nervously with the foil packet of nicotine gum while the coffee brewed. Was it too soon for another one?

She had just poured herself a cup when the phone rang. Mr. Jespersen was preparing his house for rental, and he had a question about the condition of the kitchen. Could she stop by and take a look?

Marcie sighed, gulped down her coffee, poured more into a mostly clean travel mug, and headed back out.

Although unsettled by her conversation with Mark, Fiona felt her anxieties melt away in the atmosphere of the Mercantile. She had always loved hardware stores. They represented competence, and knowledge, and an ability to cope with life's challenges in a way that she found deeply reassuring. In moments of uncertainty, a hardware store—particularly this hardware store—helped her feel equal to coping with life. Her wandering today at the Mercantile wasn't just a momentary longing for civilization. It was therapeutic.

The front of the store was for the tourists with all the usual trinkets, mugs, t-shirts, and souvenirs that seemed essential in the moment and then languished in the backs of drawers for the next generation to clear away. The rear of the store contained the aisles of hardware, and the selection of merchandise was particularly broad and deep for such a small establishment. On an island, when you needed a plumbing part, you didn't have the luxury of waiting until your next trip to the mainland.

Nancy Iverssen, who, perhaps, valued time more than Fiona did, was there in aisle six for a purpose, searching for the right spring for the latch on her paddock gate.

"Running away from someone?" asked Nancy. She knew Fiona well.

Fiona felt a tiny twinge of embarrassment. "Not this morning. Just felt like browsing around." Nancy did not appear to question this.

"Oliver still at the office?"

Fiona smiled. "Probably."

Nancy only smiled rarely, and she didn't now. "How are things going over there?"

"Oh," said Fiona. "You know. Better, I guess." She gave a perfunctory laugh, recalling her first months as a public official. They had been somewhat unnerving.

Nancy spoke absently as she picked through a jumbled bin of springs. "You've certainly had your hands full since you took office."

Fiona's cheer belied the personal cost of the past year's

events. It wasn't only her public life that had been chaotic.

"Speaking of which, have you heard about Emily Martin's new committee?"

Nancy grimaced. "Oh, yes."

"Well, I have a favor to ask."

"Shoot," said Nancy. Having found what she was looking for, she could now give Fiona her full attention.

"Do you think you could volunteer for it? For the committee, I mean? It would be nice to have someone keeping an eye on things in case I can't always be there."

Nancy gave her a wry look. "You don't ask much, do you. I'm at a point in life when every moment counts, and I promised myself when I turned seventy: no more committees. Any committee work is bad enough, but with Emily?"

"I know, I know. And I'm sorry. But, still…."

Nancy sighed and looked at Fiona over the top of her glasses. "I suppose. But you owe me." There was a glint of humor in her eyes.

"I know. For lots of things. Anyway, the meetings are in the evenings, so you can have a quick shot of brandy before you go."

"Well," said Nancy grimly, "There's that."

"Thank you. I really appreciate it."

Despite her reserved demeanor, Nancy was fond of Fiona. "Given the year you've had, I suppose it's the least I can do."

"Oh, well," said Fiona cheerfully. "What else could possibly go wrong?"

"Oh, don't ask that," said Nancy gravely. "Never, ever ask that."

en Palsson leaned idly against the stall rails and gazed contentedly at the goat.

He loved his job. It wasn't that it was easy. He shoveled and filled, carried and cleaned. He got dirty. At eleven years old, he had few opportunities to be in full command of any situation, but in Fiona's barn, he knew what was necessary and did it in his own way. No one nagged or bossed him. He just saw a job and did it. It was solitary, but never lonely. He enjoyed the company of the goat in his care and the knowledge that it trusted him. This was just about the happiest place in the world for him.

Ben looked around at the order of the barn: at the well-filled trough, the clean stall, the freshly swept walkways, the various pieces of equipment all neatly in their proper places, and he felt a small inner checkmark of satisfaction. All was well.

"Goodbye, Robert." Ben gently rubbed the goat's soft muzzle and scratched behind its ears. "See you tomorrow." Robert turned his head away in goatly contempt. Ben smiled.

Turning the latch on the barn door, Ben shoved his hands in his pockets and took off for home. It was several miles' walk, but he didn't mind. Because he was happy, however, he deliberately chose the back way, through the woods behind the golf course, away from the road where there was the possibility of cheerful offers of a ride. Ben was feeling too good for company.

The soft breeze carried the sweet smell of growing things and the promise of summer. The sunlight was reddening, but there were still hours of light left. As he crossed the fields, Ben heard the distant voice of Amand, the Island's singing farmer. He knew the sound, knew the song, and unconsciously began to whistle along. The fields he was crossing had been those that had burned last fall, and beneath his boots, there was still the crunch of burned things, but also the scent of something soft and green. The soft new shoots that grew now were proof of the resilience of the earth.

He was approaching the woods when he heard something rustling nearby and, with a start, realized that there was a boy there, crouching in the undergrowth. It was Noah, Emily Martin's son and Caleb's little brother.

"Shhhh. Ben, don't look at me."

Dutifully, Ben averted his gaze and looked up at the trees. "Why not?"

"I'm on a secret mission."

Ben nodded seriously. He liked seven-year-old Noah, who was nothing like his older brother. Sweet, quiet, and always nice, Noah seemed as if he had been dropped into his family by aliens.

"What's your brief?" Ben asked, using what he thought sounded like the military language he had heard in films.

"To observe the enemy. And not get caught, of course."

"Right," said Ben.

"Want to play?"

"Sorry. I can't." Ben took on an air of casual responsibility. "I'm just getting home from work, and I have stuff to do." He could see Noah was disappointed, and he felt sorry. It could not be easy being Caleb's brother but just the association made Ben uncomfortable. Ben and Caleb had history.

"Maybe another time."

Noah's face lit up. "Okay! Maybe tomorrow?"

"Um, maybe. But I have to work tomorrow, too."

"Oh."

"But on the weekend, maybe. I could do that."

"Hey! Know what? Caleb's home! Mom made a special dinner."

Ben felt as if he had been hit in the chest. But unconsciously following his father's example, he kept his feelings to himself.

"Mom says that Caleb had such a good year that he won't have to go back there. He's home for good."

Noah's enthusiasm for his brother's return would be short-lived. Caleb was not a pleasant person to have around the house, but for now, all was forgiven in the excitement of his homecoming.

Caleb. Ben's adrenaline surged just at the mention of the name, and he felt the need to keep moving. "Ah. Cool," he said, struggling to place good manners above honesty. "Well…I gotta go."

"K. See ya 'round."

"See ya."

Noah settled deeper into his hiding spot, and Ben continued on his way, his earlier happy reverie replaced with thoughts of darker things.

It had been months since Ben had been the victim of Caleb's bullying, and although Ben still carried the humiliation of it, it was Caleb who had lost the inevitable confrontation. Caleb, as everyone on the Island knew, had been sent to school off-Island after he had been caught abusing a fledgling bald eagle. It was a frequent point of debate among the Islanders whether he had been sent away to reform his delinquent tendencies or to hide his mother's embarrassment. Either way, it had been a happy day for Ben when he'd learned that Caleb was gone. Hearing that he was back changed Ben's hopes for the coming summer.

Ben would never forget what had passed between them. It had been more than a fight, it had been a turning point in Ben's young life, and he knew, as well as an eleven-year-old can know, that it had changed him forever. He had found something inside himself that he knew was good, a sense of who he was and what mattered. It gave him a self-possession unusual in someone his age. Ben believed that this quality in himself was his own secret. He had no idea that even strangers could observe it.

"Your son has a remarkable presence," commented a passenger on the ferry one day, speaking to Ben's father, Pali, who was the Captain.

Pali smiled, unable to contain all the pride he felt, but aloud he said, "Don't let him hear that. Make him insufferable."

Still smiling, he looked down from the upper deck. He

could see his son's blond head among the crowd at the railing, watching as the ferry approached the home port, and he felt, just in that moment, a brief shudder of fear at the fragility of life.

It had been a busy day, filled, as was so often the case, not with actual sales, but with all the small chores that encumber a business owner. It was late afternoon when Marcie was finally able to return to the office. She gauged the point in her work day by the internal sense that it was time to switch from coffee to something stronger, and with that in mind, began the routine of closing up: shutting down her computer, washing out her cup, and turning off the coffee pot.

In the process of putting on her coat, she rediscovered the express deliveries that had come earlier. Here was the one thing in her day that should have been of prime importance, and she had neglected it in favor of inconsequential tasks that would reappear again tomorrow. Shaking her head at herself, she went back to her desk to find the letter opener and slit open first one envelope, then the other. She began reading, then rifled through the packet of documents with increasing excitement. She dropped them on the desk and sat down heavily, staring out the window.

Two offers for shoreline properties. Marcie tried to recall a time when this had happened and could not. It had never happened. Not to her. Not two in one day. And for full price.

She reached into the bottom drawer of her desk where

she hid an emergency pack of cigarettes and lit one to calm herself. Leaning back in her chair, she inhaled deeply and felt the instant relaxation flood her body. "Well," she thought. She took another luxuriant breath. "Well, well, well."

Chapter 6

The yoga with goats phenomenon had spread across the world with surprising rapidity. Photos in glossy yoga magazines showed smiling people in various poses while adorable baby goats pranced nearby, occasionally with one of them standing triumphantly atop a recumbent human as if having scaled a mountain. The captions and accompanying articles spoke of the playful nature of the practice, the charm of the little animals, and the need in modern life for the stress-reducing qualities of yoga, laughter, and play.

Roger had a curious knack for predicting cultural trends, and he had studied these articles with care. If his goal was to use specialty programs at the hotel on Washington Island to draw the yoga crowds away from his coffee shop, then this, he thought, could be just the thing.

Of course, Roger's talent for prediction was not matched by his ability to interpret the details of implementation. When he had seen the coming trend in boutique coffee, he seized the opportunity and opened a coffee shop in Ephraim, but without the bohemian style and amenities that made such places so appealing. COFFEE, as Ground Zero had been known at first, had had no actual name, no music, and no charm. Roger had presented it with the kind of atmosphere that might be expected in a laboratory, with bright fluorescent lighting, stark white walls, and a menu that might kindly be described as minimalist. He greeted his customers with a menacing glare if he greeted them at all, and although this approach had left local clientele undaunted, it was frequently misinterpreted by tourists. In the end, it was Elisabeth's influence that had turned Ground Zero into a warmer, more welcoming place.

It should not have been surprising, then, that Roger's approach to goat yoga might be lacking in some of the particulars.

From the beginning, Roger had planned to introduce goat yoga to the hotel's activities. He had read about it online and in yoga magazines, and it seemed like something he could do. He didn't have any goats, but, he reasoned, how hard could it be?

Roger hadn't fully grasped that the goats themselves were the key variables in the practice. Goat yoga required sweet babies, or, perhaps, cute little pygmy goats. Their frolicking was intended to be fun to watch and stress reducing. There were no actual yoga poses with goats, but if one of the tiny creatures happened to leap upon someone's back, it was charming. Charm, however, was a concept that Roger had no facility for understanding. The problem, as he saw it, was logistical. How could he manage the care of goats on top of everything else? He suspected—rightly—that Elisabeth would be unenthused.

Roger was on his return from one of his visits to the mainland when it suddenly, and somewhat belatedly, occurred to him that he actually knew someone on the Island with a goat. This, he thought, might be the solution to all his problems.

Fiona finished her day as she had begun, sitting on her own porch steps and listening to the sound of birds.

The sun was almost down, the time when the geese were noisily arriving at their migratory stop for the night. There were many thousands, in large groups and small, calling out in their sharp voices as they flew in V formation, taking turns in leadership at the point, the formation shifting as they flew. The cacophony was a sign of spring, and but as she listened, gradually the calls faded into the distance and disappeared. In this new silence, Fiona looked up.

In an empty sky, one flock flew alone without calling, very low overhead, their wings making the only sound, a rhythmic rush of air and feathers. It seemed not of the world, and yet, was so completely a part of it. Fiona watched in wonder and listened, the moment transcendent as the big wings beat their cadence upon the air, the creatures themselves, perhaps unconscious of their majesty, intent only upon their deeply felt purpose. How often, she thought, in fulfilling our own tasks, do we miss the miracle of the ordinary beauty of what we are.

Chapter 7

After a quiet dinner, Fiona made her way to the living room and stood at the window, thinking. She was still troubled by Mark's comments, and she asked herself why they had struck her so strangely and so hard.

How was it that she was in love with a man about whose life she knew so little?

In part, perhaps, it was because his constant travel meant that they had spent so little time together; but what time they'd had was the happiest of her life. She had never seen Pete lose his temper. Being with him was easy and fun. He was intelligent. He didn't get upset about small things, he was observant and insightful about other people, and he made her laugh. He was not what some people would call kind; he didn't wear his thoughtfulness on his sleeve, but he was the most considerate person she had ever met and deeply and heroically dependable. She had seen him angry only once.

He was not a man without passion, however. In fact, as she thought about it, he was every bit as intense a person as she was. She had seen him so closely, and under such critical circumstances that she was certain about his nature. But the intensity of his emotion was usually so fully disciplined that it gave her pause. What else was hidden beneath his cultivated control?

The things she didn't know—the things she had so recently told him she didn't care about—were things that must reveal important details about his character, and the more she contemplated this, the more she knew it was true. His sincerity and integrity she really could not doubt; he had proven himself to her many times over. But, she knew there were things he wasn't telling her. Could she just ignore these deep, crucial details about who he was?

The musical frog sound of a Skype call interrupted her thoughts, and she flew to answer it.

"Speak of the devil," she began.

"Really? What were you saying? Something idolizing, I hope?"

"Just thinking about you, actually, but there may have been a tiny bit of idolatry."

Fiona toyed with the idea of telling him about her conversation with Mark, but she didn't know how to talk about it. She started, instead, with something to amuse him.

"Emily came by the office today. She wants me to join her new committee."

Far away, Pete raised his eyebrows. "A committee?"

"Yes. It's 'The Committee for the Concerned.'"

She was gratified that he did seem amused.

"And what is dear Emily concerned about?"

"It's hard to say. Me, probably."

"Perhaps you should counter with a Committee for the Nonchalant."

Fiona couldn't help laughing. "Perhaps I should."

"Or the Committee of the Indifferent. 'Tut, tut. The world

as we know it is ending and we are concerned.' The question is: *are* you concerned?"

"Emily is always concerning. Particularly when she's wandering around the Island looking for things to be concerned about."

Pete winced in agreement. "True. Well, it should provide scope for entertainment while I'm away."

"That's one way of looking at it."

Fiona looked at his image on the computer screen, sighed, and turned the conversation to more pleasing topics.

Attila the least weasel emerged from one of his hiding places to begin his usual evening excursions along the edges of the room, only to discover that his usual jar lid of snacks was missing. Fiona, in her distraction, had forgotten to put it out for him. Although this was a clear violation of protocol, weasels don't waste time on recriminations. He made his way along the edges of the room and slipped away into the darkness to do his own hunting. He smelled mouse.

Engrossed in her conversation, Fiona didn't even notice.

Chapter 8

Jim Freeburg, the Island's new fire chief, stood with one of his men gazing at the remains of an outbuilding at the golf course. It had been aluminum, but the fire had started inside, gutting it.

Since accepting his new position, Jim had attended several training courses off the Island, and although he was a man of good sense and had been a volunteer, he had no real experience. His service in the department had been inspired by a sense of obligation; no one else had been willing to take the job. Since he was not yet an expert in fires, he had to depend, where possible, on the combined experience of his volunteer company, which was considerable. Jim had no idea what could have started this. He could imagine that there had been plenty of flammable things in there.

"Well, he said, "it's obviously a total loss. Are they insured?"

The young man shook his head. "No idea. Probably."

Even so, the extent of the destruction would be hard news for the owners. Few Islanders had much financial margin for error.

Jim, however, had a more fundamental concern. Normally, the Island had only one or two fires a year, but recently the number had taken a rather sharp uptick.

He thought back to the grass fire last fall. Everyone had assumed it was just an accident, but with no fire chief, there had been no serious investigation. And there had been Fiona's barn before that. The insurance investigators, eager to get back to the mainland, had merely shrugged and issued a check. Were these fires just coincidence? Or was there a pattern here that he should be paying attention to? Jim frowned to himself. This was not a theory to discuss with his men; there was no point in starting gossip. But he wished he had more expertise. He realized, with some misgivings, that the one person whose discretion he could count on was Fiona Campbell, Chairman of the Town Board.

She was also the one person on the Island he didn't want to see.

The fire was the talk of the Island, and Fiona had nothing to contribute to the conversation. She felt enormous relief that it was no longer her responsibility to supervise the workings of the Fire Department, and although she was kept informed, she was confident that Jim would handle everything.

But Fiona well knew that lack of information was fuel for gossip, and that working at the town office put her in the way of too many speculative conversations. Not wanting to be drawn into saying anything that could come back to bite her, Fiona felt it best to stay out of the fray for a bit and work on her research project at home.

She had been deeply engrossed when she answered a knock at the door to find Roger standing on her porch. Nothing with Roger was predictable, but this, nevertheless, surprised her. Roger, as everyone on the Island knew, was not of a particularly sociable nature. Before she could utter a word of greeting, he spoke.

"How much would it be to rent Robert?"

Roger was dressed in his usual crisp, white t-shirt, his hair rumpled as if he had just risen from a restless night. Fiona occasionally remembered to notice that he was a handsome man, but his manner was so off-putting that it tended to be a distraction.

More or less accustomed to Roger, Fiona looked at him with as bland an expression of curiosity as she could summon. "I can't say I've ever thought about it," she said with mild understatement. "Why would you want to?"

"For goat yoga."

Fiona raised her eyebrows. "Ah," was all she said. Then, after a moment, "Would you like to come in?"

"No," said Roger.

Without missing a beat, Fiona returned to the business at hand. "By the day, or by the hour?"

"Probably by the day. By the time we trailer him and get him over to the hotel, we might as well make it worthwhile."

Fiona nodded, her face now perfectly expressionless. "Might as well."

During the long silent pause that was usual for a conversation with Roger, Fiona stepped out onto the porch. She took a deep breath of the spring air and turned back to him.

"What, exactly, does goat yoga entail?"

"You do yoga, but with a goat."

"The goat does yoga?"

"No. It's just…present."

"Ah," she said again. Fiona was trying to imagine this, but without success.

"Are you sure you recall his…personality? I mean, Robert is not exactly—" She searched her mind for the right words. "—enthused about human interaction."

"What do you mean?"

Fiona felt strangely embarrassed. It had occurred to her that there was a certain intersection between Roger's personality and the goat's. "He's not friendly, really."

She frowned slightly and tried to look into Roger's eyes. He looked away into the distance.

"I'm not even entirely sure that he likes me. I think he likes Ben, though," she added as an afterthought.

"That's a good idea," said Roger thoughtfully.

"What is?"

"Ben. He could be…sort of…in charge. Of the goat."

Fiona nodded slowly but without quite understanding. She wondered whether Elisabeth was aware of this plan.

"Could be. He'd be good at that. Or, at least, as good as anyone could be. But he could only work after school."

Roger seemed undeterred. "Most of the workshops would be during the summer or on weekends anyway." Struck by a new thought, he actually looked at Fiona. "How much does Ben get paid?"

Fiona told him, and he nodded as if in agreement, and

continued nodding as if seeing the whole plan laid out before him.

"Makes sense." He stopped and looked at her again. "But the rental. We didn't discuss that. How much?"

"Gosh," said Fiona, truly at a loss. "I have no idea."

"Would $100 a day be all right?"

Things were progressing more rapidly than Fiona was quite able to follow. "That's way too much."

"Not really," said Roger, launching into analysis with his usual thoroughness. "Let's say we have two classes a day at first… probably we'll end up with four. It will take a while for word to get around, because goat yoga will be a draw for the hotel, but let's say we start with four or five people per class. At twenty dollars each, that's a minimum of eighty dollars per class. Our overhead is low since we already have the space, and the classes will actually enhance revenue for the hotel. Eventually we'll probably reach capacity with twenty people per class. That's when we'll raise the rates. But, let's say for the sake of argument we stick with the twenty-dollar fee, so that's, at a minimum, once we're hitting our stride, four hundred dollars per class. Times two—or four—a day."

He looked somewhere in the direction of Fiona's face. "Actually, a hundred is probably too low."

Fiona looked back, feeling dazed. Roger's optimism seemed to her somewhat unwarranted. "Why don't we start with thirty and see how it goes?"

"Seventy-five," said Roger.

"Really?" Fiona hesitated in this backwards negotiation. She could always use the money, but this would be taking advantage. "How about fifty?"

Roger frowned, pursed his lips, and took a deep breath. "Well, all right, if you're sure. At least at first."

He started to leave, then turned back. "But we'll hit capacity sooner than you think. Then we'll have to re-negotiate."

He got into his truck and drove off. Fiona was left standing on the porch, gazing after him and thinking about the effects of enthusiasm. It was the longest conversation they had ever had.

The offers on the shoreline properties were accompanied by the usual flurry of paperwork, and Marcie dealt with it all as a matter of routine. The buyers were both companies, rather than individuals, but in different locations. After her first ponderings at the coincidence, Marcie shrugged it off. The sellers were very happy with her news, particularly since the offers had come in at full price. She was delighted, too, after a slow season, to have the commissions. With no buildings to inspect and no contingencies on the offers, the sales went through quickly and smoothly.

She was congratulating herself on the happy resolution of the business and toying with the idea of treating herself to a little something in celebration as she pulled up to her office. It had been good to have the sales, but she was looking forward to a more normal, quiet day. Instead, the first things she saw were two more express envelopes with two more offers.

Marcie studied the contents of the offers and frowned. What on earth was going on? This seemed like too much to be coincidence, but the properties were not adjacent. Did it matter? She needed to think.

She reached into her desk drawer for the consolation of her emergency pack and found only one cigarette remaining. It was a bad time to be trying to give up smoking. She made a mental note to re-stock.

Chapter 9 ✤

Oliver closed his book with a snap and tossed it aside. He had read versions of it many times before, and after only a few chapters he could already predict the pattern of the plot. He stared around the room with restless dissatisfaction.

Living alone was increasingly difficult for Oliver. He had never had a roommate, but in Milwaukee, when he had worked for a large accounting firm, the daily encounters with his colleagues had left him longing for the peace and quiet of his apartment. Now matters were entirely reversed. He had come to dread the end of the day and the silence that awaited him at home.

He told himself that this was what he had wanted—to get away from his old life—but it was becoming increasingly clear that he had merely exchanged one form of loneliness for another.

He did not know exactly what he should do about this, but he had an inkling that moving again would not solve the problem. He suspected, in fact, that wherever he went, the problem would be there, too. Changing location was just a way of hiding from himself.

Oliver thought about his life. He had made a few weak

efforts to be sociable, but it didn't come naturally to him. Perhaps, he thought, his loneliness was self-inflicted. He had come to the Island to take charge of his life. What was he doing about that now?

Although Oliver was a book person, his tastes were neither deep nor sophisticated; he merely wanted a good story. He could occasionally find something at the Island library, but he had already read most of the books in their collection, and he was too impatient to bother with interlibrary loans. When he went there, it was usually to encounter other people, not to find a book. He had to admit to himself that so far, this strategy hadn't been particularly effective. He needed something more, and he knew it wasn't something he could get from books.

It was a day filled with the hope of spring. The air was sweet and almost warm, the robins had returned to sing at dawn and peck at the hard earth for food, and the trees were purple and red with their new buds. The school year was winding down, too, and this was a reason for another kind of anticipation.

Ben frequently stopped by the Mercantile for a snack after school before heading to Ms. Campbell's to work in the barn. He was a creature of routine, and he enjoyed the friendly conversations he had with Tom, the manager, and the opportunity to roam the aisles, just looking. These explorations often reminded him of little things he needed for the barn, and he was pleasantly engrossed in thoughts of some new tools one afternoon, when he was surprised to encounter Caleb lingering in the candy aisle.

It had been good to have Caleb off the Island, whether atoning for his sins or being rewarded for them, Ben didn't care. All that had mattered was that he was away. Now, Ben felt the familiar tightening of his heart and stomach at the sight of him. Should he look right at him or look away? He couldn't allow Caleb to think he was afraid, and he couldn't be seen obviously avoiding him. Ben's confusion was so overwhelming he could barely think. Suddenly, in the midst of the maelstrom of his feelings, he heard Fiona Campbell's voice behind him.

"Ben! I didn't expect to see you here." He turned around, and she smiled at him, not seeming to notice Caleb at all. "Are you on your way to my house? If you don't mind leaving now, I could drive you over."

Ben had been so completely caught up in his dilemma that it took him a moment to reply. "Uh, sure. I guess so. I have my bike, though."

Fiona walked toward the cash register, drawing him along as she spoke, and keeping up an easy conversation all through her transaction. "Oh, that's no problem. We'll just throw your bike in the back seat. You know, I've got a project I'm working on and could use a hand, so getting a little extra time from you will be helpful. I really need to get it done."

Ben spoke hesitantly, slightly dazed. "Um…yeah. Okay. I can do that."

"Here, let me get that for you." Fiona spoke to the clerk.

"I'll pay for Ben's, too."

"Oh, no, that's okay—"

"I insist." Firmly, kindly, and talking the entire time, Fiona paid the bill, including Ben's candy bar, and led the way out of the store to her car.

When they got to her house, Fiona's interest in her project seemed to have dissipated.

"Oh, well," she said, vaguely, when Ben asked about it. "Maybe it's not the right time."

She smiled at him, and her whole face lit up in a way that Ben noticed. She was pretty, he thought.

"Come on in and have a snack before you go see Robert. Elisabeth—Mrs. Mason—has been trying out cookie recipes for the new hotel. This latest batch is amazing."

It wasn't until that night, when he was lying in bed thinking over the events of the day, that Ben realized with a jolt of insight that he had been deliberately rescued.

His gratitude blossomed then, deep and real, and he was aware of just how good it was to have friends.

When Elisabeth heard of the plans for goat yoga, she was silent for a long moment. No one knew better than she that Roger's approach to life could be somewhat idiosyncratic, and she could imagine that no matter how well-planned, this project would have certain inevitable repercussions. She had qualms, but she was nothing if not practical.

"The first thing we need to do is figure out whether there are any regulations about having an animal on the hotel premises. I will contact the health department."

Roger's expression did not change. "Thank you," he said.

"At the very least I imagine he needs some kind of health certificate." She frowned, thinking. "Has Fiona ever taken him to the vet? There's no vet on the Island, so it would have been something of an ordeal. I think I'd know about it if she had, but he must have vaccinations and things."

She turned a brisk, business-like face to her husband. "Do you know?"

"I will ask," he said, dutifully.

"Good."

The telephone rang at the front desk, and Elisabeth went to answer it.

Although they had inevitably crossed paths, Jim and Fiona had not met privately since the night of the grass fire last fall. He had thought, then, that his love for her was over, that his feelings had dissipated into the air with the smoke. Instead, he had since found that they lingered, making the prospect of seeing her a thing to dread.

It didn't help that he had come to admire—and even to like—his rival, Pete Landry, but the mischievous character of Fate was something Jim had frequent occasion to ponder. If Pete had never come to the Island, if Fiona had never laid eyes on him, what might have happened then? The answer to the question changed with his moods and, although he was not a man to dwell on his feelings, still, things were hard for Jim these days.

He knew that sooner or later he would have to speak seriously with Fiona about his concerns, and that the conversation would necessarily lead to more meetings. Were they dealing with an arsonist? He supposed that having such a specific agenda—something to distract them both from what had happened between them—would help. But, still, the dread clung to him, even in his sleep. He would awaken feeling a deep and painful angst, not knowing at first what was wrong. And then it would all settle around him like a cloud.

The truth was, he wanted to see her, and this realization bothered him as much as anything else.

As more offers for property came in, Marcie's suspicions were fully engaged. There were always different buyers and, so far, none were contiguous with the others. But there wasn't a great distance between them, either, and they all faced west for the sunsets. This was the most desirable real estate on the Island. By now, there were enough parcels to have significant consequences for the Island, and Marcie didn't know what to think. On the one hand, she didn't like to look a gift horse in the mouth: the commissions for these sales already exceeded all those of last year. On the other hand, she did live here, and it wouldn't do to have the entire Island populace up in arms against her. Marcie needed advice.

As the former Chairman of the Town Board, now retired, Lars Olufsen had the advantages of both experience and a newly disinterested perspective on local affairs. It was not that he had no opinions—after all, Island life would lose much of its flavor if no one took sides—but he was no longer involved in the political rough and tumble. Most important, he was a native Islander, and therefore without the suspect motivations of an outsider.

For privacy's sake they had met in her office. If they were overheard, the news would be all over the Island in a matter of minutes. Marcie had made coffee in her trusty pot, carefully scrubbed for the occasion, and poured it into matching mugs with the name of her real estate company—once emblazoned, now sadly faded after many washings—on the sides. They sat across from one another at the round table Marcie used for signing documents with her clients.

Lars listened, drinking his coffee as Marcie told her story. There was a plat survey of the Island spread out between them, and Marcie had marked out the properties in question with a hot pink highlighter.

"They're all different buyers?" asked Lars when she had finished.

"Two are the same, but the rest are different. There are now eight properties in all; seven buyers."

"Can you tell where the buyers are from?"

"Not really, no. I looked it up, and one of the law firms is in New York, but the others are all over the country. Also," she added, "the envelopes come from different places, although sometimes on the same day."

Lars frowned, looking down at the map, and then looked up again at Marcie.

"What would you like me to do?"

"Well, I'm not really sure. I mean, don't get me wrong. I want to sell the property. This is all great for me. But there's something odd about this. I mean, three of the places weren't even on the market so far as I know. I don't even know why I was involved, but the buyer paid my commission on top of the price."

Lars looked down at the map again. He knew, of course, who all the sellers were. None were Island natives, and none lived on the Island year-round. He knew instinctively what Marcie knew: these property owners' interests would not be the same as those of the locals. And the pattern of the purchases left very little doubt that someone was accumulating a good length of the Island's shoreline. But for what?

Lars was still looking at the map as he spoke. "If it's to build a big house, why the separate buyers and anonymous offers?"

Marcie looked at him with raised eyebrows and compressed lips and shrugged.

"It's pretty common in real estate for wealthy or famous people to hide their identities in these kinds of transactions. It's to keep the prices from being hiked. But still…I don't know. Do you think some Hollywood star is wanting to build a house on the Island?" Even amidst her doubts, Marcie's eyes gleamed at the prospect.

Lars, who had reached the stage of life when the stories in the supermarket tabloids were about people he'd never heard of, merely frowned and shook his head. "I guess we need to wait and see whether more offers come in." Lars pointed to the places on the map between the bright pink highlights. "Are these properties on the market?"

Marcie shook her head. "No. But I'm kind of tempted to contact the owners and find out if they've been approached."

Lars nodded. "If you can, it might be a good idea. Doesn't hurt to know what's coming." He paused. "Of course, if you ask any questions at all, it will kick off the gossip."

Marcie shrugged. "I guess it's only a matter of time, anyway."

"True," said Lars Olufsen. He took a drink of his coffee and wished he had added some of that powdered creamer. It would have helped mask the flavor.

Unpleasantness was a kind of a hobby with Stella DesRosiers. Among her peculiar gifts was the ability to seize opportunity and turn it to her favor. Stella, whom nature had endowed with neither a warm heart nor any particular fondness for her fellow creatures, had always found that she needed to make her luck, unlike the detestable Fiona Campbell, who seemed to stumble into one lucky break after another. Stella could not see the hard work Fiona put in, nor her struggles behind closed doors, and therefore Stella assumed that Fiona's life was easy. This limited view fed Stella's sense of being a victim in an unfair world.

All of her plotting, waiting, bitterness, and envy did not make Stella happy, but it had been a part of her life for so long that she knew no other way to live, nor was she even aware that her life had become so small and mean. Even the little pleasures of keeping her house, decorating in her favorite purple, collecting little figurines, and keeping her things just so had faded over the years as her resentment toward Fiona grew close to obsession.

As Stella's worst traits became exaggerated, the variety and quality of her daily life diminished. She no longer baked, or did crafts, or cared much about the housekeeping she had always prided herself upon. Her frequent volunteer work and involvement in community organizations—undertaken primarily for purposes of control rather than any sense of kindness or obligation—had mostly dropped away. Instead, she sat in a chair in her parlor across from the television, shades drawn, smartphone in hand, generally allowing her resentments to fester.

For everyone else on the Island, the last election for Chairman of the Town Board, which had brought Fiona Campbell into office, was ancient history. But not for Stella. Her capacity for rancor was deep and long, and although she had always been mean, there was something about Fiona that sharpened her nastiness to a fine point. She had hated Fiona from the beginning: for her looks, for her easy acceptance into the Island community, and, most particularly, for purchasing the property adjacent to Stella's own.

Stella had long been planning to buy, but her decision to offer a lower bid had cost her the opportunity. Fiona had swept in, seemingly from nowhere, and naively offered full price, unknowingly pushing out Stella's offer. This Stella could never forgive.

And then there had been the election.

The memories of the humiliations Stella had suffered in the wake of Fiona's arrival on the Island simmered unceasingly in the febrile swamps of Stella's brain. Nothing she had tried had brought Fiona Campbell the kind of ignominy she deserved. Nothing had driven her off the Island.

But, Stella had another quality nearly as potent as her bitterness. It was a grim determination to exact her revenge. And while she waited for her opportunity, she fed her resentment and vituperation by obsessively following Twitter.

Chapter 10

He had been spending a lot of time on the Island, busy with the hotel, but Roger liked to get back to the mainland to keep an eye on Ground Zero. On these occasions, he would leave the hotel in Elisabeth's very capable hands and go back to their place—Elisabeth's house and gallery—on the mainland for a few days.

He arrived at the shop one morning at his usual unearthly hour to discover that one of the yoga groupies had set up camp in his parking lot. There was a bright blue pup tent accompanied by a pickup truck. Some lawn chairs and various pieces of equipment were neatly arranged a few steps from the door of Ground Zero.

Roger walked up to it and stood for a moment taking it all in.

"Hey!" he said loudly.

There were some sounds from inside the tent.

"HEY!" he said again.

He heard a zipping noise, and a sleepy head emerged from between the flaps, peering into the pre-dawn darkness. The head appeared to be in the non-verbal stage of waking, and it merely gazed up at Roger in a state of wonder.

"Get this tent out of here," said Roger, blandly. "It's taking up space for my customers." This was a great deal of speech for him.

By this time, the camper, a young man with a ponytail, was beginning to gather his wits. He looked around at the empty parking lot.

"There's nobody here."

"Get out," said Roger.

"Oh," said the camper. "Don't worry. I'll be packed up by opening time. It's six, isn't it?"

"Get out."

For the first time the camper looked discomfited.

"Oh," he said again. There was a pause. "Okay." And the head disappeared back into the tent.

Roger stood there a moment assessing whether this was a satisfactory outcome and, determining that it was, turned and went to unlock the door of the shop.

The next morning, when he arrived, the camper was there again, but this time, he was up and already in the process of breaking camp.

Roger just stood and looked.

"Almost finished," said the camper by way of greeting.

"Get out," Roger explained.

The camper stopped his preparations and looked directly at Roger with a guileless face. He was a young man, probably in his early twenties, and there was something in his eyes that reminded Roger of that kid who worked for Fiona.

"I thought I just couldn't be here when you opened."

Roger was rarely in the mood for conversation. He just

looked at the camper in silence but managed, nevertheless, to convey his message.

"Not even when you're closed?" There was a tiny note of pleading, mixed with disbelief that anyone could be so unreasonable.

"No."

"Oh," said the camper again. "I just thought it would be okay."

Roger's expression was unchanged. "No."

And having issued what he assumed was the final word, he unlocked the door and went inside the shop.

M arcie was watching the page views of properties obsessively now, but she was well aware that if someone were seeking out property owners who hadn't already decided to sell, she would have no indication of what was coming.

She told herself that she didn't object to selling, of course. But the truth was that Marcie's worries about the reaction of the community were beginning to outweigh her greed. *If* something besides mere coincidence was at work here. Even though it was the answer to so many of her white zinfandel-induced dreams, it all seemed so unlikely.

Following Lars's advice, she had spoken to the owners of the adjacent properties that were not on the market, and two had already been approached. They couldn't tell her more than the name of the lawyer and an area code. Neither were interested in selling, but the offers had been so high that they were in the process of reconsidering.

These conversations and her talk with Lars had not allayed her fears. If anything, they had encouraged them, and Marcie's anxieties were growing by the hour. Could this really be one purchaser? It had to be. If it were one big house it might be all right, but how on earth would she be able to convince her fellow Islanders to permit a major development on their western shoreline? Once she had sold the properties did it even matter? She needed more than advice and guidance; she wanted moral support, and Lars just hadn't been much comfort. Marcie was desperate to talk to someone, and her desperation made her careless.

Chapter 11

"**G**ood morning, Fiona!" Emily Martin had a little singsong quality in her voice that was intended, probably, to be charming, but succeeded primarily in being annoying.

Fiona usually checked the Town's rented mailbox on her way to the office, and mornings were the time when her capacity to deal was Emily was at its lowest. She pondered the burdens of civilization as she spoke.

"Good morning, Emily," she said, politely.

"You know, I've been wanting to talk with you. My goodness, you're difficult to reach. You really ought to check your messages more often."

Fiona opened her mouth to reply that all three of Emily's calls had come in the last twelve hours, and she had been bracing herself to call once she got to the office, but Emily was still talking. Fiona tuned in mid-sentence.

"…there are, of course, so many things one could be concerned about." Emily's eyes were alight. "This fire at the golf course, for instance. My neighbor says someone might have set it! So frightening! So dangerous to life and limb! And the expense! Really, someone needs to pay for these damages… once we catch him, of course."

Fiona noticed the "we," but in the flood of Emily's words, it was simplest to let it go.

"Still," continued Emily. "I don't suppose there's much we can really do about an arson investigation."

"Except, of course, to be concerned," said Fiona, helpfully.

"Well, yes." Emily sounded doubtful. "Oh, well. We'll think of something!"

"No doubt." Fiona excused herself and escaped to her car.

"Damn," she thought to herself, too late. She hadn't contradicted Emily's assertion of arson. That would be fast fuel for the rumor mill.

She was already driving away when Emily came running out of the post office waving a piece of mail Fiona had dropped in her haste.

"Oh, well," Emily told herself. It would be no trouble to drop it off at Fiona's house across the street. She glanced at the paper in her hand. It was a brochure from a town across the state, advertising its annual literary festival. A slow smile began to spread across Emily's face. Of course! A literary festival. This would be just the thing. It would draw tourists, enhance local culture, and she, Emily, could choose the program! The scope of possibilities raced through her mind. She could see herself holding a microphone at the front of a room filled with people, leading the discussions, introducing the speakers, graciously hosting VIP receptions. The other members of the committee faded from her mind.

Everyone would thank her. She just knew they would.

At last, the Committee for the Concerned had a project.

After a solitary night in Elisabeth's empty house down the road, Roger arrived earlier than usual at Ground Zero to find not one but three new tents—different from yesterday's—in his parking lot. He stopped for a moment to look at the scene before him, then unlocked the door and went inside. He reappeared a few moments later with a metal pot and a spatula, stood just outside the shop, and began banging them together.

A series of exclaimed expletives could be heard, and heads popped out of tent flaps.

"What's going on?"

"Get out," explained Roger.

"It's 3:30 in the morning," said one camper.

Roger, who had neither the time nor interest required to conduct a disquisition on private property, running a business, or other niceties of civilization, lifted the spatula and continued his banging.

Shaking their heads at man's inhumanity to man, the campers retreated to their tents to begin the process of departure.

The conversation after yoga was dominated by the story of Roger and the parking lot campers, which had spread without Roger having said a word.

"What made you use this particular, er, method?" asked Mike.

Roger shrugged. "I heard it worked for bears."

Mike nodded the polite nod of a cocktail party conversation and drank his coffee, but his eyes revealed his amusement.

Terry gazed at Roger with admiration. "Got to get out in front of situations like this or before you know it, you'll be overrun."

One of the Lutherans chimed in. "It's like Canada geese. You let one or two stay on your property, pretty soon you got hundreds. You gotta chase 'em off."

Roger scowled, but since this was his usual expression, no one took it as an indication of his opinions.

Joshua looked thoughtful. "Maybe that's the key to this: get out in front if it. If one of us were here at the time of day when campers might be showing up, we could stop them before they set up." He turned his light-filled gaze on Roger. "I'll stop by around six tonight and see what's happening." Joshua knew better than to pose questions to Roger. Bald assertions worked best.

Marcie stopped by the grocery store on her way home from the office. She had been running on caffeine, nicotine—mostly from cigarettes rather than gum—and wine from a jug, and she thought maybe she'd make herself a decent dinner for a change.

Real estate agents know a community's secrets. Who's buying; who's selling; who's come into money; who's looking for a quick sale; whose heirs are secretly enquiring about the value of the family property—these are questions that cut to the heart of human interests.

This inside knowledge made Marcie an asset to anyone interested in local gossip, and she was used to being pumped for information both subtly and not so subtly. It sometimes amused her to know what she knew and to know it while speaking to someone who desperately wanted to know it too. It made her feel as if her work was worthwhile. This was the chief reason for Marcie's long career in real estate and had served as an incentive for her discretion.

In her current circumstances, however, instead of the lofty feeling of superiority she enjoyed when she knew something others did not, she felt instead a gnawing desire to tell someone. Lars had only been useful to a point, because his delicacy had been too perfect. This time, although she did not put it this way to herself, she didn't want advice.

She wanted to feel important by telling.

She was standing in front of the frozen food section debating whether to buy a prepared dinner or to actually cook something, when Stella DesRosiers pushed her cart around the corner and stopped next to her. Marcie smiled civilly and nodded, and they stood side by side, each thinking her own thoughts.

Stella, a past master of the gossip game, was well aware of Marcie's value and, as a general matter, made good use of any such encounter. She had no particular target in mind, but one never knew how a little piece of information might come in handy.

"It's hard to cook for yourself, isn't it?" commented Stella, casually. "I just never really bother much when I'm on my own."

Since Stella was entirely on her own, this remark was somewhat odd, but Marcie didn't notice.

"That's so true," she said. "Lately, I haven't been bothering much, but I just feel I need to do a better job of taking care of myself. Last night I was too tired to cook and ate an entire box of crackers. Can't live on wine and coffee!"

Stella gave an utterly mirthless chuckle in response.

"Sometimes it's hard being alone."

This remark hit a chord with Marcie, just as it was intended to.

She nodded sadly, thinking with regret of her second husband. He'd been the best of them, and she wished she had done things differently.

"You know," said Stella, with a studied offhandedness, "we single girls should stick together more. Maybe you should come to dinner sometime. It will give me a reason to make an effort. My pot roast recipe is from my French grandmama, and everyone who tries it wants to know my secret."

Secret recipe or no, this prospect could not have held less appeal for Marcie. All she wanted to do at the end of the day was to come home, kick off her shoes, pour herself some wine, and watch something mindless on television.

"Oh, yes, that would be nice," she said vaguely, even as she mentally cursed the forces of civilization that were boxing her into this corner.

"We single girls," she thought, resentfully. She cast a glance at Stella's dumpy figure and dowdy clothes. As if she and Stella had any traits at all in common.

"We certainly should do that sometime."

Stella had never intended for her invitation to be accepted, and she would have been disappointed if it had been. Her goal was entirely different. By making Marcie feel guilty, Stella could get her to do something she would normally hesitate to do.

"How about this?" Stella pretended to look at her watch. "Why don't we finish up here, and we can stop off at Nelsen's for a little drink before we go our separate ways?" Her smile appeared guileless. "Make the evening a little less lonely."

Marcie sighed to herself, and, just as Stella intended, realized that she must accept this lesser of two evils.

"What a nice idea," she lied, civilly. "Let me finish up my shopping, and I'll meet you there in fifteen minutes."

Stella smiled again.

That evening, as promised, Joshua stayed after closing the shop in order to keep an eye on the parking lot.

He stayed until dark and, satisfied that all was well, went off to join his scuba diving class at the Y.

Stella was thoughtful after her drink with Marcie. Who could be buying so much property on the Island, and why? How could she find out? And most important: how could she use this information to her advantage? Stella may have been malicious, but she wasn't stupid, and she knew that this kind of research required a sophistication she did not possess.

Knowing about the purchases before the rest of the community had many advantages, and she would keep Marcie's little secret to herself for now. A thousand wheels were turning as Stella baked her frozen pizza and settled in for a fine evening of machinations.

Chapter 12

The morning yoga practice was delayed somewhat by the presence of so many tents in the parking lot. Despite Joshua's vigil, they had appeared, as if by magic, sometime after midnight.

Roger employed what had by now become his customary pot banging method, and Joshua stood by to translate, if necessary.

"But we're supposed to be able to camp here," said one camper, who felt, after having been wakened in such a fashion, that he had a grievance.

"What makes you think so?" asked Joshua.

"The article."

"What article?"

"The one in our 'Avocado Toast' group on Reddit. It says—" he paused to search his memory, "'A plentiful parking lot has room for camping, for those who want to ensure a place in class.'"

Roger's face, never particularly revealing, now took on a look that might have been amazement. The Angel Joshua, who, long before this, had assumed the role of diplomatic relations on Roger's behalf, now hastened to step in.

"There's been a mistake. Camping is not permitted here."

"Dude," was the young man's comment. "Are you sure?"

Joshua nodded regretfully. His store of patience was one of his angelic traits, second only to his extraordinary beauty. "I'm sure."

This scene was reenacted on a daily basis and with increasing numbers of tents. Roger, not famous for his willingness to tolerate his fellow beings under any circumstances, began to be more irritable than usual. This was a condition his customers found undesirable, and after the morning's practice, the conversation turned to methods of pest control.

"Are you sure it's not the same guy? They all look alike."

"You can tell by the tents," commented Terry helpfully. "There are different tents every morning." Heads nodded at this piece of insight.

"I think we need a sign," suggested Joshua, who had watched that morning as a dozen different tents were disassembled and packed away in Japanese station wagons at varying stages of entropy. The holes from the tent stakes were beginning to show as pock marks in the asphalt.

Roger frowned and stared off into the distance.

The others exchanged glances. They knew that look. A sign, they all felt sure, would be forthcoming.

Fiona was discussing goat yoga logistics with Elisabeth on the phone after returning from the barn. It was a cold, rainy day. Fiona sat in the snug little kitchen, savoring the warmth of the room and her first cup of coffee. Chatting this way with Elisabeth was almost as nice as having her there. Her serenity was disturbed only by an occasional whiff of goat from her person when she moved a certain way. She was looking forward to school ending, when Ben would be there to take care of the morning chores.

"The vet comes here several times a month," she told Elisabeth. "She's seen him before, but she has nothing available for weeks, so we'll have to take him to Sister Bay. The difficulty, of course, is getting him there. I don't know about Robert, but the idea of two ferry rides with him on one day seems more than I can handle."

Elisabeth listened with only half an ear as she arranged and rearranged little cards on a gallery map on the table in front of her. In the midst of the frenetic preparations for the hotel's grand opening, there was a new show coming to her gallery, and she was thinking about the placement of paintings. She had become accustomed to the idea of goat yoga and decided to face its problems as they came. That, she knew, would be soon enough. She took a sip of her coffee and moved the largest card to one wall.

"Well," she said jokingly, "you and Robert could always stay overnight at the gallery. Roger's there one or two nights a week anyway."

There was a lull in the conversation during which she realized with some alarm that Fiona was actually considering this.

Fiona shifted in her chair and tilted her head as she contemplated this idea.

"He could stay in your shed," she said musingly. "I could bring along that galvanized trough and some food, and he'd be pretty comfortable." She paused as she pictured what would be required for this kind of excursion.

"I wouldn't want to put him in the car, though. He's kind of...pervasive. I don't think I'm up to this on my own. Do you think Roger would bring him over? He has a trailer, right?"

Elisabeth had been caught off guard; she stopped her arranging and stared off into the distance. Fiona traveling with a goat? There was a time when Fiona would have laughed out loud at the thought of even owning a goat, much less transporting him to stay at someone else's house. Under most circumstances, she would have told Fiona outright that she was crazy. But somehow, given Roger's involvement, this seemed both unwise and unfair. Staying over had, after all, been her own idea, and this, she knew, would be only the beginning of her goat-related challenges. She sighed inwardly.

"I suppose you could ask him," she said cautiously, her brain racing with strategies for the execution of this scheme, all the while picturing Robert seated in her dining room wearing a napkin around his neck. She wished she had put her foot down about all this from the beginning. Her sigh was audible this time. It was too late now.

Fiona was pacing energetically the length of the kitchen. She heard the sigh and had noticed by now the silence on Elisabeth's end of the phone. "You seem awfully quiet," she said in a somewhat accusatory tone.

"I was thinking."

"This is all Roger's idea. He has a responsibility here."

"I do see your point," said Elisabeth, rather vaguely, in Fiona's view.

"I'd better call Roger right away before he makes any other plans," Fiona said briskly. She was realizing that Elisabeth's attitude was not all that could be desired. "I'll check back with you later."

"Terrific," said Elisabeth rather faintly, and she was left staring blankly at her arrangement as Fiona ended the call.

She had spilled her coffee and would have to re-cut all the cards.

B en had promised to hang out with Noah. He was acutely aware of Caleb's presence on the Island, and the close association was very uncomfortable, but he reassured himself that Noah was unlikely to bring Caleb along.

The difference in age between Ben and Noah would have made their friendship unlikely in most other places, but on the Island, the choices of companionship were necessarily limited. Ben was more conscious of these distinctions than Noah, and as the older of the two, felt a certain sense of responsibility.

The sun had made a watery appearance. They met on their bikes in the school drive and spent some time swooping around the open space, their conversation casually drifting with their bikes.

After some time, Ben's interest began to fade.

"Let's go somewhere," he called to Noah.

"Okay. Where?"

"How about over to the Karfi docks?"

"What's there?" Noah's family was relatively new the Island, and he was just beginning to be allowed to explore on his own.

"People—you know, tourists, boats, stuff like that.

"Doesn't your dad work there?"

"No, he's at the main ferry docks, on Detroit Harbor."

"Oh." Noah looked uncertain.

"Come on. It's fun watching the boats come and go. I know the crew, maybe they'll let us ride along."

Noah was content to be led. "Okay."

They made one more sweep around the parking lot, like seagulls swirling on the currents of spring air, and headed out for an adventure.

Chapter 13

On the appointed day, Roger arrived promptly at the house to help Fiona take Robert to the veterinarian. There had been a spring snow squall the day before, but now it was a spectacular day; sweet, but cold, brilliant with sunshine and an almost summery blue sky. The snow had mostly melted from the grass, but it still fell from the trees in soft, wet, clumps and lay on the tightly furled leaves of the lily of the valley that grew in abundance around the house.

Fiona was ready with a neatly assembled pile of goat gear, including two bales of hay. Her own small, elegant bag looked as if she were planning a whirlwind trip to the Plaza Athénée rather than a ferry ride with a goat. She was wearing jeans with some rather splendid suede half-boots—of which she was enormously proud— a beautifully tailored jacket, and a cashmere wrap tossed dashingly over one shoulder. Roger, who was not known for his fashion sense and had never evinced even the faintest awareness of style, nevertheless felt some concern for what he thought of as her lack of preparation for goat transport.

Together, they had remarkably little difficulty in persuading Robert to enter the trailer. They had placed a plank of wood against it, and Robert had pranced up merrily like a child anticipating a trip to the amusement park, settling into the transport crate. Roger and Fiona exchanged glances with raised eyebrows, having expected hours of struggle to carry off this achievement.

"I thought something would go wrong with this," said Fiona, eyeing Robert's delighted foraging in the bales of hay they'd loaded up for him.

"There's still time," said Roger.

There was a short line at the ferry of about half a dozen cars. Robert seemed comfortably ensconced in his crate, casting malevolent looks at anyone who came near; the fact that these looks were generally unseen did not in any way lessen their intensity.

As they patiently waited their turn to board, Pali approached the truck. Reluctantly, Roger rolled down the window as for an arresting police officer.

"Morning," said Pali, peering in through the window as they waited to drive aboard. He was accustomed to seeing just about everything. Unless it grew there, or could fit in an airplane, pretty much everything on the Island had to come—or go—by ferry. A goat on a trailer was no big deal.

Nevertheless, Pali was fully aware of Fiona's views on the subject of goats in general and Robert in particular, and he seemed to be expecting an explanation of some kind.

"We're off to the vet," she said, feeling uncomfortable, as if she'd been caught in an indiscretion.

"Is Robert well-tethered, do you think? Wouldn't want him to slide overboard." Pali was joking.

Fiona had a fleeting image but dismissed it quickly before

temptation could develop.

She jumped out of the truck to show him the eyehook in the bed of the trailer and the sturdily chained tether that kept Robert's crate in place.

"Looks good," said Pali. "Ok, then, we'll put you forward in the middle. Plenty of room for you today." He walked ahead of them as they drove onto the ferry, and using well-practiced hand gestures, guided them into place. It was the Captain who determined the placement of vehicles on board, tucking the small cars into the corners, and balancing the loads when there were big trucks and tankers.

Perhaps it was the jolting sound of the truck on the metal deck, or the sound of the ferry engines, or merely a contrarian disposition, but whatever the reason, no sooner had Roger pulled the parking brake than Robert began his soliloquy.

"WHAT??WHAT??WHAT??WHAT??WHAT??WHAT ??WHAT??WHAT??WHAT??WHAT??" he demanded. His voice resonated against the metal construction of the ferry with the acoustic clarity of a nineteenth century concert hall.

Fiona and Roger traded looks, her face pale with embarrassment, his in its normal expression of cold fury.

"How did this go when you brought him over the first time?"

Roger frowned, searching his memory. "Like this."

"You could have warned me."

Roger shrugged, "I assumed you knew."

"BAAAAAAAAAAAAWB!!!!!!" said Robert at ear-splitting decibels. "BAAAAAAAAAAAAAAAAAWWB!!!!!!!!!"

Pali glanced back at them and continued the arrangements

of the cars on his ship, unable to keep from grinning. Fiona got out of the passenger seat and went around to the edge of the truck bed.

"Robert, hush!" said Fiona, *sotto voce*, as if he were uttering insults at the cotillion. She moved around to the rear of the truck so he could see her, thinking that perhaps her presence might comfort him. Roger had emerged from the truck and come around to stand next to her.

"WHAAAAAAAAATT??????WHAAAAAAAAAAAAAA AATT???" said Robert.

They were attracting looks from the other passengers. It was past the time of year when people chose to stay in their warm cars rather than to stand on the deck or mingle with other passengers. It was a beautiful day for being out on the water, and Robert's conversation was deafening. The expressions on their faces varied from amusement to pure poison. Even muffled by car doors the volume was ear-piercing.

Desperate to quiet him, Fiona leaned over the edge of the trailer, catching her cashmere wrap on one of the sharp edges. "Damn it," she breathed.

"HAHAHAHAHAHAHAHA!!!!!" said Robert.

"It's remarkable how apt his verbalizations are," observed Roger, imperturbably.

Fiona pulled off her wrap impatiently and tossed it over the edge of the trailer bed.

Roger peered into the crate, only to be met with an icy stare by Robert.

"BAAAAWWWB!" screamed Robert.

"BAAAAAAWWWWWWWWWWB!!!!!!" he repeated, in

case there might be some misunderstanding.

The ferry engines shifted as they began to pull away from the ferry.

"BAAAAAAAAAAAAAWWWWWWWB!!!!!!!!!!"

By now, Fiona, normally able to see the humor in situations, was desperate to stop the clamor. She was acutely aware of the looks they were receiving from other passengers, and their implied censure flustered her.

"Quiet!" she said sternly to Robert, who was refusing to look at her.

"Whatwhatwhatwhatwhatwhatwhat," he said now, more quietly.

"What's wrong, Robert?" Fiona asked in her most soothing tones. "It's okay. Don't worry. It's okay," she said, trying to calm him with repetition. She leaned closer to him over the edge of the truck.

"BAAAAAAAAAAAAAWWWWWWWB!!!!!!!!!!" he yelled.

Fiona involuntarily ducked her head and pulled away; nature's way of preventing deafness. She turned to Roger for help. "What should we do?"

Roger studied the animal as if he were a Petri dish. "I don't think that it matters, really," he said seriously. He turned to Fiona. "What did you have in mind?"

"BAAAAAAAAAAAAAWWWWWWWB!!!!!!!!!!!" said Robert. They both flinched.

"Maybe if we let him out of the crate," suggested Fiona, now willing to consider anything. "Do you think he would stay in the trailer?"

"BAAAAAAAAAAAAAAAAAAAAAWWWB!!!!!!!!!!!!!"
Fiona and Roger instinctively covered their ears with their
hands.

"BOB," added Robert, chewing reminiscently.

Roger looked at Fiona and shrugged. "How the Hell
should I know?" he asked amicably.

"We have to try something." By this time Fiona was
climbing over the edge of the trailer.

"You might just be giving him what he wants," said Roger,
who was inclined to deal with the problem by returning to the
truck and turning up the volume on the radio.

"I'm not sure that I particularly care at the moment," said
Fiona tartly. She unlatched the crate and sat back as Robert
emerged. He stepped daintily on the ridges of the trailer
bed, clearly pleased with the results of his efforts, and looked
around. Fiona heard a murmur of commentary from some
nearby passengers.

"Whatwhatwhatwhatwhatwhat?" he said. He began nibbling elegantly on the fringe of Fiona's cashmere wrap.

"He's going to eat the whole thing," said Roger attempting
to extract it from Robert's grip.

"Oh, just let him have it," Fiona said resignedly. "Maybe
it will keep him quiet."

"But it's cashmere! It's practically cannibalism," said Roger,
genuinely appalled.

"Not technically," said Fiona, pondering for the briefest
moment the ways in which life with Elisabeth had changed
Roger.

They both looked at Robert, who was chewing contentedly,

his yellow eyes sparkling. After ensuring that Robert was still tethered, without a word they returned to the comfort and relative quiet of the truck.

The whispers that had begun were focused more on the property sales than on the fire, but the talk of both phenomena spread with more rapidity than any flames. The rumors may have started at a card party, or possibly at Nelsen's, but they had most likely started at the grocery store's meat counter, where Islanders met to discuss the news of the day.

Speculation ranged widely and was accompanied in some quarters by a rising sense of excitement. An enthusiastic buyer, whatever his motivations, was good news for property owners in general and for those who had been wanting to sell in particular. Real estate that had been lagging on the market for years might now move more quickly.

For most of the Islanders, however, the purchases created deep anxiety. What could be the intentions of the buyer? No one cherished hopes that the land was being accumulated undeveloped as an investment. No, whatever was being planned must be some kind of commercial development, one that threatened to change the character of the Island forever.

"Some development company is planning to come in here, you just wait and see."

"It'll have bright lights and traffic and bossy people running around thinking they run the place."

Looks were exchanged as they envisioned an invasion of Emily Martins.

"Sure would be great for business, though. Think of that, now."

"I'm against it. I came here for peace and solitude."

"We'd probably lose the astronomy people and the star watchers. Darkness is in short supply these days. They come to us for that."

"Do you think it could be for one big house? That wouldn't be so bad."

"Well, guess we'll just have to wait and see."

In the meantime, there was plenty to talk about.

The visit to the veterinarian had been remarkably uneventful, and Roger and Fiona arrived at the gallery with some relief. Elisabeth had come from the Island the day before to open up the house, and she and Rocco had greeted them in the drive. Rocco loped around them in circles as the three of them lead Robert down the ramp and ensconced him comfortably, Fiona hoped, in Elisabeth's small shed.

"What is this?" asked Elisabeth, eying a scrap of soggy material lying in the bed of the trailer. "It looks like cashmere." She eyed Fiona accusingly.

"It used to be my scarf," said Fiona. "I bought it years ago in Paris."

Roger and Elisabeth exchanged glances. Elisabeth decided

that it was best to let the subject pass.

"Pretty color," she said, lightly. And then, sensing the need to change the mood, "Come on in. Let's have some lunch."

She picked up Fiona's bag to carry it in, and Roger followed her as she led the way into the house. Fiona followed more slowly. An uncharacteristically faint, sad bleat came from the shed, but she ignored it and held the door for Rocco before she entered the kitchen. Robert had already had his lunch, but Fiona had not. Being hungry may have made her less patient than she might otherwise have been, but she resolved that she would not put herself through another day like this. She would ask the vet about goat tranquilizers for the trip back.

Chapter 14 ❖

Fiona first heard about the properties being bought from Eddie. The goat tranquilizers had made for a quiet trip home, and after Robert had been settled in the barn, Fiona headed to Nelsen's to catch up on the news. Pali and his wife, Nika, were there, having stopped in for a warm-up after a very chilly ball game. The bar was busy.

"How many properties are we talking about?" asked Fiona.

"The number seems to be growing daily. I think a dozen, now, all along the western side," said Pali. "And the golf course got an offer, too."

"Really." It wasn't a question. Fiona squinted into the distance thinking. "I can't imagine any scenario in which this can be a good thing," she said, looking back at Eddie.

He shook his head. "There's a mixed response. There are those who see opportunity in it, but there's a man-the-barricades kind of atmosphere building already among everyone else."

Nika spoke up. "There has to have been a lot of money spent. Somebody has deep pockets...unless....are we sure it's one buyer?"

"Well, that's just it," said Eddie. "They're all from different law offices around the country. No individual names. But how can that many sales—all using the same method—be a coincidence?"

Pali nodded. "Seems unlikely."

Fiona's thoughts were racing. This was terrible news. The things she loved most about the Island were dependent upon its rural character. "Well," she said, "the good thing is, nothing can be built without the approval of the Town Board. And you can be damned sure we won't be giving it, whatever this is."

Pali nodded at Eddie's silent inquiry.

"Look at it this way," he said, as Eddie poured another round. "Now Emily's committee has something to be concerned about."

Chapter 15

With the goat paperwork completed and in Elisabeth's reluctant hands, Fiona was in a particularly happy frame of mind. Pete was coming back, and she was planning, this time, to talk with him frankly about her worries.

His comings and goings tended to be somewhat sporadic, but in some ways, it made his absences more bearable, because Fiona felt as if his arrival were always imminent.

He had called via Skype to tell her the news.

"I've got a plane rented next Tuesday. I'll fly in from Chicago."

"That makes me happy."

"Pick me up at the airport?"

"I could do that."

"Fingers crossed for good weather."

"Done."

Fiona heard his plane before she saw it and watched as he landed on the small grass field. The plane bounced once, probably on a ground hog hill, and then taxied toward the hangar where she was waiting near her car. She didn't like watching him land. She knew he was skillful, but she didn't like small planes very much and the process made her nervous.

Her anxieties made her even happier to see him, however, and they lingered over their greetings.

A white sign with crooked stick-on letters was posted on a tree next to the parking lot at Ground Zero. Its message was simple.

"NO CAMPING," it said.

The sign, however, had no effect, and the morning after its appearance, there were just as many tents as before.

Joshua, who had come expecting the problem to have been solved, looked over the parking lot with his benevolent gaze.

"Dude," he said, in a gentle tone of reproval. "Can't you read?"

The camper was not in the least embarrassed. "We thought it was an old sign."

Joshua sighed more deeply than usual. "It's a brand-new sign. And it says no camping. That's because there's no camping permitted here."

"Oh," said the camper. He was going back into his tent when he turned. "Any chance you could open up a little early so we could get some coffee?"

"Not a chance in the world," said Joshua.

He was beginning to think that Roger's approach to the situation would be, at least, more satisfactory.

"Oh," said the camper. "Okay."

Stella DesRosiers had questions. Particularly now that the rumors had begun, she felt an urgency to find out what was going on, and who was behind it, before everyone else. Knowledge, Stella firmly believed, was power.

She hadn't the funds to hire a lawyer or financial expert, nor the insight to do the work herself. But it occurred to her that there was a legal expert she knew rather well, who happened to have a lot of time on his hands: her disgraced nephew, Dean Hillard, former legislator, now serving time in prison for a long list of felonies. Research, she knew, would keep him busy.

Calling people in prison was always inconvenient. She would write.

Chapter 16

The smell of smoke was all over the Island. People noticed it and went outside in the dark to see if they could determine where it was coming from.

Jim had already received a page, and the fire fighters were converging on the firehouse, still not completely certain where they were needed. As they drove to the station, they used their senses to triangulate. They could, at least, put together an idea of where it wasn't.

After long minutes, a call came in. It was the Karfi ferry dock.

Fiona received a call, too. Once again, she felt relieved that this was no longer her responsibility but in Jim's very capable hands. Still, after she hung up, she was incapable of thinking of anything else. It was as if she were there: seeing the trucks, the flashing lights, the men silhouetted against the flames, smelling the smoke mixed with the diesel of the engines, hearing the garbled cackling of the radios.

It wasn't until the call came telling her that the fire was out, and that everyone was all right, that she was able to go upstairs to bed. Pete was already asleep when she climbed in next to him. She lay awake for a long time, thinking.

Fiona dreamed that she was walking around the outside of a barn, listening to the sounds of the animals. She could hear many goats inside, and they seemed restless. She opened the door to see, and they were all milling around outside of their stalls. She saw, in the middle of the floor, a lantern. It was lit, and the flame flickered dangerously close to the goats' careless hooves. As she moved toward it to prevent an accident, the very thing she had feared happened before her eyes. The lamp was kicked over, spilling oil everywhere, the flame quickly following the flow of the oil, the animals careless, and then fearful, crying out words in their fear. Fiona chased them all away, out of the barn, just as the straw inside caught fire, and the barn began to ignite. Soon the entire building was engulfed in flame, and then the woods were burning too. People came to watch and eat cake. Fiona looked out the window from above the burning trees and saw on the forest floor one huge beech tree, lying on its side, the fire burning all through its center like molten lava running up and down the length of the trunk. She reached out to touch it, but it was enclosed in glass.

Fiona awoke to the smell of coffee. Pete had already been for a run, and she found him at the kitchen table, freshly showered and reading the Island newspaper. The pleasure of his being there struck her anew.

In a gesture of solicitude that was part of their usual routine, he brought her a cup of coffee as she sat down, kissing the top of her head as he did so.

"The historical society is sponsoring a talk by the divers who found Robert de LaSalle's *Griffon*. It sounds interesting," he said, pouring himself another cup. "Also, there will be a display at the library of 'Lace Handkerchiefs Through the Generations' including photographs of the original owners." He came back to the table and sat down across from her.

Fiona's smile was facetious. "Don't want to miss that."

"Certainly not."

"Have you been to our library?"

"I have. It's a noble effort."

Fiona smiled again. "Yes. People here are serious readers, but there's never been the money to do much."

"You have money now."

"Well, maybe. But that doesn't mean we should spend it."

"I suspect that won't be the public view."

"No," said Fiona. "Probably not. People complain when the government is over budget, but if there's anything set aside, they are itching to spend it."

There was a pause as she considered her next remark. She took a breath and plunged in. "I have to meet Jim this morning. About the fire."

From across the table, Pete looked into her eyes. Although Fiona had not told him much, he knew the story. "It's your job," he said, blandly.

"Yes."

Pete continued to gaze at her. "He can handle it."

Fiona compressed her lips and nodded. "Yes. Yes, I know."

He tilted his head and gave her a wry smile. "It's okay, you know."

Fiona smiled back, relieved. "I know."

"More coffee?"

Fiona had finished her first cup without even tasting it. "Yes, please."

He got up to get it for her.

Later that morning, Fiona and Jim stood next to the ruins of the old building looking down into the charred remains. It hadn't been much more than a shed, built of wood on a hundred-year-old stone foundation. Its loss wouldn't slow down the operations of the ferry service to Rock Island, but it wasn't entirely inconsequential, either. It meant no maintenance equipment on-site, and the inconvenience of hauling things from one ferry dock to another on the opposite side of the Island.

In a city, former lovers, enemies, or someone who remembered an embarrassing moment could be dismissed into eternal invisibility. Not so on the Island, where proximity meant that relationships never ended. Every step out in public meant the likelihood of meeting an uncomfortable someone, and the best anyone could hope for were the diminishing effects of time and memory.

Although he had moved on in his hopes, Jim's feelings for Fiona had not really changed, only shifted into a place that bore a little less weight on his heart. There was freedom in certainty, and that helped, somehow. For her part, Fiona felt regret to have caused pain to someone she liked and admired and was somewhat abashed at their few moments of affection.

"The fire started right here." Jim indicated a corner of the foundation.

"What caused it?" It was early morning, and the mosquitoes were out. Fiona waved her hands around her head and was glad she'd covered her arms.

"Well, I know enough to know what I don't know, and the science is quite complex…" his voice trailed off.

Fiona looked at him, thinking of the loose talk she had heard. "You think it was arson." It was not a question.

Jim nodded his head slightly in a sign of vague acquiescence. "I'm trying to stay open-minded, but it's possible. Maybe even likely. I've put in a call to the state investigator's office. Thought you'd like to know."

Fiona nodded. She felt the physical reaction of dread, but she was not really surprised. His request for a meeting had signaled something was out of the ordinary and, in any case, like so many of her neighbors, she had her own suspicions. The number of recent fires definitely seemed disproportionate.

Jim was looking at her face, scrutinizing her reaction. "Just seems like a good idea."

Fiona nodded again. "I agree." She looked rueful. "The rumor mill is already turning."

"I know."

They stood together in silence, looking into the ashes of the burned building while waving away the mosquitoes, each contemplating the possibilities to come.

After the meeting with Jim, Fiona felt the need to wind down a bit, so she headed over to the hotel for coffee and a chat with Elisabeth.

"How's Jim?" asked Elisabeth, promptly.

Fiona took a deep breath and kept her voice light.

"He seems fine. Doing a great job as chief."

Fiona had no intention of delving into deep feelings, nor did she intend to discuss Jim's theories about arson. Even discreet Elisabeth might be tempted to mention it, and she wanted to hold off on alarming the public for as long as possible. Besides, Fiona had come expressly to distract herself from feeling sorry about Jim. "So, when is the Grand Opening?"

Elisabeth allowed the conversation to move on. "Picking a date has been tricky. I don't want to conflict with the tea party."

"I'd have thought you would want to. The tea party people and the hotel party people really aren't in the same group."

Elisabeth gave Fiona a mischievous look. "The Island's too small for that kind of segmentation and you know it. There will be plenty of overlap. Your problem is you just can't get over your bad experience."

"On the contrary. I treasure my tea party adventures."

Fiona smiled happily at the memory of Elisabeth dumping an entire plate of tea sandwiches, buttered scones, and jam onto Stella's antique tablecloth. It had been so deliciously out of character for Elisabeth, and so richly deserved by Stella. Fiona's favorite part had been seeing the egg salad with chives clotting a particularly delicate piece of lace. It was an image she often summoned in the presence of Stella, just for moral support.

"Speaking of which," said Fiona, breaking out of her reverie, "Stella, apparently, has joined the Committee of the Concerned."

"That certainly is concerning."

"Well, particularly since I'm fairly certain she wants me dead. I saw her at the store yesterday."

"So, what else is new? Did you speak to her?"

"Nope," said Fiona cheerfully. I just pretended not to notice when she gave me dirty looks."

"That's the only way, I suppose."

"So far, yes. Short of death, anyway. Preferably hers. But I'm counting on some kind of technological advance to make her invisible."

"You don't want Stella invisible. Seriously. Think of the trouble she could cause."

Fiona drank her coffee. "Maybe I could be invisible."

"That might be better. But until then, you'll just have to cope."

"There's always scotch."

Elisabeth shook her head in mock despair.

"So...the opening..." prompted Fiona.

Elisabeth, who loved planning parties, launched happily into all the details.

"Here's the place. This is where the fire was."

In the way of boys to find their way to wherever trouble might be, Ben and Noah were irresistibly drawn to the site of the latest fire. All that remained was the stone foundation. They stood, straddling their bikes, regarding the charred remains of the little wooden shed that had been there only the day before. All that was left was the stone foundation. The adults working nearby, and the tourists on their way to the small ferry that took them to uninhabited Rock Island for camping or birdwatching, ignored the boys. After all, they were doing no harm: just looking.

"What do you think caused it?" asked Ben, more rhetorically than anything else. Noah obliged by not replying, only staring wide-eyed at the destruction.

"Jim says it started over there, in that corner," added Ben. He was in awe that Jim knew so much, and he hoped to impress Noah with his own knowledge.

Noah only nodded silently, one finger in his mouth as he chewed on a nail.

Ben was silent again, too, and merely stood looking for a few moments. In the end, though, there wasn't much to see.

"Come on," said Ben. "I'll race you to the beach."

They took off together on their bikes, leaving the smell of smoke far behind.

Pete had been back for almost a week, but Fiona still hadn't broached the topic of her concerns. They were sitting on the porch together. He was deeply engrossed in his reading while Fiona held her book and stared into space. She was thinking about Mark's comments on human nature and whether they applied to Pete.

The more Fiona thought about his character, the more intrigued she became by what Pete did, and where, and with whom. He worked for an energy company, yes. But what about before that? The Navy, he'd said, but he'd never wanted to discuss it. Was this the source of the discipline? And what, exactly, did his present work entail?

For her, one of the key details of their interactions with one another was that she felt that she was a better person around him. She liked herself with him. His admiration, his respect, and his love were, she knew, a reflection of her own character. At every instinctual level, her trust in him and respect for his judgment were fully engaged. But still, she needed to know.

She could imagine how he would react if she brought up the subject. She could see the look of amusement in his eyes, as if he had always known she would ask. She could even imagine the sound of his voice as he spoke to her about it. But for some reason she didn't fully understand, she couldn't bring herself to ask him. Instead, she found herself watching him, silently, as if she could know the answers to her questions simply by the way he moved.

"What are you thinking about so seriously?" he asked, catching her now in one of these moments.

Fiona only smiled and shrugged. "Just drifting."

Pete looked at her skeptically, but with a characteristic glint of humor in his eyes. She knew he didn't believe her, but that he wouldn't pressure her to answer.

It would have been a perfect moment to begin a conversation, but for some reason, she couldn't bring herself to do it.

Pali had stopped by the ferry offices to fill out some paperwork. It was a beautiful early summer day, and Pali wanted to be in it. Instead, he sat at a desk leaning his head on his hand, feeling like a kid stuck at school.

It was a task he detested and, by way of comfort, he congratulated himself for having a job where so little of this kind of thing was required. Maybe some coffee would help. He got up to get himself a cup, passing by the office manager's desk on the way.

Heather was an efficient, no-nonsense woman, but she had a radiant kindness that she bestowed on any creature in her path, human or animal.

"I made cookies last night. They're right there, next to the pot. Help yourself."

"Thanks," said Pali.

She spoke to his back as he poured.

"I suppose you heard about the fire over at the Karfi dock?"

Pali spoke over his shoulder. "Yeah. The old shack."

Heather licked an envelope. "Burned right to the ground."

"Not much valuable in it, at least."

"Not really, no. But it was so close to the main building, and all those cedar trees; a little wind and couple of sparks the wrong way could have been a disaster."

From the moment he heard the news, Pali had been thinking: another one. "What started it? Do you know?"

"No idea."

"Seems odd."

She shrugged. "People are saying arson, but I don't think that's very likely. These things happen."

Pali frowned. "I guess."

That afternoon, Pali walked around the ferry dock, looking at everything and thinking. This was the dock for the ferries to the mainland, the Island's lifeline. For all practical purposes, everyone and everything that came on the Island came through here, and every Islander was acutely aware of their dependence on it.

Improving the security of the facilities was something he'd been discussing with the owner in a vague theoretical fashion for some time, and as the larger world continued on its path toward madness, federal officials had begun to push.

Now moving ahead seemed like a good idea. He'd give him a call on the way home.

Chapter 17 ✣

In the kind of petty squabble that is usual in small town life,
certain members of the Ephraim Chamber of Commerce
were unhappy that what they chose to think of as Roger's
tent city was impinging on their business. That these
members happened to own camping grounds and hotels may
or may not have been relevant, but since the Chamber and its
members were community leaders and major donors to the
police department, their displeasure would not be ignored.

When an officer arrived one morning to discuss the situation, the yoga practice was just wrapping up. A dozen middle-
aged men were slowly rising from their Shavasana, sitting on
the floor with slightly dazed looks and putting on their shoes
and socks.

"We've had some complaints about the tents in your
parking lot," began the officer. "You must know that camping
is not permitted in parking lots in the village."

Roger simply gazed at the officer as if he were on exhibit
in a museum display case. The policeman, who knew Roger,
waited patiently for a response.

The class exchanged uneasy glances, and the silence length-
ened as Roger continued to stare. Roger was not uncomfortable with silence, but other people usually were.

Joshua felt it necessary to step in. "We know," he said at last, with supernal patience. "We even have a sign. We have been trying to get rid of them, but they keep showing up."

The policeman was unimpressed. "Maybe you should build a fence," he quipped. No one laughed, but policemen are used to that.

He finished writing out a ticket and ripped it from his book.

"Here," he said, extending his hand toward Roger. "You can contest it if you want. Date's set at the bottom."

Roger reached out his hand and took it.

"Have a good day," said the policeman politely, and he went out, the storm door slamming behind him.

Roger stood looking after him for a moment as everyone in the shop watched in suspense.

Then he turned and went into the back room.

The rest of the men looked at one another alarmed.

"You don't think…" began Mike.

"Want to bet?" asked Terry. "He's back there right now thinking about how much lumber to buy to build a fence."

They all nodded.

"Do you think he knows he'd have to go before the board for a permit?"

They all shook their heads.

"That kind of thing can go on for months: waiting for permission, submitting designs—"

"—getting rejected and submitting more designs."

"Asking for public comment."

"The scheduling alone could take six months."

"And do you know what Roger would be like all that time?"

There was silence. They all knew.

"I'll talk to him," offered Joshua.

"Thanks, man."

"Yeah, thanks."

In a gesture he managed without affectation, Joshua tossed his golden mane to keep it out of his eyes. The first rays of morning sun shone on him, making him appear like a biblical image from a Sunday school poster.

"Sure," he said. "No problem."

He held up the coffee pot in his hand. "Anyone need a warm-up?"

Ben had a great friendship with Jim, whose primary job was not Fire Chief, but game warden with the Department of Natural Resources. Ben's love for animals and the outdoors had first inspired him to seek Jim out, but it was their rescue of Robert that had sealed their friendship.

Jim was a patient and knowledgeable teacher, and Ben always wanted more information. He knew that Jim was one of the rare adults who would admit to not knowing something, and he respected that. He also knew that Jim could be trusted. Perhaps because he had been raised in a household where honesty was a priority, Ben was drawn to integrity.

For his part, Jim hoped to find distraction in Ben's company. The meeting with Fiona had gone all right. He had noticed somewhat dispassionately how attractive she was, and then brushed it aside. Fiona hadn't indicated that she felt any awkwardness between them and, to an observer, their conversation would have appeared ordinary and business-like.

But just as Jim had begun to relax, she had turned her head, and he had caught the scent of her hair. His instantaneous reaction had left him almost breathless, and the hangover from this moment had stayed with him since.

Even in the swirl of his feelings, he had savored the experience of speaking with a thoughtful colleague. She had understood his suspicions and shared them and agreed with his plans to investigate. He hadn't fully realized how hungry he was for a meaningful conversation—one that wasn't comprised solely of the superficial banter that Island men reserved for one another.

Ironically, Ben's conversation had more substance than that of many of his elders. During his walks with Jim, Ben normally was asking one question after another on the subjects of wildlife, nature, and Jim's work as a ranger. Jim found these discussions always engaging and occasionally challenging.

They were walking together along one of the many trails in the woods along the lakefront when they encountered an illegal deer stand hidden in along the edge of the woods.

"How do you know it's illegal?" asked Ben, as they worked together to take it down.

"Because I know the landowner, and she doesn't permit hunting on her land."

Ben was silent for a moment. "I don't like hunting."

Jim glanced at the boy but said nothing.

"I used to think it was okay, but it bothers me."

"Why is that?"

"One minute, an animal is there, alive and beautiful, and the next, somebody comes along and just shoots it. It's not right."

"Eating and being eaten is a natural part of life," said Jim quietly. "You eat meat, don't you?"

Ben's face was alive with a sense of injustice.

"But people don't just kill to eat. I think some of them kill for fun."

Jim was silent. Ben was right, of course; there were a lot of people who thought nothing of an animal's life, and their casual cruelty was perfectly ordinary. Jim had to deal with it frequently in his work, and it disgusted him.

"I understand what you're saying, but we cull the herd in part to keep it healthy," he said. "You get too many animals in one space and they begin to starve."

Ben frowned. He knew all this. "But why do we only cull deer? Why not other animals?"

"Here on the Island, the deer are the only animals whose population grows unchecked."

"What about squirrels?" asked Ben.

"Well, they have natural predators here. I'll bet you can tell me what they are." This was an attempt to change the tenor of the conversation, and for the moment it worked.

"Eagles, foxes, coyotes…hawks." Ben looked at Jim. "Snakes?"

"I don't think any of the snakes on the Island are fast enough to get a squirrel. That nice fox snake we saw the other day probably eats mice and frogs, with maybe some baby birds or eggs now and then."

They had finished disassembling the stand and carefully stacked the pieces near the trail. Jim would come back for them later.

Ben looked thoughtful as they continued their walk. He couldn't be put off easily. "Mr. Olafsen shoots squirrels."

"A lot of animals can be shot legally any time: squirrels, possums, skunks, woodchucks, weasels…."

"Why?"

Jim took a deep breath as he thought about this. "Most people think they're pests, and the law is designed to protect humans and property."

"So that's culling, too. Just because we think they're pests, we get to kill them." Ben looked unhappy.

Jim was sympathetic, but he answered crisply. "We're the top of the food chain. We make these decisions." He looked directly at Ben, his tone changing. "I don't always like it, either."

Ben was frowning. "Why? Why is it okay sometimes? Why is it a crime to kill an eagle, but not a squirrel?"

Jim was frequently impressed by the way Ben thought things through.

"For one thing, it's a question of rarity. We don't have that many eagles. For a while there, they were verging on extinction. Now, they're making a nice comeback. But squirrels are everywhere. They're probably a good snack for an eagle, though."

Jim saw Ben's unhappy face, and they walked for a while in silence.

"What we need are wolves," said Ben. "That would take care of the herd."

"But wolves kill, too, right?"

"Not for fun!"

"Maybe not." Jim thought for a moment before speaking again. "Can you keep a secret?" Asking this, he already knew that Ben was extremely good at secrets.

Ben nodded.

"Well, the public doesn't know this yet, but we may have one."

Ben turned to him with excitement.

"A wolf? Here? On the Island?"

"I think it's possible, yes. I've seen some suggestive evidence, but I can't say anything officially until I'm sure, and I'm going to need to say something soon, both for the wolf's sake, and the public's. It doesn't happen often, but wolves can be dangerous."

He turned to Ben and looked very seriously at him.

"It's okay when you're with me, but I don't want you walking alone for a while, got it?"

"Okay, got it." Impatiently, Ben returned to what interested him. "How would it have gotten here?"

"It would have had to swim or walk across the ice."

"Wow."

"Yes, wow. We don't have many wolves in the county. Too many people."

"Is it...killing deer?"

"That's what you wanted, right?"

Ben looked pensive. "Maybe...I...don't know."

Jim gave a brief laugh. "I call that the beginning of wisdom."

❖ *Chapter 18*

From Fiona's earliest days on the Island, she and Nancy Iversson had been friends. They each saw something of themselves in the other, and the fact of their both being women alone in a tiny, closed society had naturally drawn them together.

Nancy was the last of one of the Island's most respected families. Her farm had been established by her ancestors in the nineteenth century, and she took great pride in its productivity and immaculate appearance. Running a farm is hard work for anyone, but for a woman alone it could be a burden almost beyond bearing.

This had never been true for Nancy. The farm was powered by her sense of calling and her deeply felt love for the place. Running this farm, she firmly believed, was what she had been put on this earth to do, and that sense of mission had burned brightly throughout her life.

As she got older, Nancy felt her energy waning a bit, and she considered herself fortunate to be able to engage the services of others when required. Even now she kept her hand in, and her competence and drive still put many a young man in her shadow.

Fiona had admired Nancy's courage and frankness from

the start, and as he came to know her, Pete did, too. Nancy sparkled around Pete; she liked him and admired him, and Fiona felt that this approval was the ultimate imprimatur. The three of them became good friends.

Her proximity with Pete and Fiona's love for one another, however, was not altogether positive for Nancy. She had been lonely over the years and had mostly shrugged it off. She had never married—she liked to say that she had never met a man she couldn't work circles around—and this story of her indifference to love was part of her almost legendary reputation. But Nancy could not see Pete and Fiona together without wishing with all her being that she had been able to find such a partnership. Their ease with one another, their jokes, their passionate respect were what she would have wanted, had she been able to find it.

Perhaps out of loneliness, perhaps from her pleasure in Pete and Fiona's company, Nancy had decided suddenly to begin hosting dinner parties. Fiona, who enjoyed these events enormously, noticed that the invitations were most likely to be issued when Pete was in town, but she didn't mind. She was used to his popularity.

Fiona was continually fascinated by the way he had been so easily accepted into Island society. At first glance, Pete would seem an unlikely fit with local sensibilities; although Fiona was often spoken of as a city girl, Pete's background was far more cosmopolitan than hers. He had, however, a gift of making himself welcome wherever he went.

He was not a particularly outgoing person, but he had a quiet confidence mixed with a natural enjoyment of life that seemed to radiate from him no matter what the circumstance. He had a quick wit and was good at making people laugh. When combined with his curiosity, a genuine interest in what was going on around him, and an almost palpable respect for others, these qualities gave him an irresistible magnetism. People just wanted to be near him. Fiona, who had, after all, been an Island resident first, often felt that she was merely part of Pete's entourage, but she felt no resentment, only a kind of secret delight.

Tonight, they were gathered around Nancy's table with Nika and Pali. Nancy was a good cook and showed a surprising penchant for formality. Her table was set on a hand-embroidered tablecloth and glittered with her grandmother's crystal and china and, Fiona noticed, sterling flatware that seemed to be in the style of a hundred years ago.

Pete commented on it admiringly.

"My grandmother came here from Chicago in 1921 when she married my grandfather," said Nancy. "She was from quite a wealthy family and brought all the things a Gold Coast bride should have: crystal, china, silver, an entire trousseau of hand-stitched linens…They were just ordinary farmers, but apparently she used her beautiful things every night." Nancy paused reminiscently. "It won't surprise you that I have rarely taken it out of the cupboard, but lately I've decided I might as well." She laughed a trifle sadly. "I think my grandmother would approve."

"What must that have been like?" asked Pete, "to come from a life of affluence in Chicago to the Island in the nineteen-twenties?

"If it was hard, she never said so. They weren't rich, to be sure, but my grandparents had an almost mystical love for one another. My mother used to say that as a child she almost felt left out."

Nika smiled gently. She loved Pali the same way. Was it mystical, she wondered? It did seem like a miracle to her, when so many of her friends were complaining about their husbands, to have a man she loved and admired after so many years. Pali caught her glance across the table, and they had a silent moment of communication unnoticed by the others.

"Would you have been able to live on the Island back then?"

Fiona tilted her head to one side as she considered. "Probably not," she said, looking slightly apologetic. "I've barely made it as it is."

"It was hard, that's for sure," commented Pali, "But then, life has been hard for most of history."

"Things may be easier, but when you think about it, many of us live meek and inadequate lives in this century," said Fiona. "We're too dependent, too squeamish about life and death, and filled with comfortable prejudices."

Pete looked at her with interest. "Are you speaking of your own life? I've never thought of you as either meek or inadequate." His expression held both affection and a genuine understanding of her nature. "Or dependent, for that matter. In what ways would you describe yourself as 'meek?'"

Watching them both, Pali smiled at this. Meek was not a word anyone would use to describe Fiona.

Fiona looked sheepish. "Well, compared to you, I am, certainly. But there are a few things I don't really like to admit I'm afraid of."

Everyone around the table looked at her expectantly.

"You can't stop there, you know," said Nancy. "Come on, out with it."

Fiona took a deep breath. "Well, guns, for instance. Guns scare me. I know it's not the usual view around here, but when I was in Chicago, I spent too much time reporting on crime not to be frightened of them. And small planes. I hate them." She looked over at Pete. "I hate that you fly in them."

Pete's face took on a more serious expression. "I didn't know that."

"Well, frankly," said Nancy, "I'd be afraid if I didn't have guns. Would never have been able to sleep at night, alone here." She looked at Fiona appraisingly. "I think you ought to have at least one, living alone so much as you do." Nancy gave Pete a meaningful glance.

He appeared not to notice.

"I can teach you, if you like," she added. "Ben and I have target practice regularly. You could join us any time." She turned to Nika and Pali.

"He's getting to be quite a good shot, and he's very responsible."

Fiona leaned across the table. "Do you shoot, Nika?"

"I used to. Used to go hunting with my dad. But not really anymore."

"She can shoot, though," said Pali. "She's got a deadly aim."

Nika laughed. "I got a sharpshooter certification in Gun Club when I was in high school, but that's a long time ago. I don't think they even have gun clubs in schools anymore. Can you even imagine?"

Nancy stood up and began clearing the table. "Well, if you're going to have a gun, the real danger is not knowing how to use it properly." Nancy looked around at her guests. "Who wants pie?"

Young Rex, her Labrador pup who had been lying quietly at her feet, got up and followed her into the kitchen. He certainly wanted pie.

Chapter 19

Fiona's election to public office had not accorded her sufficient celebrity to change the name associated with her property. It had been "the Old Goeden place" for more than a hundred years, and a mere few seasons' residence were not sufficient to change Island habit. This wouldn't have been noticed except that suddenly, the Old Goeden place was figuring prominently in Island gossip. By now the rumors of arson were everywhere, and the fire at Fiona's barn more than a year ago was included in the speculation.

"I don't remember ever having so many fires. Something's not right."

"More like somebody's not right. Fires like this don't set themselves."

"Started with the barn at the Old Goeden place."

"Think so? That far back?"

"Not that far. Only a year or two."

"I hear that Martin kid is home. The one that got caught with an eagle."

Heads bobbed. "Never liked that kid."

"Spoiled, that's his problem."

"Thought he was at military school or something. When did he get back?"

"Not sure. Saw him at Mann's the other day."

"Hmm."

"He was here last fall, when we had that grass fire."

"Wouldn't put much past him."

Everyone fell quiet as they considered this. No one disagreed.

After the dinner party, Pete and Fiona were the last to leave. When the door closed, and they set off together, Nancy stood at the door listening to the happy murmur of their voices as they walked down her long driveway. The sudden sparkle of Fiona's laughter floated back to her on the breeze, and a cold desolation crept around Nancy's heart like an icy mist. After the laughter and camaraderie of the dinner party, the house felt more than usually quiet.

Maybe, she thought to herself, if she hadn't been so consumed by the farm, she might have been able to leave the Island and find someone. But there had never been any time. Maybe if her brother had returned from Vietnam, he would have shared in the work, leaving her free to lift her head and look around. But he had not returned, nor had any news of him.

Normally able to shrug off circumstance, lately she found she could not. The contrast of Pete and Fiona's good luck with her lack of it shook her to her roots. For the first time, Nancy's solitary life felt like a deep and shattering loss. She felt no resentment toward them. She shared in their joy. But the contrast with her own life had never been so clear. "Why?" she asked herself. "Why now, after a life of purpose and contentment?" But she could not find an answer.

Nancy did not believe in regret. Life didn't wait for you; you needed to straighten up and get on with it, and that's what she endeavored to do.

She supposed she was getting soft in her old age. She reached down and scratched Rex's head as he stood beside her.

Young Ben had been right in his advice to get a dog: having Rex helped. His love and youthful joy were a constant source of pleasure.

But still, there was this emptiness.

Pete put his arm around Fiona's shoulder as they were walking down Nancy's driveway to the car, and she leaned her head against him. The spring peepers were in full voice, and although it was a clear night, the soft mists rising from the warming earth somewhat obscured the stars.

"In the winter, I forget how beautiful spring is," said Fiona. "I actually love the snow and the cold. I find it invigorating. But the change of season is so dramatic that it feels as if it's a different place, and then I realize that I love that, too."

They both breathed in the damp air, sweet with the scent of young things. It was the time of year when, in stillness, the sounds of plants growing could be heard as a soft, persistent rustle, a ceaseless twisting and yearning toward sky and sun, even in the waning light. In the distance, they could hear the lake, too, its waves slow and steady in the evening air.

"Want to walk by the shore?"

"Of course."

It was still early, and by the time they arrived at the beach, the sun still sat above the horizon, colored red by the heavy, moist air. As they strolled among the rocks at School House Beach, they were each immersed in their own thoughts.

The late spring night was prolonging the sunshine, and the colors of sunset were gathering and shifting with the waves. The nights were still lengthening, and the sun seemed to lie against the water with a soft shimmer that made it difficult to distinguish where one stopped and the other began.

Pete was collecting rocks to skip, a skill he had developed to fine art. He had a mind that needed always to be doing something, and his perfection of small things like this were a part of his character and of his well-being.

Fiona's head was full of dreams. Her term as Town Chairman would be coming to a close, and she was eager to relinquish the steady stream of meetings and obligations that holding office entailed. She wanted to write a book; to travel; and she was ready to leave the Island. Not forever. She was bonded irrevocably to the place. But she needed to be in the World for a while, if only to be able to appreciate the mystery of what was now home.

Pete was suddenly behind her, his hands on her arms as he turned her around to face him. She stumbled on the rocks and fell against him laughing. He kissed her and looked into her eyes with great seriousness.

"I have," he said, with just the smallest glint in his eyes, "a small, earnest question."

Fiona, smiling, was unprepared for what came next.

"How about I teach you how to shoot? It's not good to be afraid of things. It's limiting. I worry about you."

Fiona wondered what he would say if he knew how much of her fear was about him. She glanced at him and then back at her feet. "If it were a worrying contest, I would win hands down."

He looked contrite. "Maybe so. But still."

"I'm not sure. I need to think about it."

Fiona knew that this was another perfect moment to ask him her questions, to learn about what drove him, and why even his own remarks suggested that she should be worrying. But here, on the beach, with him so near, her fears receded. It was when he was away that she worried most—when what he did and where he went created an emptiness that she filled with anxiety. Did Pete have something dark hidden away that he had not told, and she had not seen?

She knew that asking would make it seem again as if she did not trust him. And that wasn't it. Not really. But as they grew closer, it seemed more important than ever that she should know.

They walked in silence on the stony beach, their feet slipping occasionally as the rocks moved beneath them, and gradually the light diminished to a faint, rose glow.

All it once, with an odd sense that they were being watched, they both looked up, scanning the woods that came down to the shore. At first they saw nothing, and then, without shifting his gaze, Pete silently put his hand on Fiona's arm, and she saw what he saw.

There, just at the edge of the cedar trees, about twenty yards off, were a pair of glittering, golden green eyes. The eyes did not belong to a deer, which usually showed white or red, and they were too close to the ground. The shape wasn't right, either, but Fiona could not identify exactly how she knew.

Pete made a faint questioning motion with his head. Just as faintly, Fiona shook hers. The three sets of eyes gazed at one another for what seemed a very long time, and then the golden ones slipped away back among the cedars. Still watching, Pete and Fiona listened for the rustle of retreating steps in the woods, but the wind had come up, and the rush of the waves and the moving leaves made it impossible to discern any other sound.

Keeping their silence, they made their way back to the road cautiously and quickly, watching and listening. They were wondering what it was that they had seen, and whether it was still with them, silently trailing them along the path.

Chapter 20

Ben had learned his passion for baseball from his father, but it was enhanced by the simple reality that there wasn't that much for an eleven-year-old to do in the summer. He played on a team, and now that the weather was improving, he felt the sweet, nostalgic joy of a new season, when all hopes would be fulfilled.

Ben's good eye and accurate arm had earned him a position at shortstop, and he'd had a particularly good afternoon drilling double plays. Although he wouldn't have thought of himself this way, Ben probably did a little too much thinking, and the focus on throwing the ball and catching it was a relief to his busy mind. He felt good. He was humming under his breath and looking forward to dinner when he noticed Caleb loitering near the backstop.

Caleb stared at Ben, and Ben stared back. Ben had been embarrassed by his reaction the last time they had seen one another. This time he had to hold his own. He looked directly at Caleb, then walked past him on his way to his bike. It wasn't running away, he assured himself. He had been going to leave anyway.

Caleb followed Ben to the bike rack.

"That's a pretty crappy bike, you know that?"

Ben unconsciously straightened his shoulders but didn't

turn around. He continued the process of tucking his glove into his bike bag. Ben's bike wasn't new, but it was nothing to be ashamed of. His dad had helped him purchase it from the hardware store last year when the end-of-season rentals were offered for a discount. It was not, however, equal to the high-end titanium bike that Caleb's parents had purchased for him in Chicago.

"Your dad such a failure he can't even buy you a decent bike?"

Ben's temper rose, and he made a sharp intake of breath, but he continued to ignore Caleb's taunts. He knew Caleb's purpose, and he did not intend to give him the satisfaction of reacting.

"You're such a little dill weed. Little Island boy." Caleb laughed nastily. "Probably never even been to a decent city. Little dork."

Ben was angry, whether it was the insult to his bike, or his father, or the Island, he couldn't say. It didn't matter; it was an attack on all his loyalties. He could feel his heart beating faster, and the urge to retaliate was growing. Ben got on his bike and summoned all the self-restraint he had learned. He looked at Caleb and smiled.

"Hey, nice to see you, too, Caleb. You take care, now." He spoke with all the patronizing kindness he could muster, as if he were the adult and Caleb the child.

Caleb shouted an obscenity.

Ben felt a sense of satisfaction. He had gotten under Caleb's skin far more effectively than if he had engaged in his insults. As he pedaled off, Ben was astonished at how good it felt—almost as good as throwing a punch.

But not quite.

Chapter 21

Fiona dreamed that she was trying to choose between two calendars that had been presented to her by some invisible being. There was a bright calendar and a dark calendar. She knew she could only choose one. She yearned for the mysteries and beauty of the dark calendar, but she found it difficult to think of never having light. She reached her hand out to touch each of them, to feel how it would be to have only one or the other. Unwilling to choose, she backed away.

She looked up and saw, deep in the darkness behind her, the glittering eyes of a wolf. She felt no urgency and no fear, but she knew that the wolf was waiting, and that somehow her decision would alter his path.

Fiona and Pete stood in the back pasture of Nancy Iversson's farm late one afternoon. It had been a warm day, with the sweet taste of early summer in the air.

Fiona was standing with her feet planted, listening carefully as Pete talked her through the procedure. "Tell me what you do first," he said.

"Check the safety. Then check the chamber."

They had spent two evenings together as he had instructed her in the fundamentals of gun safety, ammunition, and the pros and cons of various guns. He had borrowed a number of them from friends on the Island so that she could see and understand. Pete was a good teacher: calm, clear, and able to streamline and simplify complex information. Fiona paid painstaking attention. The guns frightened her.

Pete's patience seemed infinite.

"It's good to be a little scared, but not too much. You can't afford to undermine your own confidence, but you also need to be extremely clear about what you have the capacity to do."

"The possibilities of all the bad things that could happen keep coming into my mind."

"Use those possibilities to think out your strategy. How can you prevent a worst-case scenario from actually happening? What steps can you take to be safe?" He looked at her politely, as a teacher to a student. "Tell me your worst fear."

Fiona just stared at him. How could she tell him that her worst fear involved him? That his expertise was too perfect, too practiced? That she was wondering what kinds of shooting he actually did?

"Articulate what scares you most," said Pete calmly. "Then we'll talk it through."

When she continued to be silent, he changed his tactic to take the pressure off. "Just think for each individual instance: What could make that possible? How would that happen? What can you do to stop that from happening?"

She remembered Nika's remarks at dinner; she had

expertise in shooting, but Fiona didn't find it alarming. So why did the subject arouse so much uncertainty about Pete? The answer was obvious: because he never spoke of it. It was the vagueness about where he went and what he did that allowed her to imagine that anything was possible. She chastised herself for her feelings, but she couldn't shake them, and when he looked at her, so reasonable, so calm, and so understanding, she felt even more embarrassed at what she feared.

Now she was standing here, ready to fire. The target was set up on a bale of hay that stood against a hill. She braced herself as he had taught her, one hand cradling the other, her thumb on one hand linked to the finger of the other.

"Are you ready? Remember: breathe as you fire."

She nodded, steadied herself again, breathed, and fired. The recoil on this little Smith and Wesson was slight. It was Nancy's favorite gun.

"Okay. That was good. Steady yourself again. Check your stance. Breathe."

Fiona followed his directions. After six shots, she put her arms down, flipped the safety on the gun, and looked up.

"That's some pretty fine shooting," he said. "You were close to the center each time; a nice little cluster. You have a knack for this."

In spite of herself, Fiona felt a little rush of delight. Shooting was fun.

Chapter 22 ❖

When the phone call came, it marked, as these calls always do, the end of an era. Life, from that moment, would never be the same. There would be happiness again, even joy and some peace, but always touched by an edge of grief and regret, sometimes jagged and sometimes worn away. And though it might recede from time to time, it would forever be nearby, ready to snag the heart.

Each new grief has its own character, and each represents a new and diminished world. For children, the world they are born into is the world as it should be. The nostalgia of old people for the old days is a nostalgia for a time when their worlds were still intact, all the loved and even the unloved people of childhood still there, vibrant and looming, unchanged and seemingly unchangeable. The slow shifting of life's landscape—as, one after another, the human landmarks of life pass away—leaves an increasingly alien world, where the elderly no longer feel they belong, and where there is little real comfort from those who have the capacity to console. There is only the condescending kindness of the young, who carry their youth with an unearned air of superiority. Surviving these changes requires an attitude of acceptance and determination.

Fiona thought of all this as she stood on the rail of the ferry, heading toward the mainland. The call had come a few hours before. It had been her father, his voice its usual calm, but with an undercurrent Fiona recognized with alarm.

"It's Uncle Victor," he'd said. "He's asking for you."

Pete had offered to come, but Fiona did not feel equal to the pressures of an introduction at this moment.

Now she was headed to the small town in Pennsylvania where her uncle lay dying. The flight from Milwaukee was not until early the following morning. She did not know if she would be there in time.

Chapter 23

Shortly after she graduated from college, Fiona received a rare phone call from her Uncle Victor.

"Why don't you come to visit me in Paris this summer? I'll pay your way."

Fiona hesitated. She had arranged an internship at a major newspaper, and it would be an important experience for her resume.

"I don't know, Uncle Victor. I'm supposed to work for the Trib. I'm starting next week."

Uncle Victor harrumphed. "You know what I think about journalism. But never mind that. You'll probably work your whole life. Now is the time to enjoy yourself a little."

"But I do enjoy working, Uncle Victor."

He harrumphed again. He would never admit it, but this was one of the reasons he admired his niece. "They say old fools are the worst. I'm not so sure. Well, you think about it. Let me know by the end of the week."

Fiona hung up, feeling regretful.

By the end of the week, however, with the help of daily calls from Uncle Victor, Fiona had come to see things his way. Why not take a summer to have fun before her working life began? Uncle Victor was not a particularly warm person, but he was intelligent company, and the allure of an all-expense paid trip was, in the end, irresistible.

He flew her to Paris first class and had one of his people meet her at the airport with a car. It was her first trip abroad. She emerged from the buzz of customs, baggage, and little sleep, into the exhaust-scented air of Charles de Gaulle airport in the early morning and felt, in every way, the foreign quality of life. The whole world looked and sounded different. She sat back in the car and watched the traffic, noting the unfamiliar cars and the sounds of the their horns, the graffiti everywhere, the snippets of green near apartment doorways, the billboards with ads for unknown products, the chirpy sounds of morning radio mixed with a new language and French music.

She entered the lobby of the luxury hotel where a room had been booked for her. It was scented with flowers and the morning's coffee, and she found that she liked being addressed as Madame.

She spent her days on her own, wandering the city according to whim. Sitting alone in a café on a beautiful day, watching others interact, or seeing a great work of art without someone to share it with had been painfully lonely. But it had also been a time of great personal discovery. Her conversational French was polished on the scorn of French waiters, and her growing intimacy with the city paralleled a growing understanding of herself.

In the evenings, Uncle Victor would be waiting in the lobby of the hotel to take her to dinner. They went to the best restaurants in the city, some of them famous, some only tiny corners in obscure neighborhoods. Afterward, they would sit in a café until late in the evening, chatting or reading the papers.

Her Uncle Victor's comfort in the world intrigued her, and she admired him for it. On the occasions they went to a museum or cultural event together, his comments were sensitive and knowledgeable. He taught her how to look at paintings, how to appreciate music, how to taste wine. He was not doting but treated her like a respected peer.

Looking back, Fiona saw that the summer she had spent with Uncle Victor had changed her life. She would always be grateful to him for that.

Ben and Pali were playing catch in the backyard after dinner. Even though it was June, the night was cold, and the ball stung when it hit the glove.

As they threw, the rhythm of the ball hitting their gloves seemed almost like a pulse, and its steady beat had an oddly soothing quality that often drew out conversation. It wasn't necessary to think about throwing and catching, so the mind was able to roam. Each throw seemed to be the moment for speaking, suspended momentarily by the catch, so the conversation had an almost syncopated rhythm that was punctuated by the ball. Speak, throw, catch. Speak, throw, catch.

"People are bad," said Ben, seemingly from out of nowhere.

Pali caught the ball, and threw it back, but said nothing.

"They lie, they do bad things, and they don't care about who they hurt."

Pali caught.

He threw. "That's often true," he said. Catch.

"But you have to remember that not everybody is like that." Throw. "Your friends, Jim, Fiona, and Nancy for example. They're not like that." Catch. "Your grandparents. Your mom and I are not like that." Throw. "You know a lot of people who try to do what's right."

Ben was in no mood to be comforted.

Catch. "What good does it do to be good when everybody else is bad?" Throw. "You do all the work, and the bad people just get the benefit of it." Catch. "You save the world, they go around trying to wreck it." Throw.

Pali felt at a loss. Ben was too young for cynicism. He held the ball a moment while he spoke.

"The battle between good and evil is the fundamental struggle in life. Good and Evil; Life and Death; Justice and Injustice. Even animals are in a struggle to survive, and not everyone can win."

He threw. "It's all a fight, Ben, and you have to be on one side or the other." Catch. "There's no sitting it out." Throw.

Catch. "But why? Why does it have to be so hard?" Throw.

Catch. "Maybe it wouldn't be worth it if it were easy. Maybe struggling is what we're meant to do." Throw.

Catch.

Nika called from the door. "Pali, can you get the hose out before you come in?"

"Sure." Pali set his glove down on the patio table. Ben followed him to the garage, still tossing the ball in one hand.

"Do you believe in God?"

This was another unexpected conversational turn. Pali hesitated before he answered.

"Yes, but maybe not the way other people do." He thought for a moment before asking in an oddly unfatherly way, "Do you?"

"I used to. I thought I did. Now..." he kicked at the dirt.

Pali stopped re-coiling the recalcitrant hose onto the cart for a moment, then returned to his task. "Even the angels are in a struggle between the forces of light and dark."

Ben looked up suddenly as if hearing an idea for the first time.

"Do you believe in angels?" he asked.

"Yes," said Pali firmly, as he hooked up the hose to the spigot. "I do."

He brushed his hands on his jeans. "We still have some light. Let's have another catch."

After a solitary workday, Oliver Robert was restless. He sat at his desk in the little green office of the Town Chairman and stared into space. He fervently wished for a night out on the town—a chic restaurant, a concert or the theater, and the company of friends. The cultural life of the Island did not permit a great deal of variety. He had gotten tired of the same restaurants, and the concerts—although occasionally quite good— were only intermittent.

As for friends, well, he had to admit there weren't any, and with Fiona gone from the office today, he was more isolated than usual. He could barely admit to himself that he rather missed her. It was true that his role last fall in determining that the Island's finances were in rather better shape than anyone had thought had earned him respect and helped to solidify a position for him in the community, but it was not the same as truly belonging.

He was quite aware that he did not exactly fit in. He was not an outdoorsman, nor did he want to be. The rough and tumble of male life here had no appeal. His foray into musical theater had been a success of sorts, and although he had big plans to continue, the results had been far from professional. And while there were people here with serious intellectual interests, their lives seemed full, with no room for him to join in.

In moments of personal reckoning, he suspected that he was laughed at. He was accustomed to that. He had always been laughed at. The psychic familiarity of it was deep and painful, but his wounds were mostly tucked away out of sight. No, he needed an outlet. Something to do that did not involve going outside in all weather and killing things.

He was resourceful, he thought to himself. He could think of something. He would treat himself this evening to an online search for some new books. He sighed and shrugged to himself and looked back at the work before him. He was assisting the town clerk with the tax rolls. It was just the kind of thing that engaged his accountant's heart.

But when it came time to leave, Oliver hesitated. Another evening of shopping for books and reading hadn't much appeal. Somehow the thought of going home to silence was depressing, and he was in no mood for the church committee meeting that had been listed in this week's bulletin. He turned instead to Nelsen's, where he could at least be assured of running into someone who would say hello.

As Oliver walked into Nelsen's, a few people waved in casual recognition, and he took a seat at the bar with a feeling of welcome. This was why he had come. The bartender, Eddie, looking up from another transaction, nodded his greeting, and Oliver took a few moments to contemplate while he waited.

In his old life, he'd never have gone to a bar by himself, but here he was, less than a year into his residency on the Island and drinking alone. He supposed this was how it started: boredom, loneliness, and depression. Weren't these the things he had come to the Island to avoid? He would allow himself only one drink. Then he would go home and follow up with his original plans.

"Old fashioned?" asked Eddie, already beginning to reach for the brandy. "Sweet?"

Oliver nodded. This was something else Oliver hadn't done before: drink cocktails. He had been a wine drinker, but over the cold winter, wine had seemed inadequate, and now the taste for something stronger was ingrained. Besides, he liked having a usual drink, one that Eddie assumed he would want, even if he wasn't always in the mood for it. This little ritual made him feel that maybe he did belong.

Eddie put the cocktail before him and began polishing glasses with a quick practiced style that Oliver found interesting to watch.

"Fiona be gone long?" asked Eddie.

Everyone on the Island—including Eddie—would know as much about Fiona's business as he did, but Oliver accepted it for what it was: an easy door to conversation.

Oliver shrugged. "She said it would be a few days. Her uncle isn't going to last long, apparently."

Eddie nodded. He knew all this, of course, through Island osmosis, the process by which all things seeped into the collective consciousness and were known by everyone, even though many of those things might not be strictly true.

"Shame," he said.

"I suppose," said Oliver, with the easy distance of the casual observer. "But I didn't get the impression they were especially close."

As he said this, Oliver felt a stab of poignancy at the thought of dying unmourned. Fiona's passing grief over a distant relative was regrettable, maybe even hard, he thought, but why did conversations dwell on the living and pass so lightly over the universal tragedy of mortality, of a life coming to close? This, he supposed, was a form of denial. No one wants to think about their own finite reality. Death always happens to other people. Even professional conversations about the process of dying—or for that matter, aging—always refer to "they" and "them," never to "we" or "us."

Oliver flashed through a memory of his grandmother in her last weeks. "What do you want for Christmas?" he had asked her, trying to make light-hearted conversation. She did not hesitate, speaking as her hands worked to smooth the knitted blanket on her lap. "More time on this earth." The hard truth of her reply shoved away the chatty cheerfulness he had been trying to create. Oliver could only nod. The fear and desperation of facing the end sat between them in the silence.

Feeling now his own fear creeping around the edges, Oliver pushed these thoughts aside.

"What do you do for fun?" he asked. Eddie always seemed so steady, so perfectly at ease with himself. Oliver observed this and envied it.

"For fun?" Eddie held the glass he was polishing up to the light, examining it for spots, and ran his cloth around it again as he spoke.

"I listen to a lot of music. Do a lot of reading."

"Do you hunt? Fish?" Oliver was genuinely curious. Was there at least one male here who didn't participate in that part of the local culture?

Eddie shrugged. "I don't hunt anymore. Don't enjoy it. Fishing sometimes, though. It's peaceful."

There was a summons from the other end of the bar, and Eddie went to respond. When he returned, he picked up the cloth and began polishing again.

"How'd you end up here on the Island?" asked Oliver.

"Kind of by accident, I guess. When I first came back here, I wasn't planning to stay long."

"You were from the Island?"

"Nope. Green Bay. Family used to come up here every summer, though. Went to college for a couple years. Got restless. Quit. Thought I'd work for a while and figure things out. Got a summer job. Never left."

This succinct account of more than a decade was rather admirable, Oliver thought. He respected efficiency in all its forms.

"You have to make the choice to be here," continued Eddie, still polishing. "I don't think I could live anywhere else, but it can be hard sometimes. It gets small."

Eddie's sharp eyes were evaluating Oliver Robert as he spoke. Couldn't be easy for the guy. A bit odd. Didn't fit in. Definitely not a typical Islander. "Know what saved me?"

Oliver shook his head and looked interested.

"Books."

This was disappointing. Oliver already read continually; he had been hoping for something useful.

"Not just reading, but courses. Great Books courses. Better than going to college. And cheaper." Eddie's face took on a dreamy look. "Conversations with the great minds of history. Changed my life."

Oliver was silent, thinking. Eddie was underestimating a key difference between them. He was a bartender. He saw people all the time. People liked him, confided in him, trusted him. He liked himself, for that matter. Books were all well and good, but Eddie wasn't really lonely. He was included in things. He was one of them.

This, Oliver knew, was not something he could hope for. Besides, the books, for Eddie, were a respite from people. What Oliver needed was a respite from solitude.

Sighing, he defied his own resolution and ordered another drink.

Chapter 24

Fiona dreamed that she was accompanied by the wolf. He was a silent companion who walked by her side, pausing sometimes to look back at her with his glittering green-gold eyes. Although he seemed more companionable than frightening, he was, nevertheless, intimidating, and she moved cautiously, watching him at all times. They walked together through the woods, through the fields, and down the middle of the Main Road of the Island. Tonight, in her sleep, she knew she was in a cheap hotel near the airport, and she slept fitfully, knowing the wolf lay outside the door of her room, whether to protect or attack she could not be sure.

When she woke, it felt more like it had been a visitation than a dream.

It was early on a hazy spring morning as the plane took off from Milwaukee and banked to the east toward the lake. Fiona leaned her head against the window of the plane and watched the earth below.

The lake was calm, almost smooth. There were already

many small boats, their wakes like small white arrows in the blue water, and a big ore freighter, just leaving port and heading north. Fiona thought about what it would feel like to be on one of those boats in the early sun, possibly escaping from a day at work, feeling the cool, damp air, heading out for the open water. She loved being at sea.

Further out, in its waveless surface, the pale blue water had fault lines where, she supposed, the terrain of the lakebed changed, and the flow of the water shifted to follow its ridges and crevices. The lines looked like veins or stretch marks on the surface of the water, and Fiona pondered on the link between the things of creation—of human form, of lake form, of all things. She thought of the saltwater in her veins and the fish swimming invisibly below her and, for that moment, forgot the purpose of her journey and felt strangely and inexpressibly happy.

Particularly with Fiona out of town, Ben's summer schedule was full of responsibilities, but out of kindness, he tried to find time for Noah. They met on their bikes across the street from Fiona's house at the post office.

"What do you do there, anyway?" asked Noah when Ben showed up, slightly sweaty and wearing dirty clothes.

"Lots of things," said Ben with modest pride. "Look after Ms. Campbell's goat, mainly, but other things, too. Sometimes she lets me cut the lawn or plant things for her. Once, I taught her Morse Code."

"Why'd she want to know that?"

"She said it might be useful someday."

"How'd you know it?"

"We learned it in the scouts, remember?"

"I forgot most of that stuff," said Noah.

Ben shrugged. "My dad says you remember best the things that interest you. What interests you? Got any hobbies?" Ben realized as he asked this that he knew very little about Noah's inner life. He rarely spoke, as if he were accustomed to having no one listen.

Noah shrugged. "I like doughnuts."

Ben nodded, but he found this answer very strange indeed. Ben was interested in everything.

"Want to go down the road and get some doughnuts? Joey's should still be open."

"Okay."

Ben was already on his bike and making circles in the parking lot. "Sometimes, if it's really late, the lady lets me have one for free. Let's go find out."

Noah got on his bike, wobbled a bit, and followed his friend down the road. Ben was riding fast. After a day of work, he was hungry.

Uncle Victor looked old and small lying in his hospital bed. Always thin, he had lost too much weight, and his skin was yellow. Even knowing it was serious, Fiona had not imagined he would be in this condition. She had to discipline herself not to show her shock. But when he opened his eyes, they had their old sparkle.

"My dear," he said, reaching for her hand. "You've come."

Fiona came to the bedside and took his hand, her smile a bit too bright.

"Here I am," she said in a voice that felt as false as her smile. "Returned from the wilderness."

Uncle Victor smiled faintly and leaned back against his pillows.

"I've been wanting to speak with you." He closed his eyes and was silent for so long that Fiona began to be alarmed, but she could see his breath rising, so she waited, anxiously watching him.

At last he opened his eyes again. "I'm afraid I need to conduct some business." He looked up at her. "Sit down and stop hovering over me. I'm not going to die in the next five minutes."

Fiona sat but held onto his hand. Uncle Victor had never been a physically affectionate man. Although he was famous for his charm, he had often seemed brusque and in a hurry. Perhaps this was why the sojourn in Paris had been so remarkable. Uncle Victor's admiration for her had been expressed in his respect for her intelligence and by his sharp comments on her decisions. He had not pretended to approve of her choice of careers. "Journalism is public charity work. Earn your fortune first, then publish a magazine as a hobby," he had told her.

She had laughed and brushed off most of his criticisms, but even from a distance, he had instilled in her an inner voice of self-preservation that served her well.

Her father, never a fan of Uncle Victor's, had spoken seriously to her in her youth about following her own instincts and not allowing herself to be bullied. Victor, his late wife's brother, was, in his view, not to be trusted. There had been multiple marriages—all disastrous—and Victor had managed, despite his divorces, to keep his fortune intact, perhaps because he was always involved in some new financial scheme, perhaps because of his ephemeral charm.

But Fiona had never been troubled by her uncle's approach to life or familial relations, and her blithe indifference to his advice had somehow endeared her to him above all the other cousins, who tended to stammer and shuffle their feet when he spoke to them.

"Now, I want you to listen to me." He spoke in the tone of command he had been using all his life to get what he wanted.

Fiona waited silently.

"You know I'm a wealthy man, but money is like a child. You have to watch it and nurture it. You can't just leave it in the care of anyone and expect everything to go well. Open that drawer over there."

He pointed to the nightstand just out of his reach and paused to gather strength as Fiona rose to follow his instructions and returned with the notebook she'd found in the drawer.

"You aren't like your cousins. You have sense. I am leaving you in charge, but they'll have a little share, just to keep them from bothering you. I have finance people who will do the actual management, but you will be the primary beneficiary. Money can ruin people, Fiona. Too much can be worse than not enough, but I don't think it will ruin you. The others, well…." He made a little snorting noise as he turned the pages of the notebook that could have been distaste or laughter. Fiona couldn't tell.

"I've made a few notes here about where things are and some ideas for how you are to use the money. It's all formalized in my estate. Most of it, of course, will be for your own use as you choose. I worry about you up there in the middle of nowhere. You need help."

Fiona smiled. "I'm fine, Uncle Victor. You shouldn't worry."

Uncle Victor harrumphed dismissively. "The main thing you need to know is the name of my attorney, Dirk Richards, in New York. It's there on the list. Call him when I'm dead. Or call him now. It doesn't much matter."

He coughed painfully and closed his eyes again. Fiona's thoughts flew from the serious to the irrelevant as she worked to come up with an appropriate response. Finally, urged on by the weight of lengthening silence, she spoke. "I respect your confidence in me, Uncle Victor, but I'd be lying if I said I weren't worried about how to handle this."

"Worry all you want. That's why you'll do all right with it." He opened his eyes again and seemed to be inspecting her. "You don't have to worry about making a profit. That will be other people's job. Just don't let your cousins talk you into frittering your money away on their petty wants. I've set something aside for each of them, which they can't touch except for the interest, so you can forget about it. Richards will explain all that to them."

"Now get me that envelope." He indicated the drawer again.

Fiona did as he asked.

"No, it's for you," he said, as she started to hand it to him. "There's a document in there I want you to sign. I didn't have as much time as I'd hoped to arrange things. You'll have to make do." He gave a rasping laugh. "Never really thought I'd die, to tell you the truth."

Fiona's misgivings grew as she opened the envelope. There was just one sheet of paper, with a place for her signature, her name already neatly typed below.

She read it over. It seemed an ordinary enough document, acknowledging her acceptance of the terms of the trust, which included his properties. Every instinct she had told her that to sign now, without advice or consideration, was a bad idea. But there was Uncle Victor on his deathbed, willing her to do this last thing for him.

She picked up the pen and signed.

He closed his eyes. "Now go away. I want to sleep, and I can't with you sitting there watching to see whether I'm still breathing. Come back at dinnertime. That's when all the televisions blaring around here annoy me the most. You'll be a distraction."

Fiona touched his hand. "All right. I'll see you later. Keep breathing."

She bent over to kiss his cheek.

"Take the notebook."

The wheezing sound that was his laugh followed her out of the room.

M uch to Elisabeth's disappointment, the Grand Opening took place without Fiona. The old hotel had never been better. Along with its freshly completed renovations, the place was filled with touches of Elisabeth's gracious perfectionism: shining glass, polished wood, flowers, linens, beautiful but not overdone arrangements of food, and a soft proprietary scent of citrus that entranced without overwhelming.

Outside, Rocco mingled with the guests as if they were sheep and he their shepherd. Carefully moving so as not to startle or block them, never begging for food or love, he deigned to be spoken to or caressed by those who admired him, occasionally honoring a chosen subject by rolling on his back to have his tummy rubbed. But mostly, he was on duty, and vigilant in his inspection of all comers.

The Islanders had turned out in force. The combination of natural curiosity mixed with free food and drink made the event irresistible, and like all Wisconsinites, they were driven to maximize every opportunity to enjoy good weather.

The expected crowds had led Elisabeth to set up a separate bar outdoors. Here, Roger was serving Bloody Marys from his own recipe. There was a curious buzz of people around his station, and an odd undercurrent of whispers that the casual observer noticed almost immediately.

The drinks themselves were beautiful. They were served in tall, hourglass goblets, each with a signature garnish arranged on a wooden skewer. There were a pickle spear, three cubes of sharp cheese, a small pickled mushroom, and a tiny sausage, embellished with a sprig of fresh basil grown in the hotel's new garden. The lure of these drinks was almost irresistible to anyone who saw them.

Roger stood behind the bar table, which had been draped in starched white linen, dispensing his concoction. A row of filled glasses was lined up before him, the afternoon sun glinting off them in a most appealing fashion. Roger himself had traded in his usual white t-shirt for a regular white shirt. His sleeves were rolled up, and his hair stood out in all directions as if he had run his hands through it and forgotten. He had a look of cold fury on his face, which those who knew him recognized as his normal expression, but which had a way of discouraging human interaction. You had to really want a Bloody Mary to approach Roger's table.

Eddie arrived from his small cottage nearby and walked up the drive to the hotel for a brief stop before his shift. He saw Pali and Pete standing together on the lawn and went to join them. After the usual greetings, they all stood back to watch the many small dramas being played out around the Bloody Mary bar.

"Have you tried one?" asked Pete, watching one guest surreptitiously pouring his nearly full glass into the garden.

Pali smiled and shook his head. "Not my kind of thing."

Pete nodded in agreement. He turned to Eddie enquiringly. "Perhaps you might...?"

Eddie was watching as someone took his first swallow and froze, standing in the middle of the lawn, eyes wide, unable to move.

"I think I'll pass. What's the story?"

"Roger seems to have gone a bit overboard with the Tabasco...or possibly horseradish."

"Or both."

They all nodded. Probably both.

"Has anyone mentioned it to him, do you suppose?" asked Pete as he watched a woman running up the lawn to the hotel in search of water, the glass in her hand flinging its Bloody contents as she ran.

She was the fourth such runner they had witnessed in as many minutes. Those who had not tried Roger's special cocktail looked after her in wonder or annoyance, the flying capacity of Bloody Mary droplets being the primary source of the annoyance.

"Unlikely."

Again, they all nodded.

"That last runner might have been the fastest so far," commented Eddie. "I wonder if she's signed up for the baseball team." He turned to Pali.

"She the one renting the old Gulbrandsen place?"

Pali nodded. "Think so. Want me to ask her this week?"

"Yeah," said Eddie. "Thanks."

"You have to hand it to Roger," said Pete after a bit, watching yet another guest sprinting for the hotel, "he certainly makes the glass attractive."

"Like a poisonous mushroom," said Eddie.

Nancy had been attending the same church off and on her whole life. She had been baptized here, and confirmed here, and attended her grandparents and parents' funerals here. She had once thought she would be married here, but that now seemed a distant dream from another life.

Although she knew everyone, she was finding the realization that she was now one of the older members of the congregation somewhat shocking. She still felt the same inside as she always had. She observed the young families with a certain amount of sympathy for the pressures they bore, and a great deal of envy for the years of life they still had.

Nancy was seeing the horizon ahead. She supposed that her own funeral would be here someday, and sooner than she cared to think. Still, she liked the idea of permanence, that the church would continue as it had always been, and that the Island, too, would remain unchanged. She was deeply worried about this property buying business.

After the service, Nancy joined the gathering for coffee and cookies in the church basement. She shook the pastor's hand, chose a cookie from the platter, and wandered into middle of the room, looking for someone to talk to. She noticed with alarm that her neighbor, Carole, was standing in the middle of a group of friends, weeping. Assuming the worst about

Carole's husband, Nancy went to offer her support.

"I feel just terrible," Carole sobbed. "But it was so much money, I couldn't pass it up." Looking up, Carole saw Nancy.

"Oh, Nancy. I'm so sorry. I've been dreading telling you this, but…we've had an offer on the farm…and we're selling."

"Selling?" Nancy was deeply shocked. Carole's family had owned their farm for more than a hundred years. "To whom?"

Carole's eyes shifted guiltily, and she covered her feelings by dabbing at her nose with a tissue.

"We don't actually know. We got a call—just like everybody's getting calls—and they offered us so much—Marcie Landmeier told me the offer is at least twice as much as it's worth. Probably more."

She looked around at the faces of her neighbors.

"The kids don't want the place. They have their own lives, and we're getting too old to keep things up. It's life-changing money. We just couldn't turn it down." She looked imploringly at Nancy. "Please don't hate us."

Murmuring reassurances, Nancy patted Carole's back absently while the little group that stood around them were silent. They were all as shaken as Nancy; there weren't that many old farming families left.

No one wanted to say it, but as they stood in a circle around their lifelong friend, they were all wondering who would be the next to go.

In many ways, the weekends were the worst. Oliver couldn't distract himself with work, and there were so few activities on the Island that he found himself sinking into a gloomy restlessness that was a product of loneliness and boredom. He looked at his watch. The hotel's grand opening was today, but he felt shy. He thought Eddie had mentioned stopping by before his shift, but what if he didn't know anyone there? The thought of standing around awkwardly among people he didn't know filled him with dread. No, he would skip that.

It was early in the afternoon when Oliver, almost against his will, succumbed to the lure of Nelsen's. He thought of someone's description of the human brain as consisting of an elephant and a rider. No matter how skilled the rider, if the elephant wanted something, there wasn't one thing the rider could do to stop it. And this elephant, thought Oliver, wanted to go to Nelsen's.

Oliver almost smiled.

It was quiet at the bar, and Eddie greeted him as he entered, held up a glass in inquiry, and seeing Oliver's nod, prepared a brandy old fashioned—sweet— exactly to Oliver's taste: two cherries, one slice of orange. Oliver had planned to have a beer—a departure from his usual tastes—out of respect for the early hour, but Eddie's solicitude was too much appreciated to be rejected. He set the drink in front of Oliver and reached under the bar.

"I've been hoping you'd stop by," said Eddie, pulling out

a battered paperback and sliding it across the bar to Oliver.

"Brought it in after our last conversation. It's the poetry of Paul Verlaine. Do you know him?"

Oliver shook his head and reached for the book. He felt oddly touched that Eddie would have given any thought to him whatsoever, apart from his favorite drink.

"I'm on my third course of French poetry."

Oliver looked surprised.

"I don't speak French," added Eddie hastily, with an Islander's instinctive dismissal of anything that might be perceived as being elitist. "Although I have picked up a few things, and I'm thinking about taking it up in one of my next courses. But the translations are beautiful, and the professor recommends them as being the most true to the original language."

Eddie put down the bar rag, stood looking dreamily into the distance, and began to recite the melancholy words spoken over a grave of lost love and grief.

He continued through four stanzas of the poem, his eyes fixed at some point far away. They were both silent for a moment after he finished, each buried in his own thoughts as an afternoon ballgame blared on the bar TV.

Then Eddie broke the spell with a laugh and quickly returned to his expert glass polishing.

"I surprised you. Actually, I kind of surprise myself. But the professor recommends memorizing as much as possible. That way the poems really become yours. You own them, like your own personal library that you carry with you wherever you go." Eddie smiled somewhat apologetically. "It's cool. And it's kind of like a workout for the mind. I'm memorizing really quickly now. It's a skill, really."

Oliver nodded and began paging through the book.

"You can have that if you want," said Eddie. I'm reading something else at the moment." He shrugged. "I thought maybe if you were interested, we could discuss it."

A faint light came into Oliver's eyes, and he looked up. Eddie had returned to glass washing and didn't see.

"What is it about that poem that you like?"

Eddie shrugged again, his back to Oliver as he worked. "The words are beautiful. And the images." He stopped and looked down for a moment into the soapy water before continuing. "And they remind me of a time in my life…of…someone."

"A woman?" asked Oliver, perhaps a bit too quickly.

Eddie stood perfectly still and nodded before picking up another dirty glass.

They both fell into an embarrassed silence. Eddie was not in the habit of revealing much about himself to his clientele. It broke an unspoken code. Bartenders at work needed to assume an air of professional impersonality. The patrons could reveal their troubles; the bartender's job, however, was to listen. Eddie thought, for the thousandth time, how much this role had crept into his real life. It had become a habit, and breaking it felt uncomfortable.

Fortunately for them both, the pool game at the back of the room had just ended, and the players all wanted another round. Eddie went off to refill their glasses. Oliver stood, put some cash on the bar, waved to Eddie, and putting the book in his pocket, headed out into the June sunlight.

U ncle Victor was not there at dinnertime. His death
brought to Fiona the weary mixture of grief and relief
that torments the living. She made the necessary calls, and then
stood on the sidewalk in the warm spring twilight uncertain
of what to do next. Her time with him had been too brief to
have required much of her; the real ordeal lay ahead. A robin
sang nearby, flowers bloomed in the garden beds outside the
hotel, and there was a soft, sweet breeze. It seemed wrong for
death to come on such an evening.

Remembering her nights in Paris, Fiona went alone to a
little restaurant nearby, ordered a splendid dinner, and—partly
out of tribute, partly out of need—drank an entire bottle
of Bordeaux herself. It was expensive, but she supposed she
didn't have to worry about that now. The looming prospect of
Uncle Victor's lawyer, his finance people, the paper wrangling,
and her cousins' mixture of overt and barely concealed greed
wearied her in advance. Their affection for Uncle Victor was
limited strictly to their interest in his finances, and this was
proven by their absence now, even though they all lived within
driving distance.

Fiona could hardly blame them. He had not been kind to
them. He had not played games, brought gifts, ruffled hair,
or done any of the usual things that uncles do. Only she had
been offered a trip to Europe.

As a child, Fiona had watched him and listened to him
talk, observing his elegant clothes and expensive cars, and he

had noticed her. That had been the basis of their relationship. She felt a stab of pity for a life so little mourned, with no wife, no children of his own, but it consoled her to recall her uncle's conversation that afternoon. There had been no sign of regret or change of heart. He had been as always: businesslike, vaguely affectionate, and self-absorbed. Perhaps, she thought, that was just as well. It would have been too late for regret anyway.

She wished he had left the money to someone else.

Chapter 26

Several times a week, Ben stopped by Jim's on his way home from baseball practice. Usually, Jim was there, puttering around his small property or sitting on the porch watching the water.

Tonight, for a change, neither had felt like talking, and they had walked their usual paths listening to the sounds of the woods. The sun was low in the sky, and the light was rose-colored. It was a calm, humid evening that felt for the first time like summer. They stopped by the water and were skipping stones.

"Jim?" asked Ben in the silence. "Have you ever hated anyone?"

Jim looked quizzically at Ben as he thought about his answer. He believed in telling the truth to children, but he had doubts about whether this was a conversation in which he should share his true feelings. Still, Jim sensed that this was a question with deep implications. He looked out at the water and made a decision.

"Yes. Yes, I have." He turned his gaze to Ben. "It's a terrible feeling, but in the teeth of it, it can seem like a good feeling, too. Passion for anything can feel good." He stopped for a moment, thinking. "I guess that's why hating is dangerous."

He was careful not to ask any questions.

Ben frowned, looking not at Jim but at the water. They were silent again for a while and continued with their stone skipping.

In a flash of nostalgia, Jim recalled the talks he had had with his father when he had been Ben's age. He remembered them with a clarity that made them feel set apart from real life, and he marveled that these distant events lay so close to the surface of his memory even though he hadn't thought of them for years. To his surprise, one of them leapt into his mind with a peculiar relevance. Maybe their talk of wolves had inspired it, but he felt as if he had been waiting all his life for this moment. He spoke now without thinking.

"You know, Ben, my dad used to tell me an old Indian tale about a man whose grandson asks him about a problem he is having."

Jim could almost smell the air from the night his father had told him this story. It had been October, and there was smoke in the air from the chimney of his father's hunting cabin. It had been the kind of brilliant fall day that feels as if it should be counted in a life tally and treasured. They had spent it tramping through the woods along golden paths of yellow leaves, blue sky, and sunshine. His father hadn't really been much of a hunter; he just enjoyed being out of doors, and Jim realized now just how much these kinds of experiences with his father had influenced his own choices in life. He also understood for the first time why he enjoyed these walks with Ben so much.

On that night long ago, Jim and his father had just eaten

dinner and were sitting on the porch, listening to the sounds of the woods, smelling the fallen leaves. Jim couldn't remember what had inspired the story, but he wondered whether he had asked his father a question like this one. All these memories flashed through his mind in a moment.

Ben was silent, but Jim could see he was listening.

"The grandfather said, 'Do you know the voice you hear inside you that tells you what to do? That is the voice of a wolf. We all have two wolves that speak to our hearts. Sometimes it is a wolf of the light, that speaks to us of goodness and mercy, of honesty and courage. Sometimes it is a wolf of darkness. He speaks to us of evil and deceit, cunning, and violence.'"

They had both stopped skipping stones, and Jim stood looking into the distance, unconsciously cradling one of the flat, smooth stones in his hand. Ben was watching him, listening hard.

"They walked for a long time along the path where the sunlight lay before them. The boy had been thinking, and after a while, he asked: 'Which wolf will win?' And the grandfather stopped walking so the boy would know that what he said was important. He said, 'The one you feed.'"

Jim stopped talking to skip the stone in his hand out into the waveless water.

He could see Ben, motionless, out of the corner of his eye, plainly thinking.

Then Ben, too, skipped a stone, still frowning. After a long moment he asked.

"How do you feed it?"

"By the kinds of thoughts you allow yourself to have,

what you allow yourself to feel, what you expect of yourself, what you allow yourself to do. You can feed the good wolf by thinking the right thoughts, driving away the bad ones. By spending time with other people who are feeding their good wolves and avoiding those who aren't."

Ben was looking at Jim directly as he spoke. "Everybody has bad thoughts?"

"I imagine so. No one is all good, Ben. There are only people who choose to be good...or bad, for that matter. It's all a choice."

He smiled then, adding, "But it may be more difficult for some people than others."

He watched Ben thinking and wondered—what will he remember? What stories will stay with him when he's a man and a boy is asking him for help? Will he remember this?

"We should get back," he said aloud. "It will be dark soon."

Ben nodded.

Each pondering their own thoughts, they headed away from the beach toward the trail in silence. They didn't speak during the ten-minute walk to Jim's truck, but the cranes were having an evening conversation of their own, and their haunting cries filled the evening air.

Chapter 27

J im got the phone call later that night. Joey's, one of the
Island's favorite breakfast restaurants, was on fire. It was
a full alarm for the whole department, but the building
had been quietly burning for hours, and by the time they
got the call, it was already too late. Despite heroic efforts, the
restaurant burned to the ground.

Some hours later, the state investigators were already on
site, and Jim was there to learn what he could from them.

The head of the division saw him and came over. "Hey,
Jim. You're keeping pretty busy over here."

"Hey, Andy. Yeah, we sure are. What did you find?"

"I think this one was routine. Looks as if the wiring was
bad."

"Are you sure?"

"We'll double-check, of course. Treat it as suspicious just
in case. But, yeah, I'm pretty sure."

"Right. Well, I guess that's some good news. Won't stop
the rumor mill from turning, though."

"Nope. Can't let the facts get in the way of a good story."

Andy turned to get on with his work and called over his
shoulder. "I'll give you a call before I write the report."

"Thanks," said Jim. "I appreciate it."

He stood gazing at the ruins of a local institution, thinking of all the times he had stopped in, met friends, laughed over local news. He felt a deep sense of loss.

Oliver expected to find Eddie's book of poetry rather slow going, but he was gradually drawn into its unsettling beauty. He hadn't read much poetry aside from high-school English and the lyrics of his favorite musicals. He had to admit, he hadn't ever really appreciated it before.

To be sure, the prospect of conversation with Eddie was his primary motivation in sticking with it. He carefully read through the book several times, selecting things he particularly liked and taking a few small, neatly hand-printed notes. And then he got nervous.

What if what he thought was stupid? What if Eddie, in his superior experience of literature, found his comments juvenile or superficial? He regretted now that he hadn't been a better French student in high school.

As he sat alone in his anxieties, Oliver suddenly found the answer. He would read some more French poetry—or, at least, some more information about it. He would educate himself and impress Eddie with his erudition.

In his old life, Oliver had been accustomed to buying a book online and having it appear magically on his doorstep a few days—or even hours— later. Even so, he had always preferred browsing in bookstores, but this wasn't possible on the Island. He could, however, browse in the library. True, he could stay home and find the poems online, but he preferred paper to screens.

Besides, he reminded himself, libraries had people.

His eagerness to begin launched him into action with his usual industry, and he set off immediately on his quest. He could not have explained why he felt it mattered to prove himself to Eddie. He only knew that something important depended on it.

With Fiona gone on family business, Emily had decided to press ahead with her plans. Having Fiona named as a member of the Committee was sufficient. As Emily had pointed out with perhaps unnecessary frequency, Fiona didn't actually need to be there.

The truth was that Emily preferred things this way. Fiona really could only be an obstacle. Of course, so too could the community members who were on the Committee. She needed them to provide the impression of consensus, but Emily had no intention of permitting them to interfere in her plans. The Island needed her, she firmly believed, and this required that she have a free hand. Emily wouldn't have admitted it, but she also didn't want to share credit for whatever the Committee managed to accomplish.

She looked around her living room at the people gathered there. "I'm so glad you've all made the time to be here for this important work." Emily's manner bordered on flirtatious, and her smile betrayed a self-admiration that could be perceived by the sensitive observer, even though for most people, it was merely annoying in a way they couldn't quite identify.

The group looked back at her, innocently unaware of their role as pawns. So far, no work had been suggested. They were merely a group of people who met, drank coffee, and ate some rather good cake. There was a general understanding in the group that any activity involving both Emily Martin and Stella DesRosiers was likely to wind up being controversial, but this, of course, was part of the entertainment. Being on the Committee did not in any way imply endorsement of the Committee's activities. When you live on a remote island, you have to make your own fun.

Emily looked around the room at each of them in turn.

"I've been searching for an idea for our first big project. Since it's going to be our very first, it has to be exactly the right thing. Something to show that we're serious."

The Committee members continued eating their cake and drinking their coffee without comment. So far, this was nothing new.

"What about all these properties being bought up around the Island?" asked one of the ladies. "That strikes me as pretty concerning."

Emily's face changed for the merest flicker from its bright smile to annoyance, but she quickly returned to the smile.

"It is, of course, most concerning, and very much within the purview of the Committee, but until we have more information, I'm afraid we must just wait and see."

She was struck now with a moment of sheer inspiration.

"And, after all, we want the Committee to be *proactive, not reactive.* We want to create a really lasting contribution to Island life. This cannot be accomplished by running hither and yon in response to every piece of news. No. We must create a plan and march methodically toward its completion."

There were a few polite nods.

Nancy, sitting as inconspicuously as she could manage in a corner of the room, was tempted to remark that waiting for more information was not proactive, but she let it pass. She had a sudden mental image of Emily marching down Main Street, tossing her head and twirling a baton, the Committee lagging haphazardly along behind. This vision cheered her and made her more willing to overlook minor annoyances.

Emily was still talking. "...so what I propose is an annual literary festival to celebrate the cultural life of the community. It will be in the fall," she said, lapsing unconsciously into the wrong tense, "at a time when tourism falls off, and the economy can use a little boost. That also gives us time to arrange something for this year."

"All in favor?" she asked, in blatant disregard of Robert's Rules.

"Aye," said everyone dutifully, even Nancy, who was of the seems-harmless-enough school of thought.

"Excellent!" said Emily as the crowd began to stir and rise, the rattle of their empty plates, cups and saucers being returned to the sideboard threatening to overpower her voice.

"This is so exciting! I'll be in touch this week with sub-committee assignments. Good night! Good night, everybody!"

She looked after their departing backs like a fond auntie.

There was a new sign at the Ground Zero parking lot. It was considerably larger than the original sign, but it bore the same peel-and-stick hardware store lettering that had once adorned the entrance to Ground Zero. Somewhat crookedly, it announced:

BY ORDER OF THE POLICE DEPARTMENT.
NO CAMPING.
THIS IS A NEW SIGN.

It was immediately apparent the next morning, however, that the sign was not having the intended result. There were just as many tents as before.

Joshua found himself contemplating the police officer's comment about a fence. An actual fence wasn't feasible, but what about some other kind of barrier? After his shift, he headed down the peninsula to the big stores in Sturgeon Bay. Surely, a solution could be found there.

By late afternoon he was busily setting up some big orange cones of the kind used in road construction, along with ready-made signs saying "No Parking. The message on the signs wasn't exactly right, but it was as close as Joshua had been able to find. He felt sure that this would be sufficient to deter the campers.

Despite his research, as the prospect of actually discussing poetry with Eddie loomed, Oliver's habitual sense of his own unworthiness rose up and began to corner him. In sheer defiance of it, this time with the rider in charge of the elephant, Oliver forced himself to stop in at Nelsen's, the book tucked into his jacket pocket.

Eddie was busy. The main travel season had begun, and there were many more tourists than the week before. Oliver slid onto a lone bar stool close to the door and looked around.

Eddie, whose professional instincts were unerring, looked up from the crush of customers waiting for his attention and acknowledged Oliver's arrival with a glance. While Eddie had a deeply embedded sense of fair play, he was always able to show favoritism to the locals without it being obvious. In no time at all he was sailing along the bar past Oliver.

"Usual?" he asked, as he whizzed by, returning change to an impatient tourist.

Unwilling to throw a cog in the machine with an unexpected preference, Oliver nodded and watched as, in a rather amazing sleight of hand, Eddie accepted payment, delivered a check to one patron, two glasses of extremely ordinary Pinot Grigio to another, and began, with the dexterity of years' experience, to mix Oliver's drink.

Eddie slid the drink toward Oliver during another of these event-filled pass-bys and gave a friendly slap on the bar in front of him in welcome. Oliver took a sip, settled back, and removed the book of poetry from his pocket. There would be no time for conversation until much later. That much, at least, was clear. But he was in no hurry. He had his book.

Oliver relished the sense of belonging.

The week passed quickly, but Fiona felt it had been a thousand years since she had left home. She had fulfilled her new obligations so far, pushed off her cousins' eager enquiries about the estate to Dirk Richards, and accompanied Uncle Victor on his last journey to the country cemetery where his ancestors lay.

Now she was headed back to the Island. She had arrived at the airport ridiculously early, anticipating big city security lines, but there had been no one else there. The small airport had an almost family quality, with chatty TSA agents and local policemen whose German Shepherd rolled over to be petted, leaving her black suit covered with long hairs. Her trip would require multiple flights, but despite her worries about Pete's small planes, she was a comfortable traveler so she barely minded. And, anyway, she told herself, she was going home.

Fiona loved the moment of takeoff: the gathering speed, the split second of suspense as the plane left earth. She put down her book. The plane banked to the west, gaining altitude.

She was going home. The thought filled her with pleasure. The Island would be bathed in the mists of early summer, the signs of the local establishments freshly painted, the flower pots and baskets sparse and newly planted, and although the water of Lake Michigan would still be too cold for the average swimmer, the beaches would already be filled with the muffled sounds of calling voices, boat motors, and gulls. Tourist season had begun, and it felt, always, like a new start in life. Winter was gone, a distant dream that seemed never to have happened. Everything seemed possible.

On the ground below, the seasons were well ahead of the Island. Summer was already past its first bloom, the leaves fully formed and lush. Looking out at the green hills in the misty light of the June morning, Fiona's thoughts turned to the grave on the country hillside, which must now be bathed in this same light.

She was not normally morbid, but today she felt the sorrow of the lonely body now forever in the earth. He was gone, and what remained was stilled for all time. Fiona looked down upon the clean countryside and felt the full fragility of human life.

With some effort, she shook this mood away. She was alive. This was still her morning. What grief she felt must be expressed in gratitude for the day before her. She took a deep breath and turned her gaze back to the book in her lap.

When the airline coffee came, hot and fragrant, she held the paper cup in her hands and felt grateful.

Chapter 28

When Fiona landed at last in Green Bay, she felt
the usual air travel hangover. She needed to
cleanse herself: of airport germs and stale air;
of the lifeless, processed food; and of the gray
blandness she felt from being among too many human beings.
She longed to strip off her clothes and burn them.

Pete, waiting for her, held her in his arms for a long
moment of comfort before murmuring, "Let's get out of here."

Now, Fiona leaned on the rail of the ferry and breathed
the lake air into her lungs. The weather had shifted while she
was away into a balmy sweetness. In the lengthening light
of the early summer evening, the lake was a deep midnight
blue. The sky was a paler shade of blue, filled with summer
clouds tinted pink, a bright rim of orange around the edges.
It looked, thought Fiona, like a Maxfield Parrish painting,
unreal in its beauty.

She felt, as physical sensation, every anxiety fall away,
seeing the splendid spread of summer before her, the months
lying ahead, feeling the deep soft swells of the waves moving
the ferry beneath her feet. Even her grief felt as if it were
part of this natural place, a wholesome sadness rather than a
wound. She resolved to enjoy these days of beauty without the

blemish of anxiety. The Island waited, a dark shape of land in the distance. She was home.

*F*iona *dreamed that the wolf was waiting for her as she opened her door, and they walked together into the night. They walked what seemed like great distances over rolling hills and twisting mountain paths, until they came out into an open space, and Fiona realized it was the cemetery where Uncle Victor was buried. The wolf led her to the grave and, after a long stillness, began to howl, lifting his great muzzle to the sky. Fiona watched as he howled through the night, the stars seeming to circle above him, as if he wove their movements with his song. Suddenly, she began to howl with him, sending her voice into the sky to mingle with his. She could see the colors of the sound swirling like smoke above their heads.*

She woke herself with her own sobbing. Pete held her in his arms until she fell back to sleep.

Chapter 29

L ife on the Island had not stopped in her absence. Fiona's first order of business in the morning was to listen to her messages. There were dozens of calls—some from the same people. Several of the calls expressed concerns about the fires. The rest were about the mysterious property sales.

The grocery store family was thrilled by the prospect of new business, as were the owners of the golf course, the proprietor of a restaurant, the Principal of the Island School, and the new plumber who'd been recruited to the Island.

Those opposed were not only the old families. There were calls, too, from newcomers whose sole purpose in moving to the Island had been the search for solitude and a simpler life. A major hotel or condo development was not in keeping with their vision.

Fiona began to realize that the issue would be more complex than she had at first imagined.

The first call she returned was Nancy's, and she listened with some amusement to her account of how the Committee's new literary project came into being.

Her flurried day behind her, Fiona was sitting on the steps of the porch when Pete came out and put a drink in her hand.

He sat down beside her.

"Are you okay?"

"Mostly, yes. There were a lot of good distractions, today. Kept me busy."

He nodded. "How are things with the Committee of the Furrowed Brow?" He looked off, frowning. "Wait. Isn't there a Welsh word for that?"

Fiona laughed for the first time in days. "You're thinking of Frank Lloyd Wright and 'Taliesin.' That's 'shining brow.'"

Pete kept a straight face. "Ah. Of course. I saw the opera at Covent Garden. Tedious."

She looked at him with affectionate amusement. "Between this property thing and all the fires, there will be a lot to distract me for some time to come."

"Well, they also have the advantage of being sufficiently concerning for those who traffic in being concerned."

Fiona sighed. "Even I'm concerned."

"But that's my point. Why not let those concerned be concerned, while you can be merely…slightly bothered?"

She laughed at him, which had been his intention. "Want to go to the beach?"

"That depends. Can I bring my drink?"

"Who's going to stop you?" She stood up. "I'll fill your glass and get a blanket."

It was solstice, the longest day of the year. The lake was nearly still. For six months, the earth had waited for the warmth of summer and now, in this one moment, it lay before them. Pete and Fiona lay on a blanket, watching the last fading light of the sky.

All was in shadow, but a tinge of deep rose and lavender still shaded the world, and the tops of the trees glowed orange from the last beams of sun. The thick, heavy rustle of wings flapping for balance came from the woods where the turkeys were perched high in the trees to sleep. A pair of owls conversed in deep echoing calls. The heavy roll of the waves moved against the rocky shore.

And then a flock of geese came as if from nowhere, flying faster than usual, their wings still alight by the sun, their calls arising from afar like an approaching train and fading just as quickly.

Tomorrow, even in the fresh growth of summer, the days would begin their long waning into winter. But now, in its nadir, the night moved in from the shadows and covered the earth in darkness.

One star, then two appeared overhead.

Fiona's head rested on Pete's shoulder, and she sighed in her sleep.

He tightened his arm around her, watching the stars in their eternal spinning until he, too, slept to the sound of the waves.

Chapter 30

"Look, look, look. Shhhhhh. No, don't look. Wait. Okay, look! That guy. The one in the blue shirt. He just ordered a Bloody Roger."

A wave of tittering arose from a small party of Islanders who were seated in the corner of the Washington Hotel's bar, but it was quickly suppressed. Local patronage at the hotel was on the rise, and although no one would admit it to the management, the reason was the utter undrinkability of Roger's cocktails.

Elisabeth was fully aware of the lethal quality of these drinks, but despite her best efforts, and those of her carefully trained wait staff, the sales of what the menu called Bloody Marys, but which were commonly—if somewhat furtively— known as "Bloody Rogers" were steady.

The reason was simple—encouraging their purchase had become a local sport.

After their own unwitting initiations to the Bloody Roger, patrons of the hotel bar took great pleasure in observing the delivery of the drinks, their consumption, and the inevitable dash for water or a place to spit. Occasionally, the victim was caught so unaware that he or she was unprepared for the niceties of choosing a location, and the resulting disaster to table linens and nearby diners was a source of high entertainment. These innocent imbibers of Roger's lethal drinks had come to be known as "sprinters," and being a Sprinter was seen as membership in a unique—if uniquely miserable—club.

Roger, if he was aware of these activities, gave no sign, and continued merely in his usual state of acute silence.

The silence itself was, perhaps, an indicator of Roger's lack of qualification for the job. Whereas most bartenders display a skill for banter, diplomacy, and genuine enjoyment of socializing with their patrons, Roger's approach was different. Unsmiling, silent, and with a demeanor he was convinced was friendly, but which most people would describe as fierce, he went about his work with unalloyed satisfaction. Not even the boldest Chicago visitor would dare criticize one of Roger's cocktails to his face, and since he drank only wine, he was able to continue in his belief that they were palatable.

His regular patrons, however, knew better. With varying degrees of cunning, and with their own attractive and undrink-able Bloody Rogers lined up along the table in front of them, they would draw unsuspecting visitors into conversation.

"What am I drinking?" would be the response to queries. "Why, this is a specialty of the house."

"It's probably too strong for someone from Chicago."

"Oh, definitely. You need to be an Islander for this."

These forays into reverse psychology were irresistible to the average tourist, particularly those from Chicago with a sense of urban superiority.

"I'll have one of those," was the preface to a reaction which never ceased to amuse the onlookers.

The plans for the literary festival were moving along quickly. After many conversations with Elisabeth over dates, Emily had managed to book the hotel. The questions now centered on the featured events. There were plenty of talented local writers willing to participate, but Emily was unsatisfied.

She stood one sunny afternoon in a chance meeting of a few Committee members outside the grocery store.

"We need a big name," she said, delivering an unintentional insult to the rest of the writers who would be her guests, and in a way they were certain to hear about. "Someone with prestige who can really draw a crowd."

"What about Pali?" suggested Nancy. "He's a published poet. Everyone in the area knows him."

Emily made a little face. "Oh, Heavens," she said, dismissing Pali's talent with a wave of her hand. "We need someone with stature. Someone who can put us on the map." She looked over to see Pali walking up the sidewalk.

"But you must come," she said, putting her hand on his arm. "I'm sure you'll find it helpful in your little efforts, and you might learn something!" Pali looked both nonplussed and faintly amused. He nodded briefly with a weak smile and excused himself to squeeze past the little group into the store.

Emily tried to look encouraging. "We'll all just have to put our heads together."

Everyone nodded politely. No one had any hope that anyone but Emily would be choosing the keynote speaker.

After the first tentative conversations about Eddie's book of poetry, Oliver gained confidence. If he had made a fool of himself, Eddie hadn't shown it, seeming, instead, to use Oliver's comments as jumping off points for discussion. By one way or another, their conversations had led them in the direction of Yeats, whose writing, though in English, Oliver found even more impenetrable than the French.

In this, at least, Eddie had no superior understanding since he, too, was reading it for the first time.

When Oliver came in one evening, Eddie was waiting for him. There was a baseball game on TV, and some of the regulars were clustered around it.

"Look," said Eddie, taking a rather heavy volume from the shelf behind him. "I've found this book about understanding Yeats. It's all about the Irish myth he uses, and the Irish politics of the time, and his passion for a woman he wrote about in a lot of his poems. It's very helpful. Explains a lot."

Oliver accepted the book eagerly. "I think," he said, slowly turning the pages, "I should probably get my own copy." He took out his phone. "I'll order one right now."

Eddie nodded earnestly. "I had no idea what I was reading without it."

"I know," said Oliver, somewhat relieved that it hadn't been his own stupidity. "I was a bit lost." He pulled out his copy of the poetry. "I don't even know how to pronounce the names. He flipped through the pages rapidly, looking for a place. "For example, this." He pointed to the poem in question. "How do you pronounce *Cuchulain?*"

Pete Landry had just walked in and sat down a few stools away. Without asking, Eddie poured him a bourbon.

"Yeats?" asked Pete, seeing the book on the bar. "Why are you reading Yeats?"

"For fun," said Oliver.

"For enlightenment," said Eddie.

Pete nodded solemnly. "Good for both, I suppose."

"How's Fiona?" asked Eddie politely.

"Back to the usual round of meetings."

"She okay?"

"She's okay." Pete smiled. "In her own way."

Eddie was suddenly struck by an idea. "Have you read Yeats?"

"Some," admitted Pete. "Why?"

Eddie's admiration of Pete bordered on hero-worship, and he enjoyed being able to discuss anything serious with him. "Some of it's pretty rough-going."

Pete nodded sympathetically. "All that Irish mythology. And the politics. Very insider stuff."

Oliver, suddenly feeling bold, jumped in. "And the names. They're completely unpronounceable."

"Right," said Pete, looking thoughtful. "I recall hearing some recordings somewhere of Yeats reading his poetry. You can buy them. Or maybe they're on YouTube."

"Wow," said Eddie. He had spent so much time studying the Ancient Greeks that it had never occurred to him that he could actually hear the voice of the poet himself. "That would be cool."

"Would help with pronunciation, at least." Pete reached for Eddie's book, still sitting on the bar, and began leafing through it, becoming engrossed. "Here's the classic," he said at last, pointing to a page.

"Love this," he muttered, more to himself than to the others.

"Look! Look at this!" cried Oliver, who had been gazing at his phone.

Several heads in the bar turned.

"I've got one. Here's a recording of Yeats reading!"

Intrigued, the three men leaned in to listen.

Chapter 31

A t least in part because it was so remote, Washington Island had a lack of development that put it in contrast to the picturesque tourist towns that stretched along the shorelines of Door County. There were some million-dollar houses and certainly some spectacular properties with vistas of the sunset or the sunrise, the shores of the mainland in the distance. But, there was no fashionable night life, no chic restaurant, no quaint shops, nor condominiums. There were idiosyncratic family-owned inns and resorts with varying degrees of charm and mildew, some having been in business for a century or almost, and most caught in time capsules at various points in the mid-twentieth century. There were the bars and eateries—usually the same thing—that served mostly good but casual food. There was the grocery store, and there was the Mercantile—a kind of hardware store and souvenir shop combined. There was a garage, and a gas station, and a post office.

The Island was at the end of a long drive up the Door Peninsula, with towns growing increasingly sparse along the way, and then a ferry ride across the dangerous straits known for centuries as Death's Door. This lack of commercial development could be interpreted as an expression of the inconvenience of getting there. But that clearly wasn't the reason when the ferries were busy from dawn to dusk every day in tourist season.

It was, in fact, a specific decision of the Islanders, made amid various controversies and at their own expense. The lack of development—and the refusal to permit it—meant there was very little real estate market, which made it difficult, if not impossible, for property owners to sell. It forced people in their seventies and older to continue the hard work of running their family establishments because their retirement money was tied up in the property, and they couldn't find a buyer. It meant tight budgets and a struggling economy and holding multiple jobs. Real estate languished on the market, sometimes for years.

But it also meant that there were no multi-story modern condominiums being built to block the sunset, and most important, it meant that the essential small-town character of the place—against fearsome odds—was still maintained. This was the whole charm of the Island, and it was how the Islanders wanted it. Most of them, anyway.

In many respects, the Island's off-the-grid quality created a little oasis of freedom in a world filled with regulations. Particularly in the winter, when the tourists were gone, Islanders lived by their own rules and kept their foibles amongst themselves. A drunk driver was cautioned by his neighbors. A father allowed his ten-year-old to practice driving the truck on the road. Casual drug use was accepted as a personal decision and nobody's business. Heaven help anyone who dared to report and bring state or federal agents into the picture—although when they did come, the Islanders closed ranks. This, for most residents, was a feature of the good life.

But in contrast to their generally libertarian views, the community felt no qualms about exerting its control over the use of private property. Limiting how land could be used was accepted without a flicker of conscience. Fiona couldn't help wondering how long they could hold out against the march of development.

The outside world's changes had to come to the Island eventually, and now, here they were. She could only hope there would be no blood.

Back at home, Oliver sat down at his computer and returned to the recordings of Yeats reading his poems. They had been radio broadcasts, so there was no visual, just a photo of the poet accompanied the scratchy sound recordings from nearly a century before. But, the voice was there with its singing quality, and so, too, was the spirit of the man with his Irish vowels and his confident possession of the words he had sculpted to make this music. For Oliver, it was like a visitation, and he listened for hours, feeling the presence of the great man's soul in this shadowy form.

Ben was acutely wary of another encounter with Caleb, and Noah's persistent requests to play made him uneasy. What if he brought his brother along? When Ben finally agreed to meet Noah again one afternoon, he was relieved to see him arrive alone.

"How come you're not hanging out with Caleb?" Ben was almost superstitious about the name, as if mentioning it could summon an evil spirit.

Noah's face took on the particular wounded look that only a disappointed child can have. "All he wants to do is watch TV and play video games."

Ben nodded silently, reassured. The last thing on earth he wanted was to run into Caleb again, but he felt pity for Noah, who had to live with him. His sympathy made him generous.

"There's a ball game over at the park, and I've got money for ice cream. My treat."

Noah's face lit up with anticipation. "Okay!"

They got back on their bikes and headed toward the road with Ben in the lead. "Do you know how to keep score?" he called over his shoulder.

Noah sounded doubtful. "No." His voice came out in puffs as he pumped hard to keep up. "My dad doesn't like baseball."

"Doesn't like baseball? What?! It's the greatest thing in the world! I'll show you!"

With renewed enthusiasm, Ben led on toward the park, with Noah peddling doggedly behind.

In the hotel office, an open laptop computer displayed an unpublished page on the hotel's website, complete with alluring photographs of the property.

"Yoga With Goats," it said.

"Build Your Practice With the Renowned Roger Mason."

Elisabeth, whose goat-related sense of foreboding was growing by the day, looked up from the hotel's website and gazed at her husband who was lying face down on the floor in kapotasana, or pigeon pose.

"Did you write this?" she asked.

"Joshua did."

Elisabeth nodded and restrained a sigh. She hadn't been able to imagine Roger using a word like "renowned" to describe himself. It had a diplomacy, a sense of delicacy she would not have expected in him. Of course, it had been Joshua.

"I think it's very well-phrased," she said, employing diplomacy of her own. She smiled to herself. Roger's enthusiasms were one of the things she loved about him, and she was needing to remind herself of that with increasing frequency. She consoled herself that goat yoga might distract him from bartending. Oh, fond hope, she thought.

Roger bestirred himself from his pose and came to stand over her shoulder. "Are you okay with letting it go live?" He trusted Elisabeth's judgment implicitly.

Once again, Elisabeth suppressed the impulse to sigh. She smiled at him, instead, and reached up to touch his face.

Roger, for all his flaws, was a very handsome man. "Let's do it," she said.

Roger loved his wife with a devotion magnified by his single-mindedness. In their private moments he had learned to be attentive, and even, in his way, thoughtful. He leaned his head slightly into her hand in a gesture of affection that was becoming more natural to him.

Still smiling, Elisabeth looked back at the screen. "Which button should I push?"

Roger put his arms around her to reach the keyboard and hit the button to publish. She leaned against him, and he breathed in the scent of her, filled with wonder that she should love him.

Chapter 32

*F*iona *dreamed she was a passenger in a car, sleeping. She did not know the driver, nor why she was there. When she woke, the car was driving along a very long rope bridge, very high up over water. The rope twisted as they drove so dramatically that at times she was looking straight down into the water, hundreds of feet below her. She did not know the other people in the car, and she tried not to be alarmed, but it was frightening to have the weight of a car on such a bridge, and it was frightening to look down so far at the water below. It was a terrifying beauty. She hadn't known anything so spectacular was nearby, surrounded by rich, green mountains and hills. She thought that she had never seen this bridge before, even though it was so near where she lived, and she wondered whether she should bring others to it or keep its strange beauty to herself and the few others who knew of it.*

Concerned that Roger's indefatigable approach to problem solving might lead to undesirable extremes, Joshua now counseled reliance on the police department. If they wanted the tents gone, he reasoned, then they could stop them from being there in the first place. Even Roger seemed relieved to pass on the burden and agreed that this made sense.

The police did arrive on the first night, and the second, and even on the third. But after a week, when the department had its hands full with the usual misdemeanor crises that arise during the peak of tourist season, the patrolling officer announced that he would not be returning.

"Look," he said, as the last ancient Subaru lumbered out of the parking lot. "We can't come here every night to chase these guys off. It's a waste of police resources."

"But," countered Joshua, "you said—"

"Sorry. Chief's orders. You're on your own."

Joshua watched him go with mixed feelings.

Eddie and Oliver's discussions about literature were no longer private conversations. It had happened gradually. At first a bar patron or two just began sitting closer, and then looking over someone's shoulder at the text, and soon, they were joining in the conversation and asking where they could get the book. One or two other Islanders who were not Nelsen's regulars heard about it and asked to join.

They had started with eight members in the first few weeks and grown to a dozen. Eddie, as the de facto leader, felt, at first, that this was the maximum. So long as they chose a quiet night at the bar, everyone could be heard, and they could still cluster at the corners and see one another's faces.

Talk of moving to a less public location had arisen, but so far, nothing had been done. They all liked the rough and tumble of Nelsen's, they enjoyed being able to order whatever they liked, and it was no fuss for anyone. Until the start of football season—now a distant dream—Monday nights were designated.

The public nature of their meeting place meant that random patrons—those who were not interested in the books—could wander into their conversations or interrupt to ask what they were doing. This was mostly accepted with good humor.

The side effect, however, was that more and more people began to show up to discuss the readings. They came with ancient paperback books from their high school years, with brand new editions ordered online, or with computer printouts gleaned from online searchings. Occasionally, someone brought a library book, but the library's capacity was soon insufficient to meet the needs of everyone who wanted to join.

There was no way to stop people who really wanted to participate, and no one especially wanted to. But the result had the odd effect of, one night a week, turning Nelsen's bar into a seminar on great books.

Chapter 33

The fire started with only a few noiseless licks of flame in a corner of the darkened shed. It fed itself on some old tarps, slowly increasing its consumption of the heavy cloth until its gentle nibbling grew to ravenous hunger. A small, damp patch of gasoline had accumulated nearby where the college-age grounds crew had carelessly refilled the mowers. These morsels would lead to the machines, filled with oil and gasoline and clumps of old grass clippings. From there, it would be a small leap to the boxes of fertilizer, weed killer, and insecticides that lined the wooden shelves haphazardly, and to the flags, and awnings, and other combustibles tucked away for special events, and, at some point, the half-filled gas cans. Slowly, but with growing appetite, the flames spread in search of fuel. By the time anyone would notice, it would be too late.

Nils Bjornstad was in his field surveying the broken belt on his tractor when he saw the smoke. It was in the vicinity of the baseball field. Seemed odd to have smoke coming from there. He hesitated. He'd feel like a fool if he called the fire department and somebody was burning trash. He decided he'd better go investigate.

He pocketed his keys and made his way across the freshly

plowed furrows with quickening steps, all while the fire continued its relentless quest for fuel. By the time Nils had reached his fence, the flames were already licking the edges of the machinery, and the heat in the building was rising to a flash point. In a split second, the temperature was enough to ignite the vapors in the gas cans.

Nils felt the explosion hit him like a wave. Instinctively, he turned away and raised his arm to shield his face, then, after a moment, looked back, grasped the fence and stared. Only a few seconds difference and he'd have been too close.

A moment passed before he could recover his wits sufficiently to offer a silent prayer and reach for his cell phone. Not that it was necessary. Everyone on the Island would have heard the explosion.

Jim found himself once again staring at the still smoking remains of a small building, this time a maintenance shed at the baseball field. The explosions of the half-filled gas cans had been catastrophic, destroying the roof and the landscaping equipment stored there. Jim was grateful that no one had been nearby. If there had been a game, or if Nils Bjornstad had been a moment or two earlier...well.

One of the volunteer firefighters stood nearby, surveying the damage.

"If it had been on a weekend, there might have been more people out here to notice it in time."

Jim shook his head. "Or more people with injuries." They were both silent for a moment contemplating how bad it might have been. They had been lucky.

The reports from the golf course and the Karfi dock had been conclusive: the cause was arson. This time, however, like the restaurant fire, could have been routine. It was only in the context of the other fires that Jim was suspicious: another small building in a quiet place, where mischief could be done anonymously.

He watched as the firefighters finished up, making sure the fire was completely out. In a community this small, having someone acting with this kind of malice was highly unusual, and all the more disturbing when he considered that it had to be someone he knew. He was aware that arsonists were frequently firefighters, but he hated to suspect any of his men. Like so much public work on the Island, their efforts were a sacrifice in service to the community, not a vocation. He knew them all—family men, church goers, members of the baseball team. It was unthinkable. But if not them, who?

Jim spoke to the Assistant Chief, leaving him in charge of the scene, and got into his truck to head over to speak with Bill Yahr, the chief of police. If it had been arson, the question was whether the explosion had been incidental to the high heat. Or was the arsonist deliberately raising the stakes?

The hotel's website had done its job, and registrations for the first goat yoga classes were already coming in. Preparations were in their final stages, and the hotel buzzed with activity.

"Well, Joshua, what do you think?" asked Elisabeth.

She and Roger had invited Joshua to come to the hotel for a preview of the facilities before the first session, and they now stood at the entrance to the new yoga studio. Roger had come to depend on Joshua for his opinions on things beyond his own expertise, which were, essentially, anything involving people, comfort, or communications. Elisabeth, in turn, had come to depend on Joshua for watching Roger in her absence.

Joshua's celestial gaze roamed over the room. It was an airy, sunlit space with a long anteroom that ran the width of the building, filled with built-in benches, cubby holes, and shelves. The studio itself had floor to ceiling windows along two sides, white walls, hardwood floors, and long, sheer draperies that wafted gently in the breeze from the open windows. A rack of new yoga mats, blocks, straps, and blankets, and a cart with fresh white towels stood ready at the back. There were tall potted plants artfully arranged around the room. Everything gleamed. It was a yoga dream room.

Joshua nodded approvingly. "Very nice."

Then he turned to Elisabeth with a slightly unbeatific expression. "You're going to have goats in here?" he asked.

"Just one," said Elisabeth firmly.

"At first," added Roger.

After weeks of waiting, Stella still had not heard back from her nephew. Communications in federal prison were such that she couldn't even be completely certain whether he had gotten her letter. So, when a letter did arrive, she plucked it eagerly from the pile of catalogs and ripped it open to read. She was silent for a few minutes, her lips moving over the words until she came to a sentence she had never dreamed of seeing.

Stella let out a whoop of delight. How sweet, how infinitely sweet—and to have her nephew, Dean, be the instrument of this discovery. It was positively biblical. All alone in her kitchen, she laughed. She re-read the letter and laughed again.

It had been Jake, who had once compared Stella to Medusa, the Gorgon with snakes for hair who could turn men into stone. The truth, unfortunately, was somewhat worse. Being an object of Stella's vengeance might make stone seem rather preferable.

Ben lay in bed looking at the tops of the trees through his bedroom window. Even the smallest branches were profiled against the faint light of the sky. Sometimes he could see faces there, or the shapes of animals. A few of the shapes were old friends who had been there as long as he could remember—the boy with thick black glasses, the face of an owl, the flying crow. Tonight, in the heavy winds of a spring storm, he could see the shape of a wolf. Was it, he wondered, a good wolf, or a bad wolf? And who, on this bleak, wild night, was giving it comfort?

Ben watched the movement of the shape of the wolf until he fell asleep. It followed him into his dreams.

Chapter 34

P ete was gone again, and Fiona's house echoed with loneliness.

As she looked back on their lessons, she felt almost reassured. Pete's respect for the danger and his thoughtful approach to handling guns made her feel safe and feel, too, that he could handle an emergency—not that she didn't feel that about him anyway.

But his professionalism was part of what fed her fears. As he took his turn at the target, she watched his face. It was a face she knew so well in its moods and expressions. She could detect nothing unusual there, just a dispassionate concentration. He was a superb shot, and his expertise had been honed to automaticity. She wished she could see some crack, some opening to his inner workings that would reveal what she wanted to know. She kept thinking about Mark's comments. "Men are beasts," he'd said.

Pete turned to her when he had finished firing, his eyes alight with his usual good humor. He was having fun.

"See?" he'd said, emptying the spent cartridge. "Nothing to be afraid of."

In her excitement, Stella lost no time in seeking out Emily Martin. Stella needed a showcase, a place to announce what she had learned to the community, and for this, Emily would serve a very useful purpose. It would be best—and most satisfying, she decided—to keep her big news to herself and leave Emily—for now—to focus on the larger question of the anonymous purchases. She pondered a discussion over the phone but decided that this conversation would be better in person.

"Let's have lunch, Emily," she said in a purr, and Emily readily agreed, naming a favorite spot. Neither woman particularly wanted the burden of the other in her house.

They met when the Albatross, the Island's famous little walk-up restaurant, was at its busiest, and their conversation would be protected by the noise around them.

Emily was delighted by Stella's suggestion. "Of course," she said facetiously, "I have heard something about these purchases here and there." She looked at Stella with an earnestness that played into Stella's hand. "This is definitely something for the Committee."

"Yes," said Stella, with a sly little smile. "I thought so, too."

"I'll see about calling a meeting. We can invite everyone. This is our chance to get the whole Island involved." She caught her breath with excitement. "I know! It can be the Committee of the Concerned at-large!

Emily's eyes shone at the thought of so much influence. "After all, we all need to be on the same page."

After a hurried lunch, they each departed to their respective tasks.

In addition to those she'd discussed with Emily, Stella had one that was highest on her list.

She went home to make a little call to a reporter she'd once met in Green Bay.

As more and more properties were being bought and sold, Fiona's unease grew, and she decided that it would be wise to write something for the local newspaper, declaring her support for the Island's rural heritage of solitude and quiet.

When her column appeared, she waited for some kind of reaction, but there was almost none. One or two people quietly expressed their appreciation at the grocery store, but that was all.

"Why do you suppose no one's commenting?" she asked Oliver one afternoon.

"It's so unusual."

He did not look up from his computer screen. "The light of lights looks always on the motive, not the deed, the shadow of shadows on the deed alone."

Fiona raised an eyebrow, which he did not see. "Is that Yeats?"

"People who lean on logic and philosophy and rational exposition end by starving the best part of the mind."

Fiona now regretted having engaged him. Once he began

down this road, he was impossible to stop.

"I'm sorry I asked. Forget it."

Fiona picked up her headphones and turned them on. "I'm going to read now," she said loudly over her music.

If Oliver had a response, she didn't hear it.

Sometime later, she was jolted by the ringing of her cell phone, and after a brief conversation, she rose and began to gather her things.

"I'm afraid I have to leave. Robert, it seems, has been causing trouble at the hotel."

Oliver looked up with interest. He rather enjoyed trouble.

"If you have no trouble, buy a goat."

"I didn't buy him. And anyway, I'm renting him out."

"Nevertheless."

"Is that one of your rules?"

Oliver shrugged. "It is now."

Fiona eyed him suspiciously. "You just make this stuff up on the fly."

The office phone rang, and Oliver answered it with unwonted alacrity.

Fiona, waiting to see whether it was for her, mouthed her words to him. "Well?"

Oliver Robert shrugged again, turned his back, and continued his conversation on the phone.

"No, ma'am, there is no garbage pick-up on the Island, no matter what Paul at the dock told you."

Picking up her bag, Fiona stalked out of the office. He could deal with his own set of problems.

Chapter 35 ✤

Fiona, Elisabeth, and Roger stood surveying the wreckage of the new yoga studio.

"Can't the classes be held outside?" asked Elisabeth, somewhat plaintively.

"The mosquitoes are a problem," said Roger.

She looked at him patiently. It was often necessary to be patient with Roger. "More of a problem than goat manure?"

"I would say so, yes."

Elisabeth said nothing.

"I mean," added Roger, "they all know it's goat yoga. They must expect that a goat wouldn't be housebroken."

Elisabeth's tone was acquiring a bite. "I should think they would also expect it to be outside."

"They might also expect that the goat in question be a bit more...pleasant to encounter," added Fiona.

They all turned to look at Robert, who was standing in the corner of the studio, serenely chewing one of the rolled-up yoga mats stacked on the rack at the back of the room. He sensed their interest and daintily stomped his hooves to show his approval. Elisabeth noted the resulting dents in the newly installed hardwood floor.

"We'll be going through a lot of yoga mats at this rate,"

she said wryly.

"Cost of doing business," said Roger.

In the end, Elisabeth won as Fiona had suspected she would, and the goat yoga continued on the lawn outside the hotel. At first, Roger was concerned that they needed a tent, but Elisabeth convinced him that passersby being able to see the classes was a means of generating interest, so he acquired instead a canvas pavilion with see-through mesh sides to keep out the mosquitoes. This solution seemed to please everyone, except, possibly, Robert, but he had so far kept his views on this subject to himself.

Chapter 36

F iona strode into the office one morning in an energetic mood. Sitting around and waiting for things to happen was not her style. She was exhausted by all the mystery and gossip.

"Oliver," she announced, "We need to tackle this property-buying thing. It's important. Maybe it's time for a town meeting."

Oliver perked up at once. He enjoyed town meetings; they gave him things to do.

"The problem is," Fiona went on, "if we make it an official meeting, we have to post notice and follow the legal restrictions on scheduling and so forth."

"So, why not skip the official meeting, and let the Committee of the Concerned host something?" asked Oliver. "They can organize, and I can arrange for them to have it in the church basement."

Fiona looked at him with surprise.

"Well, we have to do something," he said indignantly. "God gives every bird a worm, but he doesn't throw it in the nest."

Fiona laughed at his militant tone. "I'm glad you're on board, Oliver."

Oliver looked smug. "A wise man does at first what a fool must do at last."

"Okay," said Fiona pouring herself a cup of coffee. "Why don't you give Emily a call?

When he made the call, Fiona could hear Emily Martin's voice from across the room. Conversations with Emily tended to be somewhat one-sided.

"Well, I must say, Oliver, great minds think alike! Sooner would be best, don't you think?" She did not pause for an answer. "I'll take care of everything, don't you worry."

Oliver started to mention St. Thor's. "Yes, yes, that's the best place, probably. Unless…the school? Well, we'll figure it all out. I'll be in touch. Bye-bye!"

Oliver put the phone down and turned his head to look at Fiona.

"Missile armed."

Fiona tipped her head cheerfully. "Thank you, Oliver. You tell me when, and I'll be there."

Ben had happily accepted the job of supervising Robert at the hotel. It wasn't much different from what he did at Fiona's, except that he helped with transport back and forth. Among the fringe benefits for Ben were the warm cookies from the hotel's kitchen and the unlikelihood of running into Caleb.

Roger had built a pen with a little shed behind the main building, and after some initial explorations, Robert seemed content.

The job had very few responsibilities, and Ben found

himself with little to do. He had been raised to look for ways to make himself useful, and Elisabeth soon found a willing assistant for the many little chores necessary for running a hotel. Ben's intelligence and good manners led her to depend upon him more and more, and she enjoyed his cheerful company, just as Fiona always had.

Having Ben around, so far as Elisabeth could tell, was the primary advantage of goat yoga.

Chapter 37

The Committee for the Concerned had been able to arrange the unofficial meeting quite quickly, and only a few posters—at the grocery store, the post office, the ferry station, and the Mercantile—were sufficient to get the word out. Most of the information spread by word of mouth, perhaps most particularly by Emily's.

On the day of the event, Fiona was in the interim period between work and the evening's meeting when Elisabeth called. She chit-chatted for a few minutes in a way that Fiona, rushing around to finish various tasks before she had to leave, found the smallest bit annoying.

"Listen," she said. "You know I'd love to chat, but I have this meeting I need to go to."

"Actually," said Elisabeth, "that's why I'm calling."

Half-listening, Fiona was standing on one foot, trying to buckle the strap on her new Italian sandals. "Oh?"

"I got a call today from somebody offering to buy the hotel."

Fiona dropped her shoe and sat down on a kitchen chair. "What did you say to him?"

"Very little, actually. I just listened."

"You listened? You didn't tell whoever it was to shove off?"

"He was a very nice attorney from Nebraska. I forget his

name—Neil Somebody—who made me a rather spectacular offer."

"Please don't tell me you're considering it."

"Well, it's an amazing sum. Far more than the place is worth, frankly, and they'd keep us on to run the place. We can't just turn it down without considering it."

Fiona was stunned. Elisabeth had a trust fund. And although she lived a relatively frugal life—until the purchase of the hotel—she had never wanted for anything. She and Roger had been behaving as if the hotel was a dream come true. This must be a great deal of money to catch her attention. And if Elisabeth was tempted…

"But…"

"I know, Fiona, I know." Elisabeth sounded very calm, and very cool. "But when we make it—and we haven't yet—this will be a business decision. Nothing more."

"A *business decision?* The life of the whole Island is at stake. This is practically the last outpost of sanity in the world, and you want to take money to destroy it? Elisabeth, you're my friend."

There was a long silence, and Fiona listened as if Elisabeth had spoken words.

"I see," said Fiona, after a full minute.

Without another word, she slowly hung up the phone.

As Fiona drove up to St. Thor's Lutheran Church, the parking lot was already packed. Despite the seriousness of the topic, she felt an unfamiliar lightness at the prospect of a meeting in which she had no official part. She followed the flow of people to the church basement.

The rows of folding chairs were nearly filled, and, at the back, despite ceaseless interference and various forms of brow-beating by Emily Martin, the church ladies had graciously opened their kitchen, with coffee urns and plates of cookies arranged along the long buffet counter that separated the kitchen from the rest of the room.

Fiona saw Nancy seated at the end of a row, and slipped in beside her just as the pastor came to the front for welcoming remarks and a prayer. Emily stood nearby, visibly impatient to take over the meeting.

"Lord God, Heavenly Father," he began, "look down on this assembly to offer us grace and understanding. Help us to respect one another, and to find Your path to righteousness..." The pastor, who took his responsibilities seriously, firmly believed that his invocation was essential to the proceedings, and he went on accordingly, and at great length, with Emily fidgeting next to him.

Fiona found her mind wandering and had to snap herself back to paying attention.

"...for even as we sow, so shall we reap, and we must sow the seeds of mutual assistance and good faith..."

Fiona now felt a sneeze coming on and was desperate to suppress it. She added her own prayers that she could hold on until he finished.

"...and in Your Heavenly power and might, we seek refuge..."

Fiona was surreptitiously squeezing her nose as she bent

her head, but the tickling would not stop.

"…in Jesus's name, Amen."

Fiona hastily buried her face in her arm. "ACHOO!"

"God Bless You," chorused all assembled.

Nancy leaned over and whispered loudly in Fiona's ear. "If only Pastor John could have thought of that."

She pressed a tissue into Fiona's hand. "Here."

Fiona nodded her thanks.

Emily had already expressed her appreciation to the Pastor and was launched. Stella, looking as if she had a mouthful of canaries, sat silently nearby, facing the audience, her eyes drifting over the crowd as if searching for someone.

"As you all know, we have had someone—or some group of someones—buying up shoreline properties along the western side. I understand that there are offers being made elsewhere, too, all in the same style, but not in the same name. That's, at this point, all we really know. But we, the members of the Committee of the Concerned, are offering this forum for the people of Washington Island to discuss how to address this situation as it now, er, stands."

Several people raised their hands, wanting to speak, but Emily, who was thoroughly enjoying being the center of attention, was not yet finished.

"As of yet, we have been unable to determine who is behind the purchases, and what they intend to do with them. But you have my word that I will see to it that we find out. Ladies and Gentlemen, that's what the Committee for the Concerned is all about: helping the Island community in these moments of mutual, um, concern and confusion."

She looked around the room with satisfaction and was about to continue when Jake stood up and spoke without raising his hand.

"How many offers have there been so far?"

Marcie, who had foregone an evening of television and was seriously wishing for a glass of wine, spoke up from across the room.

"There have been six sales on shoreline properties so far, with four new offers to properties not previously for sale—"

She was interrupted by calls for her to stand and speak up. She did so before Emily could urge her.

"In addition, there have been offers made on the golf course, Schmidt's tavern, and a dairy farm. Every day, I find more offers, and they're generous, too. Usually more than the asking price."

Marcie sat.

At the front of the room, Emily Martin was fuming. People were speaking without being called on. She was the Chairman.

"Ladies and Gentlemen," she began, "For the sake of an orderly—"

A longtime resident, a retired astronomy professor, stood up before she could finish. "It seems clear that someone's intent on buying up the whole Island. If we aren't careful, sooner or later our voices will be drowned out, and whoever has all this property will have all the say."

"He who has the gold makes the rules," called out someone.

A number of people voiced their views, and the resulting chaos raised Emily's frustration. Irritably, she tried to call order, but no one was listening. Stella, still silent, sat nearby complacently.

Jake spoke up again. "Seems to me we got the power here. They can't build stuff without approval. We get to say yes or no, no matter how much property someone buys."

He craned his head to look toward the back. "Isn't that right, Fiona?"

Fiona stood up reluctantly. She had hoped not to have to say anything. Stella turned her head and focused in on Fiona with a faint gleam in her eye.

"Before anything is built, the plans must meet community approval, yes." Her experience with town meetings had taught her to use a carrying voice, and the crowd quieted down in order to listen.

"As you know, I'm worried about the possibility of a project that could change the character of the entire Island. It's true that we don't know yet who the purchasers are, or what they have in mind, but I think there has been opposition to condominiums and hotel proposals in the past, and I am inclined to agree with that view. We can't very well stop anyone from buying, but we can stop development. I think we should stand together to oppose this—whatever it turns out to be."

There were murmurs of approval. She may not have the best morals, but that Campbell woman seemed to have a proper respect for the Island.

"I got somethin' to say." A woman stood up. Fiona recognized her as Eunice Schmidt from one of the little taverns that had been passed down from generation to generation for at least a hundred years. Eunice had been a beauty in her youth.

Now, she was in her seventies, still slim, but slightly bent, with iron gray hair and a lined face. Her voice rang out. All heads pivoted in her direction.

"My husband and I been trying to sell our place for going on five years, and we hadn't got even a nibble until this all came along. That money means a difference to us. It's all fine for you. Maybe you have what you need for the rest of your life, and you'll never have to worry. What are we suppose to do?" There was anguish in her voice. "What are we suppose to do?"

Fiona, still standing, faced her, listening, as her heart fell. She had thought she had always been sympathetic to Islanders and their needs, but she realized now that she had been blind.

"We never asked for nothing. We worked hard our whole lives. Nobody ever gave us nothing. Now we just want a little rest and a little security. We want to sell what's ours and have a little nest egg. Is that what you want to take from us?"

Eunice gave Fiona a long, hard look. "I don't bear you no grudge. But don't you bear a grudge against us. People gotta live."

And with a small nod of affirmation to herself, Eunice sat down.

There was general murmuring, with everyone commenting to one another at once.

Stella, with an unerring instinct, chose this moment to speak.

"Ladies and Gentlemen," she said. "There's something important I think you should know."

Chapter 38

S till murmuring, the crowd at the meeting for the Committee of the Concerned looked with interest toward the front of the room, where Stella DesRosiers stood with an expression of deep satisfaction.

She had been looking forward to this moment, and she took the opportunity to savor it. She surveyed the room with a small, rare smile, and waited, like a schoolteacher, for the room to quiet. Fiona began to sit down but was frozen by Stella's words.

"Ladies and Gentlemen," she said again, "we have a viper among us. Someone so cunning and so malicious that she will lie to get whatever she wants. Your Chairman, Fiona Campbell, is the owner of all these properties. She is using her position to enrich herself."

The room was dead silent.

Fiona laughed. "You cannot be serious. That's not even a good lie, Stella, and you know it."

She had a sudden mental image of Stella peddling a basket of shiny red apples through the cottage window.

"Oh," said Stella with authority. "I know it, all right. I know that I have a document in my hand that proves that all of the land purchased belongs to the Victor Eldridge Irrevocable

Trust, held for the benefit of one Fiona Ainsley Campbell."

Fiona felt the room tilt.

"What did you say?"

"Do you want me to repeat it?" asked Stella, silkily.

"Yes," said Fiona. "Repeat it."

Fiona was aware of all eyes on her as she listened to Stella read the document again.

"I...don't understand."

"It's clear enough," said Stella.

Fiona was walking toward the front of the room. "Let me see that."

She reached out to take the papers, and Stella handed them over with smug condescension.

The room was silent as Fiona read. When she finished and looked up, she saw people gazing at her with varying levels of enmity. There were a few sympathetic faces, but by and large, Island culture was based on honesty. Islanders didn't like liars.

Silent for once, Emily Martin looked at her as if she were a new and fascinating exhibit.

Slowly, Fiona gathered words in her head. They were inadequate, she knew.

"These documents are from the estate of my uncle, who died a few weeks ago. I swear to you, I had no idea. I would never—"

"Ah," said Stella in that same slithery voice as before. "Anyone who has watched your term in public office can have no doubt that you set out to do this very deliberately."

Fiona shook her head in disbelief. "I don't understand this." She looked out at the room. "I don't want development.

I love the Island the way it is."

A low muttering had begun in the room, and near the back in a far corner, a reporter sat, scribbling in her notebook.

Nancy stood up and marched to the front of the room. "Come on," she said, taking Fiona by the arm. "Let's get out of here." Nancy caught Jake's eye, and, as the crowd began arguing, together they, along with Charlotte, escorted Fiona to her car and met her at home.

Fiona was mostly silent, sitting in her living room as her friends poured drinks and seated themselves. She looked around at their faces.

"I hope you know that I am sincere when I say I had no idea of any of this. No idea at all."

Fiona saw as their eyes met briefly, and then they all looked back at her in silence.

Chapter 39

Fiona dreamed that she was pulling weeds at the edge of a public parking lot. A small hose was on nearby with a small flow of water that made the ground softer and the weeds easier to pull. She thought to herself that the water might draw snakes, and just as she thought it, she saw that there were snakes moving in the water. She stepped away, but the water from the hose was now flowing over the entire road, so instead of a trickle there was a shallow flood moving down the street. She was barefoot, and at first it was easy to avoid the snakes, but soon there were so many being moved along by the shallow water—swimming and at the same time being swept along—that it became more and more difficult to avoid them.

The colors of the snakes were varied and beautiful—blue, and green, and red, some with shimmering stripes, golden heads, or yellow markings. She couldn't tell which were venomous, and she became increasingly alarmed.

She saw suddenly a snake with red and yellow stripes moving toward her, and even in her dream, the childhood rhyme she had learned came into her mind: "red and yellow, kill a fellow." As she thought it, the snake with the red stripes next to the yellow stripes struck her foot. She could feel the hot venom coursing through her, and she knew that she would die.

The morning after the meeting, Fiona's phone and email were filled with messages. There were three kinds: those of people who wanted to drive her out of office, those of people who wanted her to buy their property, and reporters who had read the story in the Green Bay paper and wanted to write their own.

Alerted to its existence, Fiona read the article with rising fury. In addition to the news of the property purchases and an account of last night's meeting, it also included the story of her election, recall, accusations of malfeasance, and other features of her first months in office. By the time she'd reached the end, Fiona would have arrested herself.

Her first task, she realized, was to find out what was going on. With shaking hands, she made a call to Dirk Richards, Uncle Victor's lawyer in New York.

His calm, lawyerly voice did not reassure her.

"I'm afraid there's not much you can do at this point, Ms. Campbell. Mr. Eldridge left clear instructions, and until they are carried out to their completion, I'm afraid we must simply let his plans take their course."

"But what are his plans? And how long will it be for them to 'take their course?'"

"Mr. Eldridge's instructions are part of a separate legal document, not part of the trust that you inherited. The trust—and you—are merely the beneficiaries of his plans."

"But this is not a benefit. It's causing a great deal of trouble."

The lawyer paused a moment and cleared his throat. "Well, er, uh, well, I am sorry to hear that, but I'm afraid there's nothing that can be done."

"As his heir, what am I entitled to know?"

"In this instance, I'm afraid, nothing."

"Nothing?"

He was politely apologetic, but firm. "I am sorry, but nothing. Nothing at all."

"Can I reject the proceeds?"

"You can refuse to accept any monies from the trust, yes. But you can't refuse the proceeds from being given to the trust."

"Either way, my name is on it."

"Either way," he agreed.

The news of a lone wolf on the Island was met with indifference by almost everyone except the farmers, and they took extra precautions to keep their livestock safe. To date, there had been some lost chickens, but that could have been the work of the usual coyote or fox. The deer population appeared to be the wolf's primary source of food.

The DNR plane and a helicopter, swooping low over the Island in search of the wolf, gave the impression that the Island was under siege, and from Fiona's perspective, it seemed that it actually was.

The reaction to Stella's bombshell made it nearly impossible for Fiona to go anywhere without feeling cold eyes on her. After putting off her shopping until dire necessity forced it upon her, she was relieved to find Nika at the grocery store. Nika's warm friendship acted as a buffer until Fiona said her goodbyes and left the store.

Pent up feelings were relieved in a flow of words.

"She pretends she didn't know, but I think she has something to do with it. You'll notice that she refused to call an official meeting. It had to be held at the Lutherans'."

Nika attempted a defense. "But that was because—"

"Oh, don't think she can fool me. I've known what she is all along. In it for herself."

"In what?" asked someone else.

"Why, in public life, of course. You know she did it just so she could lord it over Stella. That poor woman hasn't had a moment's peace since Miss Fiona Campbell moved in next door."

Nika tried again. "Well, that seems—"

"—and another thing. That goat of hers. Have you noticed how it's allowed to take up residence at the hotel? How legal do you suppose that is, having livestock at a hotel? Highly unlikely, I'd say. Highly unlikely. But some people think the rules just don't apply to them."

Heads nodded sagely.

"But—" tried Nika again.

"I'm telling you—you just can't trust that woman. All those rumors about her morals, well. No smoke without fire, you know. No smoke without fire."

Nika left the store feeling she had let Fiona down, and that she needed to offer some support. She made the short drive down the road to Fiona's and found her putting away groceries.

"Are you okay?" asked Nika, beginning to help Fiona unpack.

Fiona made a gesture of helplessness. "Yeah. I'm okay." She gave a small sound that was supposed to be a laugh. "Been better, though."

"Come on," said Nika. "Let's finish this up and sit down with a nice cup of tea. My grandma always said that tea fixed everything."

Fiona recalled a story Nika had told about family Christmases. "Was this the grandma with the gin?"

Nika started laughing. "Sure was."

The story in the Green Bay paper had been picked up in Milwaukee and Madison and soon spread all around the state. Reporters called Fiona night and day at home and at the office, and she steadfastly refused to comment.

"A little truth makes the whole lie pass," commented Oliver, after reading the latest account.

Fiona was silent as she untangled this. "Oh," she said at last. "I see what you mean."

Oliver gave just the faintest of smiles.

As news of more property purchases continued, Fiona was feeling more alone than ever. With Pete gone and Elisabeth's loyalty in question, she felt surrounded by animosity. As she thought about her situation, it seemed obvious that she needed public relations help of some sort. The first goal, she thought, was to try to get the facts out, however improbable they might be. She looked up from the papers on her desk, which she hadn't been reading.

"Listen, Oliver, I need to do something. What do you think about an official meeting?"

"Don't you mean a public hanging?"

"That's not funny."

"May I make a suggestion?"

"Please." Fiona was restlessly fidgeting with a pen.

"Before you even think of the meeting, I think you should write another op-ed."

"And say what?"

"Say what you've been saying to me. How you didn't know, it's not your plan, you have no control….." Oliver trailed off. "Etcetera."

"I'm not really sure I can convince anyone."

Oliver shrugged. "Those who do nothing make no mistakes."

Fiona made a wry face as she considered. "I suppose it's worth a shot. I've got to do something. If I've learned anything over this past year or two, it's that I can't leave attacks unanswered. Did you know that Stella is going around town accusing me of being the arsonist? It's totally crazy, but kind of scary."

"She measures others with her own yard."

Fiona stopped her fidgeting and stared at him.

"Are you saying you think she's the arsonist?"

Oliver shrugged again, his mask having fallen away in an honest conversation. "Can you think of anyone more likely?"

Fiona frowned. "No, actually. I can't."

Oliver's eyes met hers. "Well, then."

Fiona's friends were stalwart in their defense of her, but it was a thankless task. Nancy overheard a conversation at the hardware store and felt compelled to join in.

"Who's to say she's not the one starting the fires? Maybe she's trying to scare people into selling."

"Nonsense," said Nancy impatiently. "Do you have any idea how ridiculous you sound?"

"Well, she lied about the property development."

"She didn't lie. She didn't know."

"Now who's sounding ridiculous? How could she not know?"

Nancy scowled. She was fully aware of how unbelievable it all was. "Look," she began.

But she was interrupted.

"We've all known that her morals are not the best. A person with her character is perfectly capable of lying—especially with so much money at stake."

Nancy's temper was rising. "You know perfectly well there's nothing wrong with her morals. You can't believe all that malicious gossip."

"Watch me."

"She's got you hoodwinked, Nancy Iverssen."

Shocked, Nancy watched as they walked away. She didn't

believe for one minute that Fiona would lie. But she didn't have any idea how to stop people from believing what they heard. People, she well knew, would believe what suited them. They always had.

Chapter 40

Not content with his hopelessly undrinkable Bloody Marys, Roger had branched out into new forms of creativity, and there were now many manifestations of Roger's bartending catastrophes listed in his meticulous printing on the chalk board above the bar.

Although his drinks were poured generously and made of the best ingredients, they tended to have a unifying quality of awfulness whose source was sometimes difficult to pinpoint. Was it too much bitters? Not enough sugar? A heavy hand with the citrus? The flavors blended so completely that they all became part of the grim experience. An observer might have thought that the frequency of these drinks being unfinished might have given pause to an astute barkeeper, but not so in Roger's case. The results of his experiments appeared beneath his notice.

As local observers grew bored with placing bets on the speed and agility of Roger's patrons, a new source of entertainment arose which became known as The Challenge. This entailed the willing consumption of one of the host's concoctions on a dare or a bet with gleeful—but often in the end sympathetic and regretful—observers gauging the reactions of the subject. Over time, the rankings became standardized to include redness of the eyes, tear production, time to reaction, redness of the face and neck, perspiration, and quantity actually consumed. For this, avid followers kept a checklist—surreptitiously, of course.

Elisabeth was fully aware of the phenomena engendered by Roger's bartending but found herself unable to get the message through to him.

"I worry that we may kill a patron one of these days," she said to Joshua one morning after he had come for a special visit to the hotel's yoga class. "I mean, seriously, do you think someone could have a heart attack?"

"Oh wow. I hadn't thought of that." He looked thoughtful. "It's possible, I suppose. Have you discussed it with him?"

"Of course. But, well, you know Roger."

Joshua nodded. He knew.

"Have you spoken to Fiona? She usually has good advice."

His eyes held so much kindness and understanding, that Elisabeth wondered what he knew. Roger certainly wouldn't have told anyone about their disagreement, and she was fairly sure Fiona wouldn't have, either.

"Not recently."

He nodded, still gazing sympathetically at her. "You should join us for class sometime. You might find it soothing."

The truth was, Elisabeth was deeply upset about her falling out with Fiona, and much in need of soothing. In all their years of friendship, they'd never had an argument. Elisabeth had a tranquil nature, and this estrangement from her friend went against the grain. She debated what she should do, but the good friend who would normally have given her counsel was Fiona herself.

Elisabeth felt bereft.

N ow that she was working mostly at home, Fiona reflected on the way in which solitude could bring out the extremes of personality. On the one hand, when she was happy, being alone was by turns tranquil and joyous. But when she was feeling low, it was easy for her worst fears to grow and mutate out of all proportion. These were the times she was grateful to be at the office with Oliver. He wasn't exactly reassuring, but he was, at least, a voice to break through her inner monologue. She was actually missing him when the phone rang.

It was Jim Freeburg asking to stop by. The tone of his voice told her he had something serious to discuss.

It was odd to see Jim's truck pull up in front of her house as it had so regularly in the past. He came up the steps two at a time and knocked on the door.

"I hope you don't mind me coming to the house," he said. "But what I have to say isn't something I want talked about all over town."

Fiona almost made a joke that his just coming to her house would be talked about all over town, but she caught herself, realizing how he might take it. Accidental insults, she thought to herself.

She remembered the slights she had given and received in the days leading to Uncle Victor's funeral. "All of us," she thought, "bumbling through life and devastating one another." She winced remembering her own accidental insult to her cousin.

Fiona led Jim into the kitchen and offered him a cup of coffee.

"Sit down. Please."

Jim sat and watched as she moved around the kitchen. In spite of everything, being here again felt comfortable and good. Fiona put their mugs on the table and sat down across the table in Pete's usual place.

"I've been hearing some gossip around town, and I thought I should talk to you about it."

Fiona nodded, listening.

"I'm sure you've heard the stupid talk about you being the arsonist—and we don't have to guess the source of those rumors. But here's the thing: I keep thinking that it's much more likely that it could be Stella."

He scanned Fiona's face and seeing calm, he went on.

"I've always thought she was malicious, not actually capable of hurting anyone. But lately, I've begun to wonder. I mean, her hatred of you seems beyond any normal bounds."

Fiona nodded again. She had felt that, too.

"So, I can't help thinking that maybe you need to be careful. Let's say it is her. Then her proximity to you and your place could be very dangerous. I think we need to take some precautions."

Fiona frowned. Even though Oliver's worries had been along these lines, it was far more frightening to have Jim say them.

"Do you really think it could be her?"

"We have to look at everything. Frankly, at this point, just about everyone's a suspect, but Stella is the only one who seems to have a motive."

Fiona nodded yet again and said nothing, but her thoughts

were flying. Elisabeth had always thought that Stella had been the culprit in Fiona's barn fire, but Fiona had not taken it seriously. Elisabeth's instincts were usually good. Could she have been right? And Oliver, and now Jim, all asking the same questions.

Jim's face was serious. "Do you have a good fire alarm?"

"I have smoke detectors."

"Especially with you alone so much, I think we need to do a little more than that. Let's get a wireless hookup, so if the alarms are triggered, they go straight to the station."

"Really? You think that's necessary?"

With effort, Jim made his voice sound casual. "Better safe than sorry."

Fiona nodded. "Okay. I'll take care of it."

Jim put his empty cup down and stood to go.

"And Fiona—"

"Yes?"

"Don't wait."

His words echoing in her head, she watched him walk out to his car and felt shaken. She remembered the rule Oliver had cited when they had discussed this same topic.

"Beware the person with nothing to lose," he had said.

Between his responsibilities as fire chief and as game warden for the State, Jim was busy, but he felt as much obligation to Ben as to his work, so he took the time to explain the process of capturing the wolf to him.

"No one will hurt him. Our job is to protect him. He'll be tranquilized, examined, tagged, transported out, and released in an area better suited to him. And once he's tagged, we'll always be able to tell where he goes."

"Will I be able to see him?"

Jim hesitated. "Maybe. We'll have to see."

"Do you think he's a good wolf, or a bad wolf?" asked Ben flippantly.

Jim laughed. "That remains to be seen."

Chapter 41

The Washington Hotel's goat yoga classes had a unique quality that tended to surprise its participants. People came expecting some gentle romping with adorable baby goats. They did not expect a cantankerous, un-housebroken, hundred-pound animal with wicked yellow eyes who talked, head-butted them, and tried to sit on their heads.

Roger's stoic approach to these events added an even more unexpected dimension. If they thought that he would offer advice, consolation, or even a rationale for this strange experience, they went away disappointed.

Roger merely entered the room, walked to the front, or wherever he felt like being, sat down, and began his practice. There was no incense, no diffusers of essential oils, no music, and no guidance. There was just Roger, making his way through a series of very difficult poses, while Robert the goat ambled or rampaged depending upon his mood.

In the first class, when a young woman screamed and fell down after being head-butted, everyone looked to Roger to say something, but the only explanation they heard was from Robert as he muttered "WUTWUTWUTWUT" to himself and searched for someone to sit on. Elisabeth overheard the comments afterward and was concerned.

"How are classes going?" she asked Roger that evening as they were getting ready for bed.

"Fine."

"Are you sure?"

Roger looked at her with his characteristic expression. "Pretty sure," he said and went to brush his teeth.

Elisabeth lay awake that night for a long time, wondering whether she should bring in Joshua to make some sense of things.

Aided by the newspaper reports, the backlash against Fiona had been unceasing, and it had become quite clear that nothing she could say would convince anyone. She admitted to herself that, had it been anyone else, she would have been unconvinced, too. It was wearing her down.

After a particularly contentious phone call demanding her recusal, her removal from office, and threatening all sorts of legal action, Fiona hung up the phone, and immediately began flinging her things into her bag in preparation for departure. She recalled Oliver's joke about public execution, and it didn't seem funny.

All at once, she stopped her flurry of activities, sat in her chair, and buried her head on her desk.

Oliver looked up, surprised. Fiona was a passionate person, and he was used to her intensity. But he had never seen her like this. His face showed his struggle with himself. Behind his man-nered conversation and posturing was a kind heart that he rarely showed. "Never confuse your colleagues with your friends," he reminded himself, sternly. But he couldn't help himself.

"What's wrong?" he asked, at last.

With her head in her hands Fiona's voice was muffled. Oliver had to strain to hear.

"I can't take this anymore."

"What?" asked Oliver. "What can't you take?"

Fiona sat up and brushed the hair from her face.

"This. All of this."

She was struggling to maintain control of her emotions.

"I keep asking myself why. Why would Uncle Victor do this to me?"

She looked at him briefly, then shook her head and looked off into the distance.

"Uncle Victor always thought that money was the key to everything. It's not that he didn't value culture—because he did. He had the most exquisite appreciation of art, and music, literature, and wine, and fine food. But he believed that none of those things—either their creation or their enjoyment—was—is—possible without wealth. So, he made wealth the whole focus of his life—he wanted to make it the focus of mine, too."

Oliver nodded, even though she wasn't looking at him.

"He loved me. I know he did. He didn't mean to do this. He didn't understand." She was silent a long time. "He never did."

One tear fell, and she wiped it away impatiently. Suddenly, she was brisk and in a hurry. Again, she swept her hair away from her face and took a deep breath.

"I'm going out," she said. And rising, she collected her bag and left the office, leaving Oliver looking after her, for once silent.

Chapter 42

The intensity of Fiona's emotions often hindered her, and although she had calmed down significantly, she was still impaired as she hurried from her office. She strode down the long hall in a state of distraction and pushed open the exterior door with unnecessary force.

Although she was used to carrying it, her heavy bag threw her slightly off balance, and as she stepped out the door onto the cracked concrete step, her ankle turned, and she went down hard onto the sidewalk, landing on her knee, her bags flying ahead of her and falling with a slightly smaller thud.

Fiona sat back onto the ground, rocking—almost sobbing—with pain. There was no one around. Oliver wouldn't have heard anything from his desk inside, which was just as well. Fiona wouldn't have wanted a witness, and besides, she had little confidence in Oliver's capacity for dealing with an emergency.

Fiona didn't wait for her breath to return before she could assess the damage. Carefully, she touched her knee. She could move it. She looked through the tear in her jeans and gazed at the extent of the gash. It was ugly and painful but not serious. Her ankle was a little sprained, but she thought she could stand. Impatiently, she wiped the tears from her face, camouflaged them with sunglasses, and slowly stood up. Limping, she made her way to her car and the refuge of home.

Chapter 43 ❖

As she pulled into her driveway, Fiona heard a ringing sound, and after a moment's confusion, she realized it was coming from the house. Hampered by her ankle, she hurried to the door and flung it open to the high-pitched squeal of an alarm.

She took a step in, and although she could smell nothing, she was instantly aware of a faint mistiness that filled her vision. Her mind racing, Fiona realized that if she couldn't smell smoke, it was almost certainly carbon monoxide, and then, with a sinking heart, she thought of Attila. He might be tame, but he would never come when called. He would instinctively know to escape fire, but he would be helpless against carbon monoxide.

Hands shaking and wondering why her new alarm system hadn't already notified the fire department, Fiona backed out of the house and dialed for help.

It was a matter of minutes before she heard the sirens, and at the same time, her phone started ringing.

"Fiona, it's Jim. The department is almost there, and I'm on my way."

"Please hurry."

The sirens were now close enough to be earsplitting. Engine Numbers 1 and 2 and the rescue squad pulled up, followed shortly afterward by Jim's pickup with the red light flashing on the roof.

The sound of an alarm continued through the open door.

While Jim pulled her away from the house, his men raced in, pulling on their bunker coats and their masks as they went, carrying the small electronic detectors that would identify the source of the leak. For the second time in as many years, the fire department had come to save her property.

In a matter of minutes, though, the sound of the alarm stopped. Fiona heard a faint sound from Jim's comm system, and he bent his head to speak into the microphone. At the same time, one of the men appeared at the door, mask off, holding an ancient smoke detector, wires dangling.

Jim gave her a wry look. "Seems like an old detector got overlooked when they put in your new system."

"There's no carbon monoxide?"

He shook his head.

Fiona nodded, relieved.

"Wait a minute," said one of the men. "What about the mist? The mist you saw?"

Fiona looked at them, frowning. "I'm not really sure."

For the first time, Jim looked closely at her. "Fiona, take off your sunglasses."

She had a split second of wanting to smack herself in the forehead and then slowly removed her glasses.

He looked at her, a slow smile beginning against his will. "Those are the dirtiest glasses I've ever seen. What do you do? Run your fingers over them?"

He held the glasses up. "Gentlemen, here's your mist."

They all began to laugh, relieved not to have to deal with a genuine catastrophe. Sheepishly, and half apologetically, Fiona laughed and rolled her eyes at the same time.

"The mist was what had us really worried," commented the assistant chief. "Thought maybe a propane tank was leaking."

"It's really okay?" she asked, thinking of Attila.

"We went all over the house to make sure. Primary cause: faulty detector," he paused, "Secondary cause: dirty glasses."

They teased her good naturedly as they replaced their gear on the trucks, and she took it as intended. Her relief overcame her embarrassment.

Jim spoke in a low voice. "Have to admit I kind of freaked out when I realized it was your house. I'm really glad we got that system installed. Should give you some peace of mind."

He didn't mention that his own peace of mind was somewhat disturbed, however. He looked at her face and saw that she'd been crying. Now he understood the sunglasses. "Are you okay?"

"I'm fine. Just had a fall and twisted my ankle."

"Want to have one of the guys look at it?"

"No, no. It's not serious. Thanks, though."

"You sure?"

She faked a reassuring smile. "I'm sure."

Feeling utterly alone in her troubles, Fiona needed comfort. She tried calling Pete, but the Skype frog gulped unanswered in the ether.

She sat at her desk and stared at the darkened screen of her laptop. Behind her in the room she could hear Attila—mercifully unharmed— scrabbling along the edges of the room on his nightly explorations. A moment later, she felt his sharp little nails as he climbed the leg of her jeans, painfully crossed her injured knee, and popped onto the desk. He had eaten well from his jar lid, and now he wanted to play. Sadly, she reached out her hand to play tag with him across the surface of the desk. It was a game he loved, and his least weasel happiness made her feel a little better.

After he scampered off to continue his nightly rounds, Fiona cautiously stood from the desk, gasping a bit at the pain in her knee.

She poured herself a generous scotch and, still limping, took herself off for an early bedtime and the solace of sleep.

Jim and Ben were going to have lunch together, and they met by the entrance to School House Beach. As soon as he saw Jim, Ben ran to meet him.

"How come you haven't found the wolf yet?" Ben asked by way of greeting.

Jim held out his hands helplessly.

"Wolves are elusive. Want to eat at the picnic table on the beach?"

"Sure."

Unconsciously, Ben reached up to catch the branch of the old beech tree that towered over the path. Only a few months before he had been unable to reach it. "Maybe they're hard to catch because they're smart. They know people hate them."

"Maybe so," agreed Jim.

They walked down the sloping drive through the cemetery to School House Beach.

"How come people hate wolves when they love dogs so much?"

"Not everybody hates wolves. I don't." Jim grinned at him. "You don't."

"I know, but..."

"I guess people see them as a threat to their livestock. But we need wolves. They're part of our original ecosystem. It's my job to try to help strike the right balance."

"Do they kill people?"

"Sometimes. But, so do mountain lions, and we have them in Wisconsin, too." Jim frowned, searching his memory.

"I don't think anyone's been killed by a wolf around here since the nineteenth century. But there was a guy right across the lake in Escanaba pretty recently who was chased up a tree by a pack of wolves."

"But ours is all alone?"

Jim smiled to himself at the "ours." "Far as I can tell. Wolves are very good at hiding their presence, but this is a small island. If there were more, we'd probably know." He grinned. "The farmers would tell us."

They settled at the picnic table and got out their sandwiches. It was a warm day, and the breeze from the lake felt good.

Ben looked worried. "So, he's all by himself, and wolves are pack animals. That's kind of sad."

"Yes," said Jim. "It is."

He thought for a while about loneliness and then shook it off. This was not the time to get moody. He looked at the boy sitting across the table and noticed he was getting taller.

"You shouldn't worry about the wolf. He'll be caught, tagged, and released somewhere else. He's kind of been trapped here on the Island, and it's unfair for him to spend his whole life here alone without other wolves for company."

Ben nodded, his mouth full.

"And listen," said Jim. "Don't take this conversation as an excuse to be careless. A wolf in the woods can be dangerous." He looked Ben directly in the eye. "You stay out of the woods until he's gone, okay?"

"Okay," said Ben.

Chapter 44

Fiona was developing a new appreciation of Oliver. He had proven himself a loyal employee—if not friend—and his advice was always sound. She thought about his habit of spouting aphorisms at every turn. This, she realized, was his way of protecting himself. By using stock phrases, he could avoid genuine interaction with people. He must, she thought, be hiding a lot of pain and sadness. Fiona felt compassion for anyone's suffering, and with the compassion came new respect for Oliver and the beginnings of genuine affection.

She was lost in thought, walking into the ferry office to pick up a package, when Emily pulled up in her big, black SUV.

Fiona sighed. She was in no mood for Emily Martin.

As usual, Emily was all bustle.

"I hear the fire department was called to your house yesterday. Everyone's talking about it. People are wondering about your judgment, and those are the ones who like you! Now I want you to know, Fiona, that no matter what everybody says, I'm sure anyone could have made a silly mistake like that. And believe me, I have no ill will toward you. None whatever. Besides, I'm sure you didn't set those fires."

"Well," said Fiona. She took a breath to add something more but was flummoxed. "Well," she said again.

"I noticed that you're limping. Did that happen yesterday?"

"Just a sprain. Nothing serious."

Emily nodded sagely. "Well, my goodness. Glad it wasn't worse. I know I couldn't afford a sprained ankle. Between this development question and the literary festival, I'm just so terribly busy. But, after all, these are just the kinds of things that the Committee for the Concerned is meant to deal with, and it is our duty! But it's all so much...."

She sighed and then returned to her usual brisk self. "Still, the Island needs me." She leaned over Caleb to speak confidingly. He grimaced, rolled his eyes, and then stared ahead as if pretending nothing was happening.

Emily didn't seem to notice but looked at her with bright eyes that reminded Fiona a bit of Attila. An image of Emily leaping across the floor in war dance flashed across her mind. She smiled in spite of herself.

"Now, I won't keep you," said Emily, as she kept Fiona standing on her still painful ankle. "But I do have some very exciting news."

She paused expectantly, waiting to be encouraged.

"And what is that?" asked Fiona, resignedly.

"We have booked our featured author!"

Fiona was now genuinely curious. "Really? Who?"

Emily leaned in breathlessly. "Bartholomew Salazar."

She saw Fiona's blank expression. "Oh, dear. You probably aren't familiar with the elite literary scene, and don't know who he is. Well," she began, "he's—"

"Oh, I know who he is," said Fiona, sounding puzzled. "But I don't understand—"

"—that's just it. No one understands him, poor man. That's why it's such an opportunity to have him here."

Fiona understood this to mean that no one else wanted him and he would therefore be easy to get. She was, in fact, familiar with Bartholomew Salazar, and she had doubts about whether he would be suitable.

"Have you read anything he's written?" asked Fiona.

"Mom," said Caleb in a warning tone.

Emily looked blank. "He's quite famous. There are stories about him in *The New York Times, The Atlantic, The New Yorker*…everywhere. Everyone who's anyone knows him: big stars, politicians, everyone. He's writing a book."

"But—" began Fiona.

"He is a very important literary figure. It's quite a coup to get him. He will bring a great deal of prestige to our little festival." Emily preened. "I'm so happy I was able to get him." She leaned in and spoke in a stage whisper, "We'll make the Island proud. Just think if I hadn't come along!"

"Just think," echoed Fiona, smiling weakly.

She wondered fleetingly whether anyone would mind if she pulled Emily out of the truck and pushed her off the dock. Caleb probably wouldn't. He might even help.

Emily was still talking.

"…and I've been putting together the agenda for the festival. It's so exciting! I, myself, will be giving a talk entitled *Culture In The Hinterlands: How I Encouraged Reading In A Small Town.*"

She lowered her voice a bit to demonstrate modesty. "Having a sense of purpose. That's what keeps me going."

"Mom!" said Caleb, again.

She laughed, ruffled Caleb's hair as if he were a child rather than a hulking adolescent, and sighed again, this time with satisfaction. Caleb seethed.

"Better go." She looked Fiona over and gave her a gracious smile.

"It's so good to be needed. Someday, you'll know just what I mean."

She gave a cheery wave and drove off.

Stella was increasingly impatient about the slow pace of investigations into the land purchases. She was pleased with all the attention the case was getting in the news, but she felt something more was needed to increase pressure on Fiona.

Politicians are well aware that each call they receive from a constituent probably represents the views of many others, and they use the calls and letters they receive to gauge public opinion. Stella knew that it only took remarkably few such calls to convince an office holder that there was a groundswell of opinion, and in this case, she knew that it wouldn't be difficult to create that sense of public feeling with the Town Board. If each of them received only ten or twenty calls, it would feel like an overwhelming demand. The calls, Stella knew, couldn't just come from her. It would be best to include people whose opinions had not yet been heard. Accordingly, she made a few discreet calls herself.

The scratchy sound of an old recording coming from a small speaker could barely be heard above the sounds of the bar. It was Yeats reading his poetry.

> Turning and turning in the widening gyre
> The falcon cannot hear the falconer;
> Things fall apart; the centre cannot hold;
> Mere anarchy is loosed upon the world...

The words rolled on in their majesty, an Irishman's prophetic vision of humanity's slide toward damnation, and a group of men who hadn't thought about poetry once in their adult lives leaned in to hear, listening with an intensity that blocked out everything else.

When it was over, there was a long silence. Each man's thoughts turned inward, the baseball game in the background unheeded.

"What does it mean, that first part?"

"I can see it perfectly," said Eddie. "You know how hawks fly in circles? It looks so lazy and aimless, but they are hunting, searching."

"But it's not about hawks."

"No." said Oliver suddenly, the understanding flashing

upon him in that moment. "It's about us. About human beings. Lost. Searching for God. We're the falcon. God's the falconer. He's gone. It's as if God is dead."

There was another briefer silence as they all took this in.

"How did you get that?"

"I'm not sure," he admitted. "It just came to me."

The questioner was now frowning and nodding to himself, working it out. "Is God dead? Or just invisible?"

"Everything's falling apart. There's no more core holding the world together."

"Anarchy."

"Dead innocence."

"Kind of feels familiar."

Every head nodded. "Yeah. It does."

"But if God is dead, what's the Second Coming?"

"Some rough beast."

"It's Satan," said Jake. "Satan is the Second Coming."

They were all silent again, feeling the desolation of the poem, each wondering in his own way whether this was an accurate description of the world now. Satan was a new topic for most of them, and it made them deeply, elementally, uncomfortable. There was at this moment a firm reliance on the drinks in their hands.

"I like that line," said Jake musingly. 'The best lack all conviction, while the worst are filled with passionate intensity.'"

"Man, ain't that the truth."

"Hey, you know, this is interesting. I never thought I liked poetry, but I like this stuff."

Again, there was a mostly silent consensus. "I feel like

I understand something fundamental about..." he paused struggling for words.

"About the world," suggested someone.

"Well, yeah. But it's something I already knew, kind of in the back of my mind, but now...I have words for it." He paused and looked helplessly at the others. "Know what I mean?"

"But not just understanding the world. Kind of understanding yourself," added Jake. "I feel as if the poem's what I feel."

"Yeah, exactly. As if I've always thought that, but it's said in a way I couldn't have said."

Everyone thought his own thoughts.

"So, what are we reading next time?"

"Do we have to buy the book?"

"You can get most of it online, I think," said Eddie. "It's out of copyright. But I like having a book."

Several heads nodded.

As if rousing himself from a trance, Eddie bestirred himself to his duties. "Another round, Gentlemen?"

"It feels necessary," said Jake.

The first trickles of articles about goat yoga at the Washington Hotel began to appear a few weeks after the first class, and the reviews were infused with the kind of wide-eyed reverence usually reserved for expensive artwork made out of perishables.

"The unique approach of the Master's style," explained one in reference to Roger, "is such that the goat itself becomes merely an idea, manifesting itself as a challenge to the internal focus and, indeed, the mastery of each practitioner."

"Rising to new challenges is the aim of any committed practice," gushed another. "Imagine the concentration necessary for your *Eka Hasta Phalakasana* with a full-grown goat attempting to stand on your back."

A well-known yogi wrote: "No matter the level of your practice, you will reap the benefits after the first class."

Reservations for hotel rooms had a year-long waiting list, and openings for those seeking classes were increasingly difficult to come by. Roger had to open a new section to accommodate demand. He contacted Fiona to discuss raising Robert's rates.

Chapter 45

B en had agreed to meet Noah after supper, and Nika had given permission. "I want you home by sunset," she told him. Her voice rose as he started down the driveway. "And turn on your light before then."

"I will," shouted Ben.

She stood on the front walk watching him pedal off.

"And stay out of the woods!"

He waved to acknowledge her instructions and headed down the road toward the south side of the Island. They were meeting at the dunes.

F iona and Oliver were still at their desks in the town office. Both would have been surprised to realize that they were prolonging the work day out of enjoyment of one another's company. Oliver was engrossed in some tedious but esoteric bookkeeping matter, while Fiona was seated, legs stretched out and resting on the wastebasket, immersed in a story written by the famous Bartholomew Salazar. She rested the magazine on her lap and looked up.

"This is terrible. Apart from everything else, I can't understand why something as miserable as this would be given such a lovely title."

Oliver didn't look up. "You can have the ugliest baby in the world and still name her Tiffany."

"Is that one of The Rules?" asked Fiona.

"No," said Oliver. "Merely an observation."

"Imagine if Stella had been named Tiffany."

Oliver actually smiled. "Now there's a thought experiment worth having." His eyes passed over the stack of papers in Fiona's inbox. "Have you answered any of those requests for interviews from the press?"

Fiona had gone back to her reading. "Nope."

"Are you going to?"

"Nope."

Oliver started to give her a disapproving look and was about to offer a little quote but caught himself. "Don't blame you," he said.

Ben had conscientiously watched the time and rode with Noah as far as the crossroad to his house. He had no intention of risking a meeting with Caleb by taking Noah home. Instead, he stood at the top of the hill, watching Noah's small figure coasting down toward his driveway and waiting until he turned in. Then Ben switched on the light of his bicycle—a brilliant flashing beam he had bought with his own money—and took off in the opposite direction toward home.

He hadn't gotten very far when he noticed that it was getting more and more difficult to pedal. When he stopped to look, he saw the flat tire.

Ben's first thought was that he would be late and his mom would be angry. But, he thought, using his father's familiar phrase, it couldn't be helped. Sighing, he began the tedious walk, pushing his crippled bicycle along the road. The sun had set, and the summer night was descending on the Island.

Both Jim and his father had impressed upon him the importance of caution with a lone wolf on the Island, but Ben felt no fear along these roads he knew so well. He'd been walking and biking along them his entire life, and there was probably no one on the Island who knew them better. Maybe Jim, but only maybe.

Ben began to sing to keep himself company and to give himself heart for his long walk home. He heard the gunning engine behind him but didn't think much about it until it was almost upon him. When he realized something was wrong, it was too late, and he turned to see a car swerving at high speed along the twisting road.

It all happened quickly: the car's headlights hitting his face, Ben leaping into the ditch, the bike falling in the gravel on the shoulder, the driver's sharp cut of the wheel to avoid him, and the suspended moment of awareness that made it seem as if everything had stopped.

The car careened wildly onward, leaving Ben lying unhurt in the damp grass.

He listened to his breathing before moving, but eventually,

the mosquitoes compelled him to get up.

He went over to his bike, and as he moved it, the brilliant beam from the bike's light momentarily swept across the woods at the side of the road. In that instant, Ben saw the pair of glittering eyes close to the edge of the trees. He stood very still. He tried to will his heart to slow, but he could hear its beating against his chest.

Suddenly there were more headlights coming up the road, and Ben looked back to see his father's truck.

Pali pulled over in a rush of gravel and jumped out. "Ben! Are you all right?"

"I'm all right, Dad," came the calm reply, and silently, Pali felt the world tilt back into its proper place. He looked up at the sky and took a deep breath, then helped Ben get his bike into the truck.

Ben didn't think to look back until he was safely in his father's truck. But, when he did, he saw only darkness.

The ride home was silent, but when his dad had patted his knee reassuringly Ben knew he wouldn't be in trouble. He thought back to what had just happened. He saw, in his mind's eye, two things: the golden-green eyes in the woods and Caleb's frightened face behind the wheel of the car.

Sgt. Johnsson was not reassuring when Pali reported what had happened to Ben. "Since there was no contact, unless he recognized the car, we have nothing to go on. We have one other report of tires squealing but, again, no visuals."

They both turned to look at Ben.

"Are you sure you can't tell us anything more?"

Ben sounded uncertain. "Mostly, I saw headlights."

Pali's eyes rested on Ben's for just a fraction of a second, but he said nothing.

That night after Sgt. Johnsson had left, Pali and Ben sat on the porch swing, listening to the sounds of the summer night.

"Dad?"

"Hmm?"

"If there are angels, then there must be God, right?"

Pali smiled in the darkness. "That's my theory."

Ben was silent for so long that Pali thought the conversation was finished.

"I wonder if they really have wings." His voice had a faraway quality, as if he were seeing some other time.

"I think our images of angels are metaphor, not actual descriptions." Pali wondered if Ben knew what he meant but saw that he was quiet, listening.

Pali's voice was quiet, too, suddenly remembering something he hadn't thought of in a long time. It had been a trip he'd taken when he was a young man in the service.

"There's a statue in Philadelphia at the big train station, there. It's, maybe, three stories tall—maybe not quite—I haven't seen it in many years, but once you've seen it, you never forget it. It's a black stone sculpture of the Archangel Michael— standing very straight and lifting a fallen soldier out of the flames of war. The soldier hangs lifeless in his arms, his head to one side. The angel's face is solemn, he has tall straight wings—higher than his head—and they seem to be raised at attention out of respect." He looked over at Ben, who was listening carefully. Pali was quiet, remembering the image and the moment he had first seen it, morning sunlight streaming over it.

"When I first saw it, I wasn't expecting it. I was young and I'd never heard of it, and seeing it felt like a shock of electricity. It was as if...I don't know...as if I'd always known it. I recognized it even though I had never seen it before."

Pali frowned remembering the odd experience of seeing something that was new and yet mystifyingly familiar. "That's how I think of angels—like that statue."

Ben said nothing. Pali watched him, wondering about his thoughts.

"If you read about angels—and I mean serious things—the people who see them are always afraid. Terrified, even. I don't think angels are the little pink fairies with harps everybody hangs on their Christmas trees."

"What do you think they are?"

It was almost dark, and Ben was visible only as a profile. Pali turned his head toward him, his eyes both on him and far away. "I think...."

He paused for so long that Ben almost thought he'd forgotten.

"I think they are majestic creatures of God."

A mist was rising from the warm earth into the cooling air. Frogs sang, and they could hear the last twitterings of birds. A screech owl made its odd little call in the darkness, and a fox yipped from somewhere deep in the woods.

Ben took a deep breath to speak to his father, to answer, but saw that he had fallen asleep.

Eddie was returning from a supplies trip to the mainland when he spotted Pete Landry leaning on the ferry railing looking out at the water. They shook hands, and Eddie took a spot next to him.

"Didn't know you were heading back."

Pete looked sheepish. "I'm finding it difficult to stay away. I snatch every opportunity, and sometimes they're unexpected."

Not everyone liked to be at the rail on the crossing, and Eddie remembered something he'd heard. "You were in the Navy, right?"

Pete nodded. "The water never loses its magic."

Eddie nodded in acknowledgment, and they lapsed into a companionable silence.

The last car came up the ramp, the gates were latched and chained, and Captain Palsson, having secured the cargo, invited them both up to the pilot house. Following the crew, Eddie and Pete climbed the metal steps up to the helm of the ferry.

Eddie felt the sense of adventure he'd always felt heading out to sea. Pete was right: it never got old. He looked out over the blue water and felt the anxieties of the rest of the world slip off his shoulders. This was why he was still on the Island after all these years. He made a mental note to mention this to Oliver and wondered idly whether Oliver ever felt tranquility anywhere.

The captain chatted with his mates and guests as he guided the ferry past the breakwater into Death's Door. In an era of sophisticated radar and GPS, no one gave much thought to the crossing's danger anymore, but Eddie never passed this way without thinking of those who had perished here. He shook himself from his musings and joined in the conversation.

As they chatted, Eddie noticed Pali's notebook lying on a shelf nearby. He knew without being told that these were the captain's much whispered of poetry notes, and he thought how remarkable it was to know a poet.

"How's the writing going?" he asked, a bit hesitantly. "Anything new?"

Pete looked up with interest at the question.

Pali looked uncomfortable and mumbled something meaningless, but polite. He didn't really mind discussing it—in fact he was quite eager to—but he still wasn't quite used to people knowing about his poetry.

Ernie, the first mate, was an enthusiastic member of the book group and not at all shy about discussing his thoughts.

"I heard a conversation the other day on TV, and there was a reference to slouching toward Bethlehem. I got it. Never would have before. It's as if I've cracked the code. Can't help wondering how many other things I've been missing."

"You should come," he said turning to Pali. "It's tonight."

Pali looked surprised. He hadn't been planning to participate, although, naturally, he had heard about it along with the rest of the Island.

"I guess I could," he said. "Why not?"

Eddie looked pleased. "Great!"

Ernie turned to Pete. "What about you?" Pete smiled and made a noncommittal gesture. "We'll see," he said good-naturedly.

Ernie dug his elbow in Eddie's ribs. "We probably could use more guys who know what they're talking about, eh, Eddie?"

Eddie smiled. He was used to Ernie. "Never hurts."

It would not be enough merely to greet Bartholomew Salazar upon his arrival on the Island. No, Emily Martin deemed it necessary that he should be met by what she called "a small elite party" at the airport in Green Bay, and properly escorted north. The jostling and positioning for the privilege of this honor was unlike anything Fiona had ever seen on the Island, and from people who only a few weeks before had never heard of Bartholomew Salazar.

Naturally, Emily herself would go. This was a predetermined condition which no one seemed to question. But the matter of who carried sufficient gravitas, and who might be able to chat with the great man about literary matters, left Emily in a quandary.

It never occurred to Emily that she might have neighbors whose knowledge was superior to her own, and who, at the very least, had the common sense and dignity not to fawn. She was only concerned with creating a good impression on this important visitor, and reluctantly, each time she ran through the possibilities, she came to the same conclusion.

"Fiona," she said one morning, as she spotted her target

with Pete in the produce aisle of the grocery store, "I have been meaning to ask you something very important."

Fiona looked up warily from the peaches she had been picking over, her sense of self-preservation instantly at the fore. Emily's important questions inevitably led to complications.

Pete nodded politely in greeting and was silent. One of the interesting things about Pete, thought Fiona, in one of those mental asides that intrude on one's thoughts during conversation, is that he was always the same, no matter the situation: polite, respectful, and unfailingly correct. She did note, however, a slight twitch of his mouth.

"It's for the literary festival." As she spoke, Emily evaluated Fiona as her choice and felt that her instincts were confirmed: a leading public official? Check. A city person with the ease of manners necessary? Check. Well groomed? She eyed Fiona's faded jeans. Well, capable, anyway. At least she was attractive; Emily had to admit that. And a writer! Check. Yes, despite her personal and public failings, Fiona would be just the right person for this important job. Or, at least, with no one who quite met Emily's standards of metropolitan sophistication, the closest thing the Island had to offer.

"Fiona," she began, as if she were preparing a fanfare for a proclamation, "I have decided that you should accompany me to greet Bartholomew Salazar in Green Bay." She hurried to continue before Fiona could reply. "Now, I know that your popularity is somewhat…on the wane…but most of the people at the festival won't know anything about your little transactions, and if they do, I feel sure they won't really mind."

She beamed as she conferred this honor. Admittedly, the

grocery store was not the best location for such a conversation, but news like this could not keep, Emily firmly believed, and for reasons she didn't understand, Emily often found Fiona somewhat elusive.

Fiona, who was nearly immune to Emily's insults, and whose knowledge of the gentleman in question was deeper than Emily's, realized at once that her wariness had been warranted. Apart from anything else, this would mean practically a whole day in a car with Emily.

"Oh, Emily, how kind," she said with glittering insincerity. "But surely, you know I'm not remotely qualified for such an honor."

Pete leaned in to speak in a low voice. "When agitated, she occasionally misuses the pluperfect."

Emily stared at him with a small smile on her face, trying to evaluate whether he was serious.

"Oh," she said. "Haha, yes! Well, I think we can overlook that! After all, she is our most important local politician, and we must see that the Island is properly represented."

"What fun!" said Pete, smiling brightly at Fiona.

She gave him a look out of the corner of her eye and returned to Emily. "But I really don't—."

"Now, that's all set! I'll be in touch with all the details." Emily turned to go, and then turned back as a new thought struck her.

"Oh, and do wear something appropriate, dear. A dress would be nice. Put your best foot forward, that's what I always say."

She wiggled her shoulders in a way she thought must be sassy, winked, and sailed off.

Fiona contemplated throwing a peach at the back of her head but decided that her aim was too unreliable.

Pete, wisely, busied himself with examining the asparagus.

The huddle of guys with books at the corner of the bar inevitably attracted some attention. There was some good-natured teasing from those who did not participate, but if it hadn't been about the books, it would have been about something else, so nobody really minded.

Pali had been reluctant to commit any of his precious free time, but Eddie's enthusiasm was contagious. Pali was quickly drawn into the spirit of the thing and found himself looking forward to it.

The group methodically made its way through the high points of Yeats's poetry. After one play, they decided to move on. "What's next, then?" asked Jake, one evening.

Eddie raised his eyebrows questioningly and looked around at the group. "Thoughts?"

There was a long silence, as everyone waited for everyone else to say something. Pali, with long experience of meetings, simply drank his beer.

Oliver spoke. "Well, I, for one, would like to know more about Shakespeare. I'm ashamed to say it with my interest in theatre, but I've never read anything except *Romeo and Juliet* when I was in high school."

Most of the men nodded.

"I mean, he's supposedly the greatest writer in the English language, and I'm not really sure why."

"Makes sense," said Jake.

Eddie nodded, too. "Okay, then. There's a lot of Shakespeare. Where shall we start?"

Again, a long silence. Eddie looked around and took charge. "How about this: I'll subscribe to an online course with a good professor, and then I'll share the syllabus with all of you, and we can read the stuff together. It gives us a sort of unifying theme."

"Do we all need to subscribe? I really don't want to spend a lot of money."

"No, that's okay," said Eddie. "I would have gotten around to Shakespeare anyway, and we can find everything he ever wrote online for free."

"Shouldn't we have a plan for next week, though?" asked Jake, ever-practical.

Eddie frowned. "How about we start with a sonnet? I'll find something we can start with."

Shrugging good-naturedly, they all agreed.

After the meeting had dissolved, Eddie consulted privately with Pali to determine the first sonnet they would read.

"I've always loved number sixty," he said. "The one that begins:

> Like as the waves make towards the pebbled shore,
>
> So do our minutes hasten to their end;
>
> Each changing place with that which goes before,
>
> In sequent toil all forwards do contend..."

"Sounds good," said Eddie, taking note on a waiter's order pad. "I'll shoot an email to everyone."

Chapter 46 ✤

Fiona had now heard from more than half of the members of the Town Board. "We need to schedule a town meeting, Fiona," said Mary Woldt, who was well known for seconding every motion that came to the floor. "My phone's been ringing off the hook, and it's all people can talk about no matter where I go. I really do think it would be best to post a meeting. The sooner the better."

Fiona was inclined to agree. She was tired of the whole mess and wanted to get everything out in the open. She had already asked Dirk Richards to sign an affidavit attesting to her innocence of her uncle's plans, and she was ready to do what she could to defend herself. Even so, she knew that each time one of Stella's rumors made the rounds, her credibility was damaged a little more. The slow, unceasing erosion of her reputation left her with no political capital and very little benefit of the doubt.

"Okay, Mary," she said. "I'll have Oliver post a notice immediately. He'll call you when it's set."

As she hung up, she saw Pete looking at her inquiringly.

"Just making plans for the execution," she said, lightly. "You know, sharpening the guillotine and all that."

"Ah," he said. "Well, in that case, how about a walk? May

as well clear your head before you lose it."

"Too late for that." Fiona's voice was somewhat muffled as she looked for her shoes under the couch. Finding them, she sat on the floor to put them on. "As you should know, I lost my head some time ago."

He nodded solemnly, watching her. "We can stop off for a drink afterward. Eat, drink and be merry, don't you know."

She threw a sneaker at him.

From the beginning, Oliver had made it a point to avoid socializing with Fiona, citing his philosophy of "never confusing your colleagues with your friends," a rule she did not object to honoring. The Island, however, was small, and when he walked into Nelsen's, even Oliver would not be so rude as to walk out when he saw Pete and Fiona sitting at the bar with Jake and Charlotte.

Fiona, he knew, had been avoiding going out much in public out of what she called "outrage fatigue." People's willingness to express their disapproval of her had become an exhausting and demoralizing routine. Tonight, however, she seemed cheerful. He guessed, rightly, that Pete had something to do with it.

Oliver sat a few seats away, not so close as to impose, but not so far as to seem to be avoiding them, even though, in truth, he'd have liked to. Conversation was required. This, after all, must be expected by any reasonable person when sitting at a bar. Oliver had come intending to talk. He just hadn't planned to have to talk with Fiona.

"Did you see who's headlining the literary festival?" Eddie's professional facility for chat frequently came in handy.

Pete and Fiona exchanged amused glances. Eddie concluded that they had discussed this already.

"Yes," said Fiona. "Bartholomew Salazar. He's…an interesting choice."

"Who is this guy?" asked Jake. "I saw the story in the paper, but I've never even heard of him."

Fiona took a deep breath of resignation. "He's a literary insider. A very well read and maybe even brilliant man. He has lots of celebrity friends, and some people think he has a gift for finding talent. He certainly seems to have a gift for friendship. Lots of big stars, famous journalists, politicians…but, oddly, he's famous for literature, even though he's never written a book…I guess he's been saying he's been working on one for decades, but no one's seen it. And he apparently drinks too much and has a drug habit. He's been let go by several big magazines. Other than that…" she trailed off with a miserable laugh.

"So, he's a living example of the emperor's new clothes," said Jake.

Fiona went on. "He's supposedly writing a book about shrugging."

"Did you say 'shrugging?'" This was Eddie, who was busy polishing as he listened.

Fiona shrugged unironically. "That's the story."

Pete spoke up. "One of the most memorable comments from one of his skeptics was that he has 'important hair.'"

"Ummm, wow," said Eddie. "That might be my favorite insult ever."

Pete gave a brief laugh.

"Why is he coming here?" asked Charlotte with her usual charming *naïveté*. "We don't have any celebrities."

"He's being paid," said Jake.

Oliver spoke, philosophically examining the orange slice and cherry in his brandy old fashioned glass. "Maybe we're the best he can do now."

The others considered this.

"Sounds like we could do better, though."

Silently, they all agreed.

Chapter 47 ✤

Having only just arrived, Pete was already talking about leaving again. He had announced it at dinner, and Fiona had become very quiet. Now they made their way to the living room, and Pete went to the sideboard where the scotch was kept.

Fiona turned from her favorite spot at the living room window, where she had been looking out. "How long this time?"

Pete looked up from pouring her scotch to examine her face.

He handed her a glass, poured one for himself, and settled on the couch without answering. He took a drink and looked up at her.

"I really don't know. There's a new mine in Africa that the Chinese are building, and as a result there's some bureaucratic conflict brewing with my company's headquarters there. We think we're being squeezed out. I'm waiting to hear from a colleague who's over there now, then I'm supposed to go see about smoothing things over."

Fiona looked thoughtful. He didn't usually talk in so much detail about his work. "What does 'smoothing things over' mean?"

"Generally, it means finding out who is being paid bribes,

but it also means finding out the more public *quid pro quo*. Unfortunately, it's all gangs and cronyism. Meanwhile, the Chinese are building highways and bridges all over Africa, cornering the market on natural resources, importing their surveillance technology to the governments, and scamming the locals, while the rest of the world looks the other way. It's not good for anybody. Except, of course, the Chinese apparatchik."

"No wonder you're a cynic."

"Who says I'm a cynic?"

"I do."

"Oh, do you really? I thought cynics were disappointed romantics." He grinned at her. "And my romanticism is fully intact."

"Is it," commented Fiona skeptically.

"Come over here and find out."

Fiona smiled in spite of herself and went to sit beside him.

"I don't really want you to go," she said, a few minutes later.

"I don't really want to," he said into her hair. He pulled back, kissed her once more, and put his arm around her shoulders.

"What's Africa like?"

"Incredibly beautiful. Incredibly poor. Incredibly troubled."

Fiona nodded thoughtfully. "I'm not sure I like the idea of you going there."

He tightened his arm around her. "Maybe it won't be so long this time."

Atilla was always emboldened by silence. He poked his little triangular head around a corner to see if it was safe to come out into the room. His black eyes glinting, he began his ritual explorations of the edges of the room where Fiona had left a particularly generous serving of raw beef for his delectation. Attila danced with joy when he discovered it, but the room's other occupants never even noticed.

I t wasn't quite a meeting of the book club, but some of its members had met accidentally at Nelsen's, and despite the group's decision to move on to new works, they found their conversation returning to the pleasures of Yeats. They took great enjoyment in cracking Yeats's code—learning the politics of the day, understanding the mythology—and there was a particular satisfaction in being able to pick out the meanings and references of the poetry.

"This kind of reminds me of working on my first car," commented Jake at one point. "The more I take it apart, the more I learn." No one laughed. It was true.

The poet's iconic and elusive lady love, the beautiful Maud Gonne, held a particular fascination for them.

"You've got to feel for the guy. Four rejected proposals." They all agreed with this, nodding in sympathy for the poet's agonies.

"He shouldn't of kept asking once she turned him down."

"But do you think he'd have written so much poetry if he'd been happy?"

"I work less when I'm happy."

"Yah. It seems that way to me, too."

It was all-you-can-eat spaghetti night, so Nelsen's was

bustling. The televisions blared a baseball game, the pool table was busy and had two groups waiting, and the bar was filled with people waiting for tables. Eddie was frequently interrupted, but in this busy time of year, it was to be expected. The group huddled at one end of the bar near the door and carried on a mostly shouted conversation.

They were deep into a philosophical digression about the meaning of life—was it work or happiness—when Emily Martin walked in.

Emily's family drifted off into the crowd—perhaps by design—but she zeroed in on the little cluster of men, all leaning into a serious conversation at the end of the bar, and immediately had to know what they were up to.

"Hello, boys," she said. There was a tinge of flirtation in her voice, but it still cut over the noise. Several of them looked up, but the rest stared into their beers like dogs who thought if they didn't see you, they couldn't be seen.

"Mind if I join you? This must be an interesting conversation! Let me guess—politics or sports? I'm betting sports! It's baseball season, isn't it?"

The game blaring on the television above her head made this remark particularly gratuitous.

The men were silent, none wishing to continue their discussion with Emily in it.

She observed them, all bright-eyed, and changed her tone to one of mock admonition. "Ohhhh, I see. It was something naughty. Well, I caught you, didn't I?" She gave them a coy smile which Oliver instantly hated.

Normally a polite group, they turned into sullen schoolboys

with her interrogation, but Emily didn't notice. She plunged onward with her determined inquisition while Eddie took the opportunity to escape by filling orders at the other end of the bar.

It was Oliver who broke.

"We were discussing Yeats." As soon as he said it, he realized his mistake. He could have made a more generic remark about happiness—or anything else for that matter—but now he had created the entry point for her to launch the invasion. He winced in apology to Ernie, the guy sitting next to him, and got a philosophical shrug in response.

Emily's face took on an arch look. "Yeats? Yeats? The poet? Well, my goodness, aren't you all just full of surprises." She looked from one to another as if she were a kindergarten teacher with a class of precocious tots.

Another opportunity then arose, which, sadly, no one thought of until later when they were driving home, their happy evening somewhat diminished. "Not the poet," they could have said. "The baseball player." And then she would have drifted away. But, as so often happens, the perfect retort formulated itself too late to be of service.

"Well, tell me! I must know! What are you saying about Yeats?"

There was a collection of shrugs. Emily's curiosity kept hitting a wall of silence. Suddenly, light dawned.

"Ohhhh, I know. This must be the book group everybody's talking about. How wonderful!" She looked around for a barstool, but finding none and with none being offered, she leaned in.

"I adore book groups! I do! I belonged to one in Winnetka! We read so many wonderful books!" She looked with her strained eagerness at each of their faces in turn.

"But really, you know, Yeats won't do. He's so old-fashioned and so gloomy! All that Gaelic mist! No, no, no, I can't allow it. I just can't. I think you need some guidance, and I know just the person." She grimaced in false modesty. "I have just the right experience to be able to guide you in choosing the right books! I was an English major, you know."

Hearing no response from her audience she continued.

"Don't get me wrong. I think what you're doing is admirable. I really do. But wouldn't it be better to have an expert leading the discussion? Someone who really understands literature? Of course, it would! You just leave it to me. I'll be in touch to set up a time—and really, we could use a better location, too, don't you think? Good literature deserves better than a barroom."

Satisfied with this and smiling as if she wanted to pat them each on the head, Emily strode off to join her family at their table.

After a long moment, the book group gave a collective sigh, and glances were exchanged. Oliver pursed his lips and looked defeated. Eddie smiled with joyless eyes and compressed mouth, making it clear what he thought without saying a word.

"And the worst are full of passionate intensity," someone muttered softly. Those who heard smiled into their beers.

"That woman could out-annoy a nest of hornets," said Jake, not softly at all.

It had been another particularly harrowing evening at the hotel for Elisabeth. A group of yoga tourists, already having experienced an afternoon class of goat yoga with all that that entailed, had decided, *en masse*—and despite the rather frantic attempts at intervention from the waitress—to forego their usual white wine at dinner for Bloody Rogers. The results had been predictable, though borne with yogic kindness and grace.

In the aftermath, Elisabeth had given them all free bathrobes and gift certificates for a future stay.

Had they been on good terms, Fiona would have made her laugh over the incident, and everything would have seemed all right.

But Elisabeth could only shut her eyes against the memory of the scene and try to console herself with calming thoughts. Despite Joshua's advice, goat yoga was not a strategy she found useful in this regard.

Chapter 48

Fiona put down her newspaper and stared off into space, thinking. After a few moments, she asked, "What is it about winking that I hate so much?"

Pete looked up from the Dickens novel he was reading. "Winking?"

"Yes. It's terribly annoying, and there's a certain kind of person who does it."

"What kind?"

"That's what I'm trying to figure out."

"I will make a note to myself—no winking,"

"You never wink."

"No," he said. "And I can safely say I've never been tempted to. It seems almost…old-fashioned, doesn't it?"

"It's more than that. It's corny. I mean, it might be okay in certain very limited circumstances, perhaps to indicate solidarity with a child in a room filled with boring adults. But otherwise, I put winking firmly in a category with golf pants and Juicy Fruit gum."

"I can understand the pants and, for that matter, the winking, but what have you got against Juicy Fruit? And why this sudden animus?"

"It's actually all gum chewing, come to think of it. Instantly lowers the IQ of anyone who does it." She paused, thinking. "Emily chews gum. She winks, too. Emily is a big winker."

Pete nodded with mock seriousness. "I begin to understand. My sainted mother, incidentally, shares your horror of gum chewing."

He thought for a moment, captivated. "Doesn't 'big winker' sound like an insult? Get out of here, you big winker!"

He looked at her with perfect solemnity, but he had a look in his eyes Fiona knew well. She gazed at him, apparently unmoved. Smiling would only encourage him.

"I've never seen you chew gum," she said, returning to the earlier point.

"That's because I don't."

"Because of your mother?"

"Because I acquired her aversion to it. Has Emily winked at you?"

Fiona frowned, thinking. "Not that I can recall. But what is it about winking that's so off-putting?"

"Maybe it's a form of condescension."

Fiona nodded. "That might be part of it. But there's something else. Something smug about it and self-important."

"I doubt everyone who winks attaches so much significance to it."

"No?"

"Probably not. In any case, I had no idea you felt so strongly about these issues."

"I like to think deeply."

"Yes," said Pete, dryly. "I do see that. So…golf pants, Juicy Fruit, and winking. I'm making a list. Anything else?"

"Go back to your book. Sorry to interrupt."

"Thank you," said Pete. After a moment's silence he looked back up at her. "Now, see what you've done? It was all I could do to stop myself from winking."

"Please don't."

"If I fail, I blame you." He put down his book. "Scotch?" he asked, rising.

"Please. I feel I need it."

"Perhaps we both do."

An emergency meeting of the book group had been called. It was Eddie's night off, and they had gathered under cover of darkness at his tiny cottage on Detroit Harbor. The place was snug and charming and had a splendid view of the sunsets. Its rocky beach had a small, rickety pier, which Eddie used primarily for star gazing, and there was a covered porch along the back, where Eddie spent long hours reading or looking at the sky and the water.

The night was warm and sweet, but it was deer fly season, so after a few desperate minutes of swatting and swearing on the lawn, they were all driven indoors.

"Hey, Eddie," said Jake, who had seized Eddie's big, soft, swivel chair by the fireplace. "Great chair!"

Eddie smiled. "Thanks. It's my reading chair."

The room buzzed with men rather than flies as they gathered beers and found their places, cramming themselves into the kitchen and living room, some seated, some leaning against the wall.

"Okay," said Eddie, when they had all assembled, beers in hand, "I guess you all know we have a problem. Emily's been haunting the bar every night, asking when we're meeting next. It's getting so I can't turn around without seeing her." The normally easygoing Eddie was clearly irked. "We need a plan."

"She hit up my wife at Mann's on Monday, trying to find out about our next meeting."

"The woman's a nuisance," said Ernie. "The Martin woman, I mean," he added hastily. "Not your wife."

"Well, obviously, we can't meet at the bar anymore."

"Damned nuisance."

They all nodded regretfully.

"Here's the thing," said Oliver suddenly. He was holding a beer without drinking it. In Eddie's casual entertaining style, guests were simply directed to the refrigerator to help themselves and beer had been the only option. Oliver was not a beer drinker, but he felt it would have been rude not to take one. He still felt like an outsider, even though he had been present at the group's beginnings.

They all turned to look at him, and he felt strangely pleased. "Whatever we do, we won't be able to tell anyone. You know how word travels around here. One leak and it will be all over."

"We could meet at my house," offered Jake.

"We can't afford to do that. If we involve family members it will be too easy to figure out."

Hesitantly, Oliver spoke up again, feeling as if he were

issuing an invitation to a party no one would want to attend. "We could meet at my place, but I have neighbors who would notice."

"Yeah. The word will get out, and she will show up."

"You've got to hand it to her. The woman has persistence."

"She's a one-woman siege."

They all sat drinking their beers in gloomy silence. They had been seriously enjoying their book group. Emily Martin would mean the end of everything.

Finally, Jake spoke up. "Eddie, you're the obvious choice. You're single. And your place is relatively out of the way."

"It's a bit cramped," said Eddie, cautiously.

They all looked around. The cottage had yellow walls lined with overstuffed bookcases, and seemed to glow in the lamplight, pleasantly warm and cheerful. The kitchen was open to the only living space. There was a wooden table that could seat four and a small adjacent living room. There was space for eight comfortably, ten, if pressed, but even packed with people, it had the feeling of a retreat—comfortable and well stocked with any necessity.

"We can make it work."

"It will be easier to talk."

"We can take turns sitting."

"It will have to be on my night off," noted Eddie.

"Changing location won't be enough," said Oliver, feeling bolder. "We can't let anyone know that we're meeting, otherwise she'll find out. After all, 'A secret told at breakfast is all the news by tea.'" He smiled to himself, but no one noticed.

"We probably should vary the times, too."

"Even our cars will let someone know we're meeting."

"This is complicated. How are we going to make this work when everybody around here knows everything?"

"It's simple," said Jake, who had a knack for cutting to the heart of things. "We're going to have to lie."

"Keeping a secret is different from lying," pointed out Ken, who was the high-school physics teacher.

"But to keep the secret, we have to have a cover story, which is, in effect, lying."

"Lying or not lying really isn't the point," observed Mark pragmatically.

"We need to choose an inconvenient time. For her, I mean."

"And we're going to have to say we've stopped meeting—"

"—another lie."

"Look," said Eddie. "It's not going to be perfect. We shouldn't overcomplicate this. Let's make one person in charge of the meeting locations and times and communicating them to each of us. Someone who's organized."

They all looked at Oliver. He looked back at them like a startled bird.

"Me?"

The room was silent as Oliver struggled not to show how pleased he felt. "Well, okay. I can do it." Unconsciously, his business demeanor took over, his shoulders straightening, and his voice changing in volume and decisiveness. "It will help if, before you leave, you all write down the times when you are absolutely unavailable and your email addresses."

As Eddie handed out sheets of scrap paper from his desk, Oliver took a sip of his beer and tried not to make a face. The room grew silent as everyone delved into the intricacies of their schedules. Gradually, one by one, they got up to hand their papers to Oliver, and a small murmuring of side conversations began.

Oliver counted the sheets in his hand and looked up at them over his glasses, his lips pursed. "This looks like everyone. I'll look these over and come up with a time."

They all sat together expectantly.

In the silence, Eddie looked around the room at the assembled group. "Well, gentlemen," he said, "Looks like we're going underground."

Chapter 49 ✤

One morning, arriving before dawn, Joshua turned on the lights of the shop, switched on the coffee making apparatus, and went outside. The orange cones had long ago been abandoned and now sat in neat stacks along the edges of the parking lot. The campers had merely stepped over them and camped anyway.

Joshua was a man utterly unburdened by any sense of his own appearance. He had heard the whispered coffee shop nickname, "The Angel Joshua." Puzzled by it, he'd shrugged it off.

Now, in the first light of morning, he turned his benevolent gaze on the small sea of tents that had arisen overnight and waited patiently for the first stirrings of their occupants.

When the first tent flap opened and a sleepy figure emerged, Joshua stood before him, a halo of golden hair around his shoulders, bathed in the lights from Ground Zero that blazed behind him. The camper gasped and staggered back at the presence of a Divine Messenger.

Unaware of the effect of his appearance, Joshua spoke. "You need to leave," he said.

Eyes wide, the camper stared. Was he still sleeping? No, he was quite certain he was not.

"Do you understand?" queried the vision.

The camper nodded, started off, turned back and made a confused little bow, then turned again and hurried to wake his friends.

Joshua watched them, shrugged, and returned to the shop to continue his preparations for the morning.

Chapter 50 ✻

Not long after the meeting at Eddie's, the Island experienced a burst of unusual activities among certain of its citizens. Oliver had realized that the best chance of avoiding Emily was during one of her own committee meetings, so his first task was determining what committees she sat on and which of these she usually attended. This required a certain amount of subterfuge, which he rather enjoyed.

The others, meanwhile, were finding solutions to the problem of a cluster of cars parked in the same place.

Much to the delight of their wives, Tom and Andy had sudden newfound interests in exercise. Unable to convince his dog that a nice walk should be taken without her, Tom often brought his ancient lab along, and she made a delightful addition to the meetings.

Jake, who had the longest walk of anybody, soon accepted Mark's invitation to pick him up along the way. They took particular delight in arranging, by signal, to meet at various places. It amused Jake to whistle the theme music from a World War II prison escape film as he walked. The film's mood of cheerful and indefatigable resistance to tyranny seemed somehow fitting.

In aid of these clandestine arrangements, members of the book club began developing some odd nervous habits when meeting in public: touching the sides of their noses rapidly and repeatedly; making odd ticks of the head; and using gestures that suggested the choreography of a particularly creative third base coach. The need for stealth had added a piquancy to their meetings that made Emily's attempts at interference almost welcome. The book club members were unpracticed in subtlety but, as it turned out, enjoying themselves thoroughly.

Chapter 51

A t Nelsen's that night, the topic of Bartholomew Salazar had come up once again.

"He perfectly fits my father's favorite definition of celebrity," said Fiona. "Someone who's famous for being well known." She had been thinking about this a great deal lately.

"There are a lot of those around these days."

"Is it just me, or does it seem as if there are more than ever?"

Eddie shook his head. "It's not just you."

Fiona recalled the quip about Bartholomew Salazar.

"Remember, he does have important hair," she said out loud.

Eddie laughed, then went to serve a customer waiting at the other end of the bar.

Pete looked thoughtful. "It's a sad commentary on society, but sometimes these things matter. I had a friend some time ago, a very talented young conductor. But even though he was brilliant, he looked, as he said himself, like a beer salesman. For years, I urged him to get a cape and wear an earring, just to cultivate an air of eccentricity. He always thought I was joking, but I was quite serious."

"What happened to him?"

"He's a happy man. Conducts a small orchestra. He should have had a great career, but merely being excellent was apparently not enough."

He looked up. "And then there are these others—more, it seems, now than ever, although that can't be true—who have so little actual creative talent, and no training, but do have a knack for self-promotion or the right connections. They become stars."

Fiona nodded. "It's all part of the culture of celebrity."

"Greatness isn't always noticed," commented Eddie, returning. "It's tragic—and wasteful—like a single flower that blooms alone in the woods."

"It's not necessarily tragic for the flower," pointed out Fiona.

"Celebrity worship is as old as civilization," said Pete. "But technology seems to have made it worse."

"And a certain lack of discernment," added Fiona.

"Yes. That seems worse, too. Chopin was a celebrity, but he had genuine talent."

He looked at her and smiled. "It's good to be on the Island."

She looked back, but her face was serious. "Do you think so? I'm never sure whether you actually like it here or are just humoring me."

"I never humor you. Well," he cast a sideways glance at her. "Almost never. But I do like it here. Life is real here. Cut down to its essence, somehow."

"You feel that, too?"

"I do. It's hard to put your finger on exactly what it is, but yes, I feel it too." He smiled again, adding, "and of course, there is a more particular attraction."

Later, the memory of this conversation gave Fiona a great deal of comfort.

Pete left at dawn the next morning.

Even a seraphic visitation—however innocently rendered—proved insufficient deterrence to the tent people, and they continued to appear nightly in increasing numbers.

The wording necessary for the Ground Zero parking lot by now necessitated more than one sign, each nailed in vertical succession on the cedar tree that grew near the corner of the building.

DESPITE POSTINGS ON AVOCADO TOAST, read the first sign.

BY ORDER OF THE POLICE DEPARTMENT, read the second sign.

NO CAMPING IS PERMITTED ON THESE PREMISES, read the third sign.

AT ANY TIME. EVER, read the fourth.

Set beneath this array of instructions was an enclave of no fewer than a dozen tents. There was no place left for him to park, so Joshua drove back down the hill to the public lot and walked up. Multicolored and clustered together, the tents seemed to rise from the asphalt of Ground Zero's parking lot like the early morning preparations for ascension at a hot air balloon festival.

He stood at the door of the shop and looked back. All was quiet.

Roger arrived a few minutes after Joshua and entered the shop just as Joshua was turning on the lights. They stood looking at each other for a moment, then Joshua disappeared into the back room. Returning, he handed a large pot and spatula to Roger, and led the way to the parking lot.

E mily had last minute misgivings about including Fiona in meeting their guest of honor at the airport, but as much as she tried hinting—and as much as Fiona would have loved to have taken the hints—Fiona feigned innocence. A day spent with Emily was a day of penance as far she was concerned, but it had amused her to watch Emily's transparent attempts to disinvite her.

They waited together on the open side of airport security. Emily, despite having seen photos of their guest, had insisted upon holding a card with his name on it. Fiona knew that this was Emily's way of bragging about his celebrity, but she was fairly certain her efforts were lost on the public. Hardly anyone outside of coastal literary circles would know who Bartholomew Salazar was or be even remotely impressed if they had.

The airport was small, and there were no crowds, so it was easy to pick the great Master from the group of passengers emerging from security. His shock of wild white hair was falling across his eyes, and Fiona saw him brush it away in what she knew at once was a practiced gesture. He carried an elegant leather briefcase that was obviously expensive with his initials embossed in large gold letters near the handle: B.S.

He kept them waiting as he stopped to chat with another man who seemed to have been on the same plane, and then turned to them. With a world-weary smile, he approached.

"Mr. Salazar," said Emily, with a formality that was part preening, part fawning, "Welcome to Green Bay. I am Emily Martin, the Founder and Director of the Washington Island Literary Festival, and this—she indicated Fiona with a dismissive hand—is Fiona Campbell, the Chairwoman of our Town Board."

Bartholomew Salazar eyed Fiona up and down and barely restrained himself from licking his lips.

Fiona offered her hand unsmilingly. She was already tired of him. And when their guest of honor insisted that she sit beside him in the backseat of the car, she was already confident that she loathed him.

"I'm not a very good traveler, you know, and I may need someone to hold my hand." He gave her a complacent little smile. "You will do very nicely, my dear."

Fiona, who had long experience of lechery, skillfully placed her bag between them on the seat.

He, just as skillfully, pretended to discover it with a guileless, "You look crowded, darling. Let me put this on the front seat for you," and doing so, he slid into the back beside her with a smile she found utterly revolting.

As expected, his hand was on her knee in no time, while Emily chatted gaily from the driver's seat. Fiona removed his hand firmly and unsmilingly, while looking him directly in the eye.

"Oh, Emily, I've left my sunglasses in my purse. Will you please hand it to me?"

"What?! Now? In traffic? Really, Fiona, you could have thought of it before."

Fiona smiled a fierce little smile. "I could have, yes."

The purse was only a temporary stopgap. When his hand moved again to her knee, Fiona quite intentionally, but with perfect deniability, spilled her water bottle over his lap.

"Oh no! What have I done? Emily, you must pull over! Poor Mr. Salazar!"

With many exclamations, comments on Fiona's clumsiness, and apologies to "dear Mr. Salazar," Emily arranged for him to sit in the front seat, "where, you can be sure, I won't be spilling anything on you!"

She delivered this last remark with a glare at Fiona, but Fiona was busily looking for something in her purse and didn't notice.

The great Mr. Salazar was tight-lipped and grim for the rest of the way.

Fiona, however, now perfectly at ease, kept up an inane chatter that was completely out of character. Because she knew it was annoying to both Emily and Salazar, she enjoyed herself thoroughly.

As they boarded the ferry, Salazar slumped in the backseat, eyes squeezed shut against the sound of her voice and the perils of the open water.

Fiona noted that the man he had spoken with was on the ferry, too. She wondered idly who he could be.

When they arrived at the hotel, Bartholomew Salazar emerged from the car and wrapped his elegant trench coat around himself with great dignity before mounting the steps and entering the main hall.

Standing at the front desk, he allowed his glance to fall lingeringly on one of the spandex clad yoga practitioners as she entered the front door and walked up the stairs.

"Nice," he said to no one in particular.

Emily took it as a compliment to the hotel. "Nothing but the best for our honored guest!"

He gave her a lifeless smile, which seemed to suggest that there was nothing she could do that could live up to his standards.

Emily's increasingly fluttering manner suggested that she was aware of her guest's ill humor and was attempting to assuage it. Fiona watched with a certain amount of sympathy and wondered whether Emily had yet fully grasped that the great Bartholomew Salazar was a jerk.

Fiona stood by dutifully while he, his briefcase, and his hair were checked into the hotel, and then excused herself. It was time, she felt, for a drink.

With Pete gone, Fiona was almost glad to have the literary festival to occupy her thoughts. It was a distraction. She dressed for the reception that evening as she would have for an important event in the city. She knew it was unnecessary for the occasion, but she felt she needed it for her morale. If she had given any thought to Bartholomew Salazar, she might have done things differently, but she was thinking, at that moment, only of her own happiness.

Attila was bouncing in his warrior dance across the floor, stalking the raw beef she had left in the jar lid. She watched him, smiling, then grabbed her bag and headed out the door.

Chapter 52

B artholomew Salazar swept into the bar of the Washington Hotel as if he had been wearing a cape. A smattering of admiring applause greeted him, and he managed a small, mirthless smile as he brushed the famous hair from his brow. He was immediately surrounded by Emily and several members of the Committee of the Concerned.

"What can we get you to drink, Mr. Salazar?" asked Emily, still fluttering.

He looked down at her with a moue of distaste.

"Oh," he said, thinking. "I doubt the wine would be decent. I suppose…a whiskey. Preferably scotch…if you have such a thing." He looked as if he expected disappointment.

His scotch was brought. He sniffed it, cautiously. His first sip was followed by an expression that reminded Elisabeth of Rocco when she had once given him an olive. He downed it quickly.

"I think I shall require another," he said to the world at large. More whiskeys were brought, and he drank them in quick succession.

As Fiona came up the steps of the hotel, Elisabeth was standing at the door.

They exchanged cool greetings, and there was an awkward silence until Elisabeth spoke. "I was hoping I'd catch you. Could you come in the back for a moment? I need to speak with you."

Fiona followed apprehensively as Elisabeth led the way to her tiny office under the stairs and closed the door. She stood very close to Fiona and spoke gently.

"Fiona, our friendship isn't a substitute for my judgement. I have to make up my own mind about things. Just because I don't think through things as fast as you do, doesn't mean I can't figure out the right thing to do in the end."

Fiona was listening in silence, her eyes on Elisabeth's face.

"I wasn't going to sell to them—" she laughed shortly "actually to you—but I needed time to think about it, and I was angry at you for assuming I would just do what you wanted."

Fiona nodded remorsefully.

"Besides," she added, "There was no way Roger was going to sell. Money doesn't interest him."

Fiona smiled. "Maybe so, but I believe it was Roger who told me that 'not having it focuses the mind.'"

She looked down for a moment and then back at Elisabeth. "You're right, of course. I'm sorry. I was so caught up in the situation, I didn't take time to hear anybody else." She looked down again, and looking up, her eyes met Elisabeth's. "Will you forgive me?"

"Of course, I forgive you. I couldn't live without you."

Fiona looked sheepish. "Me, either."

They threw their arms around each other and, after a few moments' use of the box of tissues in Elisabeth's office, walked arm in arm out to the main hall, where the reception had already begun.

Much to Emily's annoyance, the hotel had already been half-booked when she chose the dates for her festival. Yoga tourism continued to be the base of the hotel's client list, and although Roger felt gratified at the results of his efforts, Emily felt that literary tastes and yoga did not mix. In the end, however, she was forced to accept the unacceptable and share the hotel's dining room with those she called "the non-readers."

The size of the hotel meant an inevitable mingling of the two groups. Although many of the yoga practitioners were ordinary middle-aged people, this particular meeting was for instructors, and their lithe bodies clad in close-fitting yoga gear drew the attention of the literary festival's featured speaker.

Had Salazar confined himself to looking, the rest of the evening might have gone differently, but in these matters, as in so many others, subtlety was not his method.

He sidled up to one of the yoga instructors standing near the door chatting with a colleague. She held a glass of white wine, and her auburn hair fell in waves down her back. When she felt his hand, she spun around.

"Excuse me!"

Bartholomew Salazar was unfazed. "You are excused, dear lady. When one sees a thing of beauty, the temptation to touch is irresistible." He simpered as he took a sip of whiskey and tried to put his arm around her.

She brushed him off with a few choice words.

"All right, all right. Don't get hysterical." Unrepentant, he slithered away toward the bar and ordered another whiskey. His behavior, however, did not go unnoticed.

It wasn't long before Mr. Salazar had begun to view the room with a less jaundiced eye, and he happened to see one of the Sprinters standing nearby with the hotel's special drink.

"A Bloody Mary? At the cocktail hour?" Bartholomew Salazar's tone was more in sorrow than anger. "How…quaint."

Mr. Salazar did not notice the gleam that had come suddenly into the eyes of some of the guests nearby.

Jake was one of these. He was dressed to honor the occasion in a jacket and tie—a circumstance which no one who knew him could ever recall having happened before. The jacket was a little tight and didn't button, and the tie was a bit too short, but this was beside the point. Jake had confessed himself thrilled to meet a famous writer. He was beginning to feel, however, that the great Mr. Salazar had not been worth the effort.

Jake spoke from the outskirts of the little circle surrounding their guest.

"They're a local custom. Very special here. We call them Bloody Rogers—after the bartender who invented them."

Oliver Robert looked at Jake wide-eyed, but said nothing. He, too, had been unimpressed by their guest. "Even a little man casts a long shadow," he thought to himself.

Bartholomew Salazar looked around and gathered there was little chance of improvement from the glass he was holding of what he considered entirely mediocre whiskey. Never mind that it was from a very fine bottle, much prized by connoisseurs and carefully selected for the occasion. The mere fact of it being presented to him by these yokels was sufficient to convince him of its inferiority. It was his fifth. He gazed at the faces before him with a look of ill-concealed disdain. "All right," he said rolling his eyes and giving a refined little shiver, "I may as well."

He downed his whiskey and looked around. "Where does one acquire such a thing?"

"Here," said Jake, helpfully. "Let me get it for you."

The Washington Hotel had once been the home of a Great Lakes shipping captain, and it had likely seen its share of alcoholic overindulgence, but had there been an historical record for such things, the night of the opening reception of the Washington Island Literary Festival might have taken the prize for pure spectacle.

When Elisabeth heard the yelling, she came running from the kitchen. The bar was in chaos. At first, she thought there was blood spattered everywhere, and her heart stopped as the guest of honor stood in the center of the room, holding his throat and screaming like a character in a horror film. Several people stood nearby, apparently attempting to get him to drink water as he hurled invective in every direction.

Elisabeth was ready to spring into action. "What's happened? Have you called an ambulance?"

Roger, still behind the bar, looked at her with unconcern. "An ambulance? No."

He cleared his throat and leaned over the bar to speak to his wife in a stage whisper. "I don't think he likes his drink."

Elisabeth stared at him, eyes wide, and then looked back at the scene. Not blood but tomato juice had been flung everywhere, and she could not help but notice that the expressions of some of the bar's patrons looked more amused than sympathetic. It occurred to her—not for the first time—that grown men could be like children.

Elisabeth was blessed with a cool head. She sought out Emily, who stood amidst the war zone covered with the remnants of Bloody Roger, trying desperately to console her guest of honor.

"Emily," said Elisabeth, raising her voice to cut through the tumult, "Why don't you take Mr. Salazar upstairs? I can bring his dinner up later."

With some difficulty, she was able to assist Emily in getting the infuriated Salazar out of the room and to the foot of the stairs, at which point he abandoned his rage and began the weeping stage of intoxication.

It was in this condition that Elisabeth consigned his care to Emily and excused herself to return to the scene of battle. She looked back once, toward the bar, and seeing that the waiters had begun the clean-up, she sighed, muttered a few words to herself, and headed back to see how dinner preparations were coming. She was going to have to have a word with Roger, but for now, she didn't have the time.

Eddie, who had taken the night off for the event, wandered over to Fiona. He toasted her and leaned over to make himself heard over the noise of the room.

"He certainly adds rich dimension to the word 'crapulous.'"

Fiona spent the rest of the evening recovering from the resulting hiccups.

Chapter 53

Elisabeth's usual serenity was being tested that morning. The combination of hotel guests who had come for yoga with those who had come for the festival had a bit of a clashing-of-worlds feeling, and last night's disaster had had a deleterious effect on her nerves.

To make matters worse, despite Elisabeth's most urgent protestations, Roger had insisted that Goat Yoga must go on as scheduled on this, the morning of the Literary Festival. Elisabeth thought they were tempting fate.

She was not intimidated by the guests from New York, but she was fully aware of the high stakes of their opinions. Having Robert on the premises, was not, she felt, ideal, but then, it never was. At least, thank goodness, she could rely on Ben Palsson to keep a watchful eye.

Ben appeared just as Elisabeth was supervising the breakfast preparations. He had the charming quality of freshly washed boy; he smelled of soap, his hair was still slightly damp and slicked back, and he was sparkling with an energy that made caffeine unnecessary. She smiled at him appreciatively, and Ben smiled back. He liked Elisabeth.

"Good morning, Ben! We've just taken the cinnamon rolls out of the oven, and I think we need a taster."

She handed him a warm roll in a napkin, which he accepted cheerfully and demolished politely. The kitchen smelled of cinnamon rolls, coffee, and fresh oranges. Even on a splendid morning like this, it was an appealing place, especially for boys, and Ben lingered. His regular duties at this point of the day were light.

"Anything you need?" he asked, hopefully.

Elisabeth thought quickly. "Actually, could you run upstairs and do a towel check for me?"

This simple task was one he had done many times before. It involved visiting the linen room on the upstairs floor near the guest rooms and counting how many clean towels were on the shelves.

"Sure!" he said, and, his steps light in his summer sneakers, ran through the dining room toward the front stairs.

Ben was humming a little tune to himself that morning. It was something he had just heard, and it had captivated him over the past two days, lingering in his head and heart and recurring like a soundtrack beneath everything he did.

"Lalalalala," he sang under his breath. "Laladahla."

The floorboards creaked on the stairs as he ran up, trying to take two at a time. It was still a bit of a stretch, but it was already easier than it had been a few months before. He made it to the top of the stairs in no time and moved with light steps down the hall to the linen room.

"Laladahla," he sang softly, as he opened the door.

What happened next reminded Ben later of the experience of coming upon a bird in the tall grass, when there was such a rush of wings and surprise that everything blurred beyond anyone's ability to discern the sequence of events. Suddenly there was a bird in your face, and just as suddenly, it was gone.

One moment he was moving down the hall, happily engrossed in his own thoughts, and the next, he was facing two people, wildly embracing, kissing, and making noises that reminded Ben of his dog when she was dreaming.

He didn't mean to stare. It was just that he was surprised.

At the very moment he realized what he was seeing, the two people looked up from their frenzied clutching of one another, and he found himself face to face with Emily Martin and that writer guy from the Festival.

Horrified, embarrassed, and desperate, Ben spun around and ran blindly back the way he had come, down the hall, down the stairs and out the front door.

With their father and older brother away visiting relatives, Caleb had been left in charge while Emily was at the festival. The wisdom of this might certainly be debatable, but it had made sense in Emily's mind as a sort of check mark next to a duty performed. Noah, the youngest by seven years, was still the baby and was treated as such by his family. Even Caleb had a soft spot for his little brother, and whatever his other flaws, he wouldn't let Noah come to harm.

When Caleb rolled out of bed yawning and scratching, he flipped on the television in the living room and wandered into the kitchen to pour himself some cereal. It was only after he had been lounging on the couch in front of the television for half an hour that it dawned on him that he was supposed to be minding Noah. He didn't bother bestirring himself.

"NOAH!" he bellowed. "HEY, NOAH!!"

There was no answer.

Elisabeth was in the front hall when Ben came flying down the stairs of the hotel.

"Ben? What's the matter? Ben??"

He didn't seem to hear or see her as he ran past, out the front entrance, and disappeared in the direction of the goat pen.

A few minutes later, Emily Martin appeared at the top of the stairs, her face red with emotion, her hair in disarray. She hurried down, rushed past Elisabeth without returning her polite "Good morning," and headed out the door.

Elisabeth looked after her speculatively.

"What," she wondered, "was Emily Martin doing in the guest rooms?"

Joan, one of the Literary Festival's committee women, approached Elisabeth. Emily had brushed past her, ignoring her earnest questions about the keynote speaker.

"Have you seen Mr. Salazar this morning?" she asked.

Elisabeth frowned, "Why, no, I haven't. I have a lovely breakfast, if he'd like it."

It had already occurred to Elisabeth that Mr. Salazar might

not quite be in the mood to eat this morning, but she kept her thoughts to herself.

Joan frowned now, too. "I wonder where he could be."

Elisabeth shook her head helplessly. "Would you like me to knock on his door?"

Joan looked a bit uncomfortable. "Well, maybe not just yet. It seems a bit intrusive. I'll see if he's slipped past me. Probably already out there."

Elisabeth nodded.

As Joan walked away, Elisabeth looked up toward the stars and the guest rooms, an unpleasant idea forming in her mind.

It didn't take Caleb long to realize that Noah wasn't in the house. It was too much trouble to get dressed. He simply opened the kitchen door and yelled.

"NOAH! NOAH, YOU LITTLE JERK!! GET IN HERE!!!"

It was a cool fall morning, and Caleb felt the chill. Slamming the door, he went back to the refrigerator to find something else to eat.

After ten minutes had passed, he realized that Noah still hadn't come in.

He yelled out the door again. "Noah! NOAH! GET YOUR BUTT IN HERE!" But there was no answer.

With an exasperated sigh and the kind of language that horrified his mother, he went back to his room to pull on some clothes. He would have to go look for Noah in the barn.

Ben took refuge in the goat pen. He didn't even want to think about what he had just seen, but he was deeply embarrassed, feeling somehow that he had done something wrong. He had been taught that admitting to misdeeds was preferable to being found out, and he dreaded having to tell his mother about this as he knew he must. It was not for fear of her reaction but for the sheer misery of re-living the shame.

Instinctively, he buried himself in the familiar routine of time with Robert.

The yoga class had gone more or less without incident, and now there were no real chores to be done. He had already put out fresh food and water, and the pen was clean. Ben slipped inside the gate, and Robert came eagerly to him without being called. Ben rubbed the soft head and smiled in spite of himself when the goat playfully pushed his head against him. Ben's hands smelled of cinnamon roll, and Robert snuffled and licked.

"Hey, Robert," said Ben, softly. "Hey, Robert." Ben took a dog treat from his pocket and gave it to him. Robert ate it and snuffled Ben's pocket for more, which Ben promptly provided.

While Ben stroked his ears, Robert spoke softly to himself as he ate. "Yup, yup, yup, yup."

Soothed by the animal's presence, Ben began to feel calmer. He took a deep breath. It was a beautiful day, and it was impossible not to feel better because of it.

He only had a moment or two of respite.

"Ben! Ben Palsson! What do you think you're doing?"

Emily Martin's voice was both imperious and oddly hushed, like a stage whisper.

Ben turned reluctantly.

"Come here and look at me when I'm speaking to you."

Ben was, in fact—and with great difficulty—looking at Emily, but it was almost as if this were a stock phrase she spoke out of habit. He took a few steps toward the gate of the pen but carefully kept the gate between them.

"Open this gate and come here. I said, 'Come. Here.'"

Ben squared his shoulders and lifted his head. His parents did not speak this way at home, but it was a tone he knew he must obey. Nervously, he opened the latch and began to step through, but in a flash, Emily had grasped his shoulder and wrenched him forward. Ben was frightened. The closest thing to corporal punishment he could recall was many years ago when his mother had now and then administered what she called a 'potch on the seat' for some childhood infraction. But he had been little more than a baby then. Now, he was almost as tall as Emily herself. Would she hit him?

But she merely held on as she pushed her face into his.

"What were you doing in a private area of the hotel? Who gave you permission? Who?"

Ben opened his mouth to speak, but Emily did not wait for an answer.

"You listen to me, Ben Palsson. You had better not go around telling people things you see, do you hear me?" She leaned closer and hissed.

"Don't you tell anyone."

Ben, frozen in shock, simply stared at her without speaking.

After he had searched the barn and all the outbuildings, Caleb began to be worried. Noah was nowhere to be found. Caleb went back into the house. Maybe he was hiding.

"Hey, Noah!" He called in a gentler tone now. "I'm not mad, Noah. Sorry for yelling. You can come out now. Come on out, and we can watch cartoons."

The house rang with silence.

"Come on, Noah. Mom left doughnuts. They're your favorite. Chocolate!" Reluctantly, Caleb began a search of the house. He had already poked his head into Noah's room, but this time he saw the note in a childish scrawl on Noah's pillow.

"Gone to find Mom," it said.

"Oh, great."

Caleb knew he would be in trouble. In a house where there were few limitations there was one absolute. Everyone looked out for Noah.

Feeling slightly sick to his stomach, Caleb knew he needed to find Noah before their Mom found out.

He grabbed his jacket and headed out to get his bike.

Fiona was in no mood for a state breakfast with Bartholomew Salazar and decided to go check how things were going with Robert instead. As she approached the pen, she saw Emily holding Ben by the shoulder and quietly but clearly berating him. Instinctively, Fiona moved in to Ben's defense.

Seeing her, Emily immediately backed off, attempting to compose herself into a more suitable attitude.

"What on earth is going on?" Fiona noted Emily's state of disarray but hadn't time to assess it. Ben was such a steady, reliable boy. Had Robert gotten up to something? Even if he had, there was no excuse to treat the boy this way. She glanced at the goat pen. There was Robert, busily rummaging in his food bucket and appearing perfectly innocent. This, as Fiona well knew, was not a reliable indicator of his recent activities.

She looked at Ben, whose face was a study in misery.

"Are you okay?" she asked him in a quiet aside, as if Emily weren't there, fuming.

He nodded, but his face told another story.

"That child doesn't belong here," interjected Emily testily. "This is an adult event."

Fiona looked at her with surprise and confusion. "But… it's a literary festival… shouldn't children be exposed to literature?"

"At school. At home, perhaps," snapped Emily. "Certainly not here. It's not suitable."

Fiona sensed Ben's embarrassment and deliberately kept the tone of the conversation neutral for his sake. She had frequently found Emily Martin irritating, but she had never seen her in such a state of malevolence.

"That's a very peculiar view," she said, evenly. "Besides, Ben is here because he was hired to do a job. He has responsibilities."

"Then, I am unhiring him!"

"He doesn't work for you." Fiona appeared calm, but she was angry.

Emily became her most officious self, which was very officious indeed.

"Well," she began. "I am the chairman of the festival and, as such, a client of this hotel. I demand that this child be removed from the premises." She paused a moment before adding, primly. "He's upsetting Mr. Salazar."

Fiona looked around. Mr. Salazar was nowhere to be seen.

"If that's the case, then Mr. Salazar strikes me as a man with remarkable powers if he can be so easily upset from a distance."

Fiona looked at Ben's face and realized that he should not have to be witness to any further attempts at his humiliation. As Emily stood there, almost a caricature of impatience, Fiona turned to the bewildered boy and gave him a look of commiseration.

"Ben, I think I left something in my car. Would you please get it for me?"

Ben nodded with wild relief and hastened his escape.

Emily cleared her throat and patted her messy hair. "I am expected in the Festival tent."

Fiona turned a furious face on Emily and looked her full in the eye. "We will discuss this later."

Emily's chin went up but, although Fiona could not have known, her silence was the fullest expression of her mortification.

Emily spun around and stalked off.

"Big winker," muttered Fiona.

Caleb was quite winded by the time he got to the hotel. He walked up the lawn past the tents for the festival and tried to figure out what would attract Noah's interest. Never having thought much about other people's feelings, Caleb was finding this beyond his abilities. He was about to try the tents, when he caught a glimpse of Noah's bike leaning against the fence at the back of the main building.

He came around the corner at the side of the property, where there wasn't much activity, and there he saw Noah, squatting on the ground near the corner of an old shed. Relief flooded through him.

Noah was struggling with something, and Caleb realized that he was plucking handfuls of dry grasses. To feed the goat, probably. Noah spent a lot of time in the barn at home, hanging over the fences feeding their goats. Caleb had no idea why.

Noah saw him and stood up, hastily shoving the grasses into the pocket of his hoodie.

"Damn it, Noah," hissed Caleb furiously. "You're going to get me in trouble. What are you doing here? Mom told you to stay home."

Noah looked at his brother. "Mom's here," he said.

Caleb couldn't contain his frustration. "I know Mom's here. Let's get out of here before she sees us."

"I can't. I have to do something. I'm playing war."

Caleb sighed irritably. "We can play war at home. Come on."

"No, here. I want to play here." Noah took something out of his pocket and began to tap it on the palm of his hand.

Caleb looked hard at his little brother and was suddenly struck by a shocking idea.

"Noah, what are you doing?"

Noah looked at him with innocent eyes. "Nothing."

Caleb was genuinely shaken. Not the gentlest of young men, he now cautiously reached out to touch his brother's arm.

"Noah," he said, softly and earnestly, "just listen to me for a minute."

Noah regarded his brother with a blank curiosity, his body stilled as if he were in a trance.

"Noah, can I have that?"

Noah withdrew sharply from Caleb's touch and hid what Caleb wanted under his crossed arms.

"No!"

It occurred to Caleb how easy it would be to grab his brother and take the object from Noah's hands. But he knew bullying his brother was the one thing his mother would not tolerate.

Caleb thought about his last year at military school with its schedules, and discipline, and field marches. He hated it with a passion nearly as virulent as his hatred for Ben Palsson. He would do anything not to have to go back there again.

"Okay, okay," said Caleb hastily. "I won't take it. I was only asking." Caleb frowned, thinking hard.

His mother's proscriptions notwithstanding, he knew instinctively that bullying wouldn't work this time, but he had no experience in persuasion. For all his rough talk, Caleb loved his little brother.

"Noah," he asked with sudden insight, "are you playing a game?"

Noah nodded silently.

"What is the game? Is it war? Can I play war with you?"

Noah tilted his head. "No. I want Ben. I want Ben to play."

Caleb had not expected this.

"But Ben's not here. I'm here. How about you and I play for a little while first?"

"No. I want Ben."

Caleb breathed deeply, trying to find some patience. He hated Ben. Stupid Ben. Stupid, stupid Ben.

"Okay, Noah. We can ask Ben to play. How about you and I go find Ben together?"

Noah put a finger in his mouth where a tooth was wiggling. "Okay."

Chapter 54 ❖

Fiona watched Emily leave and sighed a deep breath of relief. She was still angry on Ben's behalf, and her next task was to find him and ask what had happened. Ben had seemed embarrassed, but whether it was because of a mistake he had made or having been berated by Emily, she couldn't tell.

She was about to go to her car to find him, when she stepped in something Robert had left behind. Sitting on a bench, she wiped off her shoe as best she could, thinking all the while about this metaphor for the past 24 hours. She couldn't wait for this event to be over.

Having done the best she could, she hurried to the parking lot to find Ben.

Ben had been relieved to get away from Mrs. Martin, and knew that once again, Ms. Campbell had saved him from a bad situation. He leaned back on her car to wait for her, enjoying the heat from the metal and the autumn sun on his face.

"Hey! Palsson!"

Ben heard, then saw Caleb standing behind the yoga studio, waving his arms with Noah standing nearby, looking as if they'd just stepped out of the woods. His instinctive reaction was to pretend that he hadn't noticed, but Noah's presence pulled at his conscience. He waited, and they approached.

"Hi, Ben," said Noah, innocently.

Caleb, thrust into the unfamiliar role of diplomat, was struggling with how to communicate privately with Ben. Ben sensed something different in Caleb's manner and was puzzled by it. Caleb seemed to be trying to get Ben to look at him. Ben did look, his face serious, and then glanced back at Noah as his mind swiftly sorted through possible scenarios. Wherever Caleb went, trouble followed.

"Hey, Ben," said Noah. "We've been looking for you."

"I was...working," said Ben, feeling evasive without fully understanding why.

"Noah wanted to play with you," said Caleb in an odd voice, full of meaning.

"Want to play war with us?" asked Noah. "We can play here the hotel."

"NO!" said Caleb. And then, more calmly, "We don't want to play at the hotel. Mom's here. It will be better somewhere else. Much better."

"Why?" asked Noah.

There was still that odd note in Caleb's tone that Ben couldn't decipher. He envisioned their mother, and what he had seen, and what could happen if they were to see it. It was so strange to think, now, knowing what he knew, that Mrs. Martin was their mother. He felt embarrassed again.

"No, Noah, the hotel's not a good place for war," said Ben.

They were all silent, then stymied when Fiona appeared.

She saw Caleb and Noah and was instantly concerned.

"Will you boys excuse us for a moment? I need to speak with Ben about work."

She drew Ben away so they couldn't overhear.

"Is everything okay?"

Ben nodded. "It's okay. I think."

Fiona frowned. There were Martins everywhere she turned, and she didn't want Ben to have to deal with any of them. "What's going on?"

Ben shook his head dismissively. "It's okay. Really. Noah wants me to play war." He flashed a quick grin. "Even he can't stand Caleb."

Fiona had to smile. "Are you sure you're safe?"

He wasn't. "Yeah. I'm sure."

"I'm really sorry about what happened back there. You shouldn't have to put up with that."

Ben shrugged, embarrassed. "It's okay."

"It's really not, but listen, the yoga classes are done for now, right? Why don't you get out of here? I'll tell Roger I sent you home. Does that sound good?"

The look of relief on his face told her the answer.

"Thanks, Ms. Campbell."

She nodded and gave him the faintest little wink.

"You sure you're okay?"

"I'm sure."

Fiona stood watching as he wheeled his bike down the hotel driveway toward Caleb and Noah and watched as they stood together. Everything seemed okay.

Sighing, she looked at her watch. She had lost her taste for the literary festival. Maybe, if things weren't too hectic with breakfast service, she could grab a cup of coffee with Elisabeth. She headed up the driveway to the kitchen.

M any precautions had been taken to ensure that Robert's enclosure at the hotel was secure, but these were all dependent upon consistent application of certain principles. Latching the gate, for example, was one of these principles. When Emily had grasped Ben by the shoulder, he had been just about to latch the gate but hadn't quite.

Robert, in his goatly way, was attached to Ben. Calling it love might, perhaps, have been too much, but he was used to Ben and trusted him. So, when Ben was not there, Robert noticed. Robert, being Robert, also noticed that the gate was open.

It was in this way that Robert was able to wander out and begin preliminary explorations of the property. It may have been to look for Ben, or it may simply have been opportunity. Robert rarely wasted opportunities.

Robert noticed that the grass outside his gate smelled sweet and delicate. He stopped for a small snack and then looked around. He smelled something else he liked, and soon found his way to the magnificent old rose bushes that grew luxuriantly along the south side of the hotel. Their bloom was long gone, but this was the smell he knew. Delicious.

B en approached Caleb and Noah, waiting at the foot of the driveway. There was no way he could avoid them. He sure didn't want to go back to the hotel and deal with their mother. He recalled the phrase "lesser of two evils." So, this is what it meant.

"Are you going to play with us?" asked Noah.

Ben took a deep breath. "I guess so, for a little while."

He caught Caleb's eye and tried to discern the weird signals he was getting. Noah had moved out of earshot, squatting near the culvert and poking a stick at the frogs living in the stagnant water there.

Ben looked at Caleb. "You tried to run me over," he said in a low voice.

"No, I didn't. I swear." Caleb had the grace to look ashamed. "It was an accident. I couldn't stop. I couldn't be caught driving my dad's car."

They looked at each other.

"I'm sorry," said Caleb at last. "It was stupid." He took a deep breath and mumbled at the ground. "Thanks for not telling."

Ben gave a brief nod of the head, then looked over at Noah.

Caleb leaned a little closer. "You gotta help me. I need to get Noah out of here."

Ben frowned. "Why?"

"I've got to keep an eye on him. Please." said Caleb, a new odd tone in his voice.

"I wanna play war," said Noah loudly.

Caleb gave Ben a meaning look and nodded his head at him.

Ben, despite his misgivings, was worried about Noah in Caleb's hands and decided to play along.

"Hey, I got an idea," said Ben, his voice raised so Noah could hear. "If you want to play war, how about the cemetery by School House Beach? Lots of places to hide, and the woods are there, and the water."

Ben was thinking of ways to get closer to home. Despite his assurances to Fiona, he wasn't completely confident about what was going on.

Caleb seemed relieved.

"Yeah. The cemetery would be good, Noah. It would be really good."

Ben couldn't help wondering whether the cemetery would be the place of his own death, while Noah looked at them both, somewhat unhappily.

"Okay," he said at last, reluctantly. He set off at a trot ahead of them to get his bike.

Caleb signaled to Ben to wait. "Hold on a sec'," he said in a low voice.

"Why?" Ben didn't want to be left alone with Caleb.

Caleb spoke in a low voice. "You have to help."

"What?"

Caleb gave a brief, irritable sigh.

"It's Noah. You have to help with Noah."

"What?" said Ben again. "Why?" He looked after the small figure on the driveway. Ben did not have the word to describe how vulnerable he looked. What was going on here?

"I'll explain when we get there, but I gotta go. I can't leave him alone."

Noah turned back to them, calling impatiently. "Let's go."

Caleb shot a glance at Ben. "See you there." He ran to his bike and took off after Noah.

Slowly, Ben got on his bike, feeling he was heading toward his doom.

When Emily Martin made her belated appearance near the stage at the front of the Festival tent, she seemed, to those familiar with her, perhaps a bit more tightly wound than usual with, if anything, more hauteur.

The events of the evening before had left the rest of the festival committee feeling a bit nervous. It wasn't that Islanders were unaccustomed to drunkenness, or to bad behavior, for that matter. Generally speaking, the one thing followed the other, and they were not in the habit of casting stones—at least not about this kind of thing. And then, of course, no one could be held responsible for the Bloody Rogers except, of course...well, Roger.

Midwesterners are frequently credited with being nice. It would be a mistake, however, to conflate their bland public civility with the quality of their inner thoughts. Behind the smiles and seeming docility lies a capacity for judging the behavior of others that is as merciless as the Inquisition. The most devastating disapproval might be expressed with a mild "wow," but for those who understood, this had the full force and cultural significance of the vilest burst of obscenity.

For the Islanders, in their ethos of Nice, an invited guest—particularly one so lofty and worthy of admiration as the celebrated Bartholomew Salazar—should have been someone more appreciative of his hosts' efforts—not to mention more respectful of other guests.

But perhaps, they consoled themselves, his mother never taught him how to behave, poor man. Last night, after all, was only a party, and party behavior could be excused...usually. It had been a memorable evening, and deep down, in a place no one would acknowledge—even in private—the Islanders had thoroughly enjoyed it.

Today, however, was the main event, the reason he had been invited. Today he would be on his best behavior. Surely, everything would go better.

Robert's explorations took him to the entryway of the festival tent. He stopped to survey the scene, ducking his head as if to acknowledge adoring fans, most of whom were, thus far, unaware of his presence. Had anyone been paying attention, they might have noticed a gleam in his eye. Whether this was in anticipation of some nascent plan or the result of his partial consumption of a backpack left carelessly on the floor near the entry would be difficult to determine.

After a summer of goat yoga classes, Robert might be

forgiven for having developed the idea that prancing—not around, but actually upon—people was a fine idea much to be encouraged. In hindsight, permitting this behavior may have been a mistake.

Now, entering the tent filled with people in chairs, practicing—for all he knew—a yoga pose of which he had been hitherto unaware, Robert soon put his newly-formed world view into practice.

Those at the back of the tent were the first to benefit from his experience. The sound of hooves on the wooden floor, something between a clackety clack and a clump, created a kind of prelude for the unwary before the real chaos began.

As Robert progressed from row to row, butting his head here, leaping onto laps there, people's protests, at first muted by a sense of what seemed fitting at a public event, gradually grew less encumbered by any reticence at self-expression.

Further to the front, backs to the door, and attentive to the program they were anticipating, the rest of the audience slowly became aware of a growing hubbub of gasps, outcries, muffled curses, and the sounds of some kind of scuffle—which naturally arose as Robert endeavored to climb onto the laps, heads, and backs of various bystanders in his efforts to assist them in their poses. Out of politeness, the people in front pretended not to hear, but they had a growing sense of common shame and embarrassment. This kind of behavior was clearly a sign that rural people simply weren't prepared to participate properly in serious cultural events.

Fueled by natural reactions of surprise and self-preservation among the audience, however, the maelstrom grew. Emily, trying to speak from the front, continued doggedly—whether in denial or out of conviction that the show must go on was difficult to determine. Besides, Emily had a tendency toward near-sightedness, and was too vain to wear glasses. She soon gave up trying to speak over the yelling, and merely stood at the microphone saying, "people...people," rather ineffectually. When she fully grasped what was happening, these mild remonstrances shifted to a more assertive: "Someone get that animal out of here!"

Emily's reaction seemed to enhance the crowd's level of panic, and the shouting grew.

This general response to Robert's personal ministrations only appeared to encourage him. He seemed to feel, in fact, that it would only be companionable to join in the group's vocalizations. And so, in demonstration of a skill he had not exhibited in public since his feral ruminations, Robert began with a sort of desultory murmuring, like a singer warming up, which, after a suitable period, blossomed into a sequence of full-blown screams.

The sound had a particularly nerve-tearing quality and gradually increased in both pitch and volume, beginning with a rather nasal baritone and culminating in what could easily be mistaken for a woman's full-throated terror. Robert followed each of his screams with a satisfied chortle sounding—as Oliver told Fiona later— vaguely reminiscent of an evil duck. These musical interludes were accompanied by an exhibition of the complete range of his surprisingly broad vocabulary.

Robert's progression through the tent generated a seismic effect of human upheaval, and the pandemonium in the back rows began to spread toward the front. The rolling approach of Wave Robert gathered momentum as people leapt from their chairs, overturning them in their haste to get away.

The crowd being, by and large, unfamiliar with the manifestations of goat behavior were uncertain of the seriousness of the situation. Was it dangerous?

Meanwhile, any attempt at continuing the presentations from the podium ground to a halt, which was perhaps just as well.

It was at the high point of these proceedings that Bartholomew Salazar made his belated appearance at the back of the stage. He looked somewhat worse for the wear since last night. His perfectly tailored white shirt was rumpled, his jacket unpressed, and his famous hair was somewhat less important than usual. To those observers undistracted by Robert, he seemed, perhaps, a bit unsteady on his feet.

Most of the festival's officialdom had descended from the stage and were now fully engaged in essential goat-related activities. There was a flurry of movement as those near the front of the room, still hoping for an opportunity to hear the great man speak, tried in vain to shush the rest of the attendees. Their efforts, however, went unrewarded.

Seemingly oblivious to the pandemonium going on in front of him, Bartholomew Salazar brushed aside the frantic objections of Emily, who still remained onstage, and made his unsteady way to the microphone. He began to speak.

"Ladeeth and Gentlemen," unable to hear himself above the din, he tapped at the microphone to see whether it was on but was unable to tell.

"Hullo?" he called. "HULLOOOOO? CAN YOU HEAR ME?"

The speakers squealed with feedback, adding to the noise of goat screaming, people screaming, and metal chairs being overturned. Salazar lifted his chin and squinted vaguely out over the hall, but whether from near-sightedness or some other cause, he did not seem able to identify what was happening in front of him. In any case, he might be forgiven for not believing his eyes.

He brushed a loose strand of hair back from his face and squared his shoulders. "I am not," he announced into the microphone with great dignity, "accush—accustomed to com—*peting* with a—a—a barroom brawl. Kindly take your seats, or I shall be obligshed...oblig...OBLIGED to dish—dishcon—*dishhhhcontinue.*"

When there was no response from the audience, his indignation increased. Salazar took a menacing step forward toward the edge of the platform, the better to chastise this ignorant rabble. How dare they behave in this way when he was about to speak?

Enraged by the effrontery, he took another step, his foot becoming entangled in the microphone cord. Under normal circumstances, such a minor event might not have been catastrophic, but the state of Mr. Salazar's balance was not at its best. With the same slow motion of a tall building being brought down with dynamite, he swayed for an instant and then, in a spectacular arching movement, went over the edge of the platform head first, his flailing arms grasping the mic stand and bringing it down with him, along with the nearby amplifiers and speakers, and a decorative row of potted peace lilies.

The crashing sound of this most recent disaster was nearly lost in the chaos of the room. For those closest, however, there was a collective gasp, and while the rest of the room continued in its introduction to Robert, the front rows looked with horror at the crumpled figure of their honored guest, entangled in a combination of wires, copious quantities of potting soil and leaves, and enough bunting for a World Series game. Gradually, awareness of the catastrophe spread, and a strange silence overcame the room.

In those moments of unnatural quiet, only one creature dared to move. Robert, with the prim dignity of one who has at last accomplished a long-cherished goal, approached the great Bartholomew Salazar and carefully, with regal aplomb, arranged himself delicately to sit upon his person. As he perched his considerable weight on the great Mr. Salazar's head, Robert expressed himself with a loud and satisfied "BAAAAAAAWB!"

Mr. Salazar's comments bore a distinct connection to Anglo-Saxon tradition.

Chapter 55

As he rode to the cemetery, Ben's agitation grew. He thought he trusted Noah, but it probably would be easy for Caleb to persuade his younger brother to go along with some plan. Was this an ambush? Caleb's behavior was so odd. Ben found himself itemizing reasons for his parents to get him a cell phone. That would be one good thing, he thought, grimly. If something bad happened to him now, they would be more likely to agree. Assuming, of course, that he lived.

As he came down the road, he heard voices and saw Caleb and Noah near the entrance to the cemetery. They appeared to be arguing.

"No!" said Noah, sharply. "It's mine."

As he approached, Ben could see that Noah had something clutched in his pocket, and he wondered why Caleb didn't just take it. That would be his usual style, but he seemed constrained, somehow. Ben pulled up, leaned his bike against a tree where it could be easily reached in an emergency, and reluctantly went to meet his fate.

The sounds of a commotion broke through Elisabeth and Fiona's conversation, and after one shocked moment, they put down their cups and ran toward the tent. What they saw when they arrived left them both momentarily speechless.

People were running and yelling; several clutching injured parts of their anatomy. The neatly arranged rows of chairs were now mostly overturned, and in one case piled to create a kind of goat-proof bunker in which one woman sat and wept.

The stage decorations looked as if they had been ripped down, and the plants were lying in a jumble of root balls and potting soil. Toward the front of the tent, from deep within a huddle of people, came the sound of some of the most colorful swearing Fiona had ever heard, along with a good bit of yelling.

Emily Martin was hovering nearby, literally wringing her hands and weeping.

Fiona surveyed the devastation and then uttered a small, "Oh, no." There stood Robert calmly in a far corner, ignoring the hubbub as he thoughtfully masticated one of the tent's mooring ropes. A distinct essence of goat lingered in the air.

Fiona and Elisabeth exchanged looks, and in perfect understanding of one another, Elisabeth, pulling out her cell phone, went to console Emily, while Fiona went to remove Robert from the scene.

Caleb continued speaking to Noah in a voice of false patience that was undercut by the tension in his body. Ben suddenly realized that Caleb was acting as if he were afraid of Noah. How could that be?

"Show Ben what you have, Noah."

Noah hesitated, then slowly, he withdrew his hand from his pocket and opened his palm to show the elegant silver lighter lying there. It looked valuable and had initials engraved on it in flowing letters.

"Where'd you get that, Noah?"

Noah was silent, gazing from one to another of them.

Ben and Caleb exchanged glances.

"It's my mom's," said Caleb, reluctantly. "She used to smoke."

It was clear that Caleb wanted something to happen, but Ben wasn't sure what it was. Playing war didn't seem to be the point, that much was clear.

No longer afraid for himself, but still mystified, Ben sat down on the soft, newly mown grass of the cemetery. In a gesture his mother deplored, he plucked a blade of grass, stuck it in his mouth, and squinted up at Noah. Unconsciously, he adopted the conversational tone his father often used.

"What's going on, Noah? Come on, sit down. Want to tell me about it?"

Noah shrugged and looked away.

Caleb's impatience was a suppressed explosion, but he

knew instinctively that Ben was bringing a quality to the moment that Caleb himself did not have. Caleb might hate Ben, but he knew instinctively that right now, he needed him.

Ben leaned back on his elbows in the classic pose of boyhood. This position of seeming relaxation changed the mood. He looked over at the brothers, his eyes landing meaningfully on Caleb.

"Grass feels good."

Unable to surrender his vanity completely, Caleb, sullen mistrust surrounding him like a fog, moved slowly like a dog unwilling to obey a command. He sat on a tombstone a few feet away, managing both to comply and protest at the same time.

"What's with the lighter?" asked Ben, casually. He rolled onto his side and squinted up at Noah.

Noah shrugged and looked at his feet.

"Are you worried 'cuz your mom doesn't know you have it?"

Ben was trying hard to imagine why the Martin boys seemed so strangely tongue-tied and tense. None of it made any sense. What could possibly make Caleb afraid? It couldn't be of his mother, Ben felt sure.

"Tell him," urged Caleb. "Tell him about the lighter."

Noah flinched and looked guilty and suddenly in a flash, Ben knew. The realization shook him. He sat up and looked swiftly at Caleb, and then back at Noah, his shock showing in his eyes.

"Noah," he said slowly, "you've been starting fires with that lighter, haven't you?" There was a long, deep silence, and then a new and more horrifying realization hit Ben. He sat up, his face filled with everything he felt, and looked at Noah.

"You were going to start a fire at the hotel."

Slowly, silently, Noah looked at Ben, at Caleb, and began backing away. Then, in an instant, he turned and ran. In the few seconds it took the two older and faster boys to get to their feet, he had disappeared into the woods.

The sound of sirens approached, and a small emergency team arrived to attend to the great Mr. B. Salazar and, finally, to remove him from the scene. He had a broken leg and had some contusions, they informed Fiona, but would be all right. They put him on a stretcher and took him to a private space to wait for the helicopter to transport him to a hospital in Green Bay.

After fifteen minutes of running through the woods and calling, Ben and Caleb stopped and stood gasping for breath. Noah was nowhere in sight.

"Why are you stopping?" hissed Caleb. "We can't let him go! We have to stay with him. He's going to start another fire."

"We can't…we need to get help," said Ben. "You keep looking. I'll go."

At last able to release his pent-up feelings, Caleb grabbed Ben roughly by the arm.

"Listen, you can't tell anybody about this."

Ben pulled his arm away, unintimidated.

"That's crazy," he said. "We have to tell. He could hurt someone. He could hurt himself. He was going to burn down a building with people in it. We can't just pat him on the head and tell him to stop." He wanted to say, "even you should know that," but he stopped before the words came out. Instead he added, "Isn't that why you told me?"

Caleb looked at Ben with cold resentment. He hated that Ben was right. Every experience of his life had told him not to trust anyone with this story. His instincts were to cover up and try to protect Noah from authority, just as he habitually covered up his own misdeeds. But Noah had insisted on finding Ben. And now, Ben knew.

Caleb knew Noah wouldn't just stop, but Ben's knowing what had happened stirred something ugly deep inside Caleb in a way he didn't understand. It was bad enough that Noah plainly preferred Ben to his own brother, but it was worse that Ben was right. And worse still that Ben would tell.

It didn't matter that Ben was right. Not telling was now more important than anything else—even more important than finding Noah.

Caleb wanted to punch Ben Palsson. Hard.

As the paramedics tended to the fallen genius inside the hotel, hampered in every way by Emily's frantic attempts to instruct them, Fiona, having secured Robert in his pen, came to see what else needed to be done.

Elisabeth had already calmly supervised the clearing away of the mess at the foot of the podium, while a hotel crew rearranged the chairs.

"We need to distract the audience somehow," she said to Elisabeth.

The sound of Emily's hectoring voice could be heard from some distance. Elisabeth looked at Fiona. "I think you should take charge."

Without hesitation, Fiona turned to Pali. "Pali, you're the only one of us with any literary qualifications. Couldn't you speak? Maybe read some of your poetry?"

The irony occurred to them both at the same time, and Pali hesitated. He was not much of a public speaker, and he had been so pointedly not invited. Then the humor of it struck him, and he smiled. "Well, why not?"

"Fantastic. I'll introduce you. How much time to you need?"

Pali gave the good-natured shrug of someone who has nothing to lose and patted a sheaf of papers in his pocket. "I can do it now."

Fiona lightly punched him on the arm in solidarity and led the way to the podium.

There was still a fair amount of disorder. People were milling around and talking, many of the chairs were still overturned, and there was a certain goat-related quality that lingered in the air. It took a while for her to gather the attention of the crowd.

Fiona stood on the platform and spoke with authority. Her time in public office had stood her in good stead.

"One of the pleasures of any literary festival is discovering new writers. Ver Palsson is well known here on the Island, but his work is just beginning to come to wider public attention. Last year, Poetry magazine dedicated a feature on him and on his work. Please join me in welcoming him as he reads a few of his poems."

What remained of the somewhat frazzled and bewildered audience, seated in a tent still redolent of goat, gave an exhausted round of applause. In the back corner of the room, Fiona could see The New Yorker writer—the one who had been on the ferry—scribbling in his notebook. "What a story he's going to have," she thought resignedly.

Pali had taken off the blue ferry line jacket that was part of his uniform and stood off to the side of the podium. If he was nervous, he did not show it.

Taking a deep breath, Ver Palsson, poet, walked to the lectern, a sheaf of papers clasped in one hand.

Ben and Caleb stared at each other, their fists clenched. Ben felt his heart beating. He remembered vividly the feel of his fists pounding on Caleb's face and the taste of blood in his own mouth, just as Caleb must be doing. He itched to hit him again. But even though Ben would not back down, he knew he was at a disadvantage this time. Caleb was older and bigger, and he had a grudge.

Ben instinctively moved away, out of reach, his eyes fixed on Caleb's. They circled one another like animals. Ben's heart beat so hard he could see his own pulse in his eyes. The plan formed in his mind as instinct rather than thought. He could reach one foot out to trip Caleb. Only by bringing him to the ground could Ben hope to gain advantage. He did not dare allow his eyes to follow his thoughts, for fear of giving away his plan, and he knew he only had a few seconds before Caleb lashed out first. These realizations flashed through his mind, when something simultaneously broke through the consciousness of both boys.

It was the sound of Noah screaming.

For the briefest split-second, Ben and Caleb's eyes met, and then they both took off in the direction of the screams.

Fiona saw Oliver Robert at the back of the tent and went to stand beside him.

He gave her a brief nod but appeared riveted by Pali's presentation.

"How's it going, do you think?" whispered Fiona.

"Aside from the goat invasion and a catastrophic injury of the featured speaker? Terrific."

Fiona had to restrain herself from rolling her eyes. "I meant Pali."

"Oh," said Oliver. "He's very good." He looked at Fiona

now, his mask down. "Frankly, I had no idea."

"It wouldn't be obvious, really."

"No."

Someone in the row in front of them turned to glare, and they were silent again for a minute. Fiona gestured to Oliver, and he followed her outside.

"What do you think we should do next? He can't talk forever."

Oliver studied her for a moment, trying to decide whether he should speak.

"Well," he said, slowly. "I do have an idea."

"Out with it. Please."

"We could have a panel discussion with the book club members."

Fiona pursed her lips, thinking. "That's not bad."

"Any plan is bad that cannot be changed," replied Oliver automatically.

Fiona managed to ignore this as Oliver continued speaking.

"And Eddie—maybe as part of that, he could speak about self-education through the great books. He's quite eloquent on the subject."

Fiona began to feel hopeful. "Do you think you could arrange it? We just have this chunk of time to fill, and then the rest can go on as planned."

He was already whipping out his cell phone. "I'm on it."

Pali was still answering questions from the audience when a handful of the book club members gathered on the porch of the hotel.

"I don't mind helping, but this makes me kind of nervous. I'm used to having a beer in my hand during our conversations," commented Jake. "I don't know if I can do this without one."

Elisabeth spoke up. "I'll provide the beer."

Fiona looked sideways at her.

"Desperate times, desperate measures," whispered Elisabeth. Aloud, she said "Just don't overdo it. We've already seen the results of that."

The members of the book club looked serious. No one wanted to be like that pompous ass Salazar.

"Don't worry," Eddie assured her. "In all our meetings, it's never been a problem."

"You can count on us," said Jake. And he meant it.

Chapter 56

Ben was lighter and faster than Caleb, and he met Noah first, some fifty yards down the trail. Noah was running toward them, flames rising from the sleeve of his jacket. Stop, Drop, and Roll was the first principle of Boy Scout fire safety, and although Noah did not remember, Ben and Caleb did.

"Stop, Noah!"

"Noah! Drop! Drop and roll!"

Caleb ran toward Noah, while Ben ripped his own jacket off.

"Take it! Take my jacket!"

Caleb grabbed it and flung himself at his brother, rolling himself over the small figure, wrapping him in Ben's jacket. Noah screamed and struggled to get away.

The flames were soon out, but Noah's howling continued.

"Is he hurt? How bad is it?"

Caleb looked helpless now, as Ben moved in to try to assess.

"Noah! Noah!!" Ben tried to change his tone of voice to something more calming as he had so often heard his mother do. "Let me see your arm. Come on now," he soothed. "Come on and let me see it."

Still weeping—whether with fear or pain Ben couldn't

tell—Noah allowed Ben to take his arm. Seeing it, Ben felt a hot rush of relief. The wool and leather jacket was scorched. But there was nothing else. No injury at all.

"It's okay. It's okay, Noah. You're okay."

Noah's sobs still echoed against the rock ledges of the woods.

Ben looked over at Caleb. They were both breathing hard. "He's just scared."

Caleb stepped up. "Come on, bud. Let's go home."

Noah's weeping grew louder. "No, no, no!"

"It's okay, buddy, it's okay. Come on. Come on, Noah. Let's go find Mom." And speaking to his brother with a gentleness Ben would never have thought possible, Caleb took his brother's hand and led him back along the trail toward the road.

Neither looked back.

His heart still beating fast, Ben took a deep breath and slumped down against the trunk of a tree. He sat there for a long time, not thinking but listening to the sounds of the woods and the birds in the trees.

"Lalalalala," he sang under his breath. "Laladahla."

Following Pali's reading there was a short break enhanced by coffee and Elisabeth's homemade cookies, and then the Literary Festival went on.

Eddie, Jake, and three of the others who could be rounded up were seated in a half-circle on the stage, their discreet ceramic mugs filled with the beer of their choice.

Oliver, who had declined to participate onstage, did the introductions. His nervousness made him more affected than usual, but on Fiona's advice, he kept his words brief. "No one wants to listen to the introduction," she told him. "They want the main event."

He cleared his throat, fussed a moment with the microphone, and spoke. "I am pleased to present members of the Washington Island Great Books Club in a conversation on 'Shakespeare in an Age of Discontent.'" The title had been his idea and he felt pleased with it.

At the back of the room he could see Emily, now composed, her hair re-arranged, her lipstick fresh, shooting daggers at him with her eyes. He finished his introduction and left the stage.

Fiona met him with congratulations. "But did you notice Emily?" she asked. "If looks could kill."

Oliver shrugged. "Curses are like processions: they return whence they began."

Fiona smiled.

The distant throbbing of an approaching helicopter could be heard. It was time for Bartholomew Salazar to leave.

After his reading, Fiona gave Pali an explanation of the events of the morning, and although he was confident in Ben's good sense, still, Pali's instinct was to go find him. He was delayed briefly by someone from New York wanting to speak with him, but Pali had a father's preoccupations. He listened and spoke politely and then excused himself.

"I can give you some copies of the poems I just read," he offered. "Would that be helpful?"

He thrust his packet of papers into the man's hands and hurried off.

After some time, Ben shook himself from his reverie. He had been trusting Caleb to give an accurate report of what had happened, but he now realized that this was unlikely. It was up to him.

He thought about his morning and the odd echoes of both Mrs. Martin and Caleb telling him not to tell. He felt suddenly vulnerable. Could Caleb have circled back to find him and stop him from reporting Noah's crimes? He shook himself like a big dog rising from sleep. No, Caleb wouldn't expect him still to be here. Ben knew these paths better than anyone, and he would be safe here. He would circle through the woods and go in search of help. Reassured by this plan, Ben set off.

A small group, hands to ears, stood watching as the helicopter, carrying a conscious and colorfully expressive Bartholomew Salazar—with the hair, but without the beautiful briefcase— completed its slow, majestic rise, banked off to the southwest, and headed toward Green Bay.

Everyone was silent for a few moments as the rhythmic beat of the rotors faded into the distance, and the events of the past hour settled upon them all. Oliver Robert spoke. "Ah," he said. "Well."

As if this were a cue to shake them out of their reveries, the others began to move away, but Oliver and Fiona stood apart, still watching the sky in a contemplative fashion.

"It's true, I suppose," said Oliver.

"What is?"

"Empty vessels make the most noise." Oliver delivered this with a sigh of satisfaction and, removing his glasses, began to polish them with a reminiscent air.

Now that the festival was no longer her problem, Fiona felt an enormous sense of relief. She gave him a sidelong glance. "Well," she said, "Empty vessels and goats."

Chapter 57

Ben made his way through the wooded paths with a sense of urgency, both for his own protection and for his worries about where Caleb might be taking Noah. Would they go home and risk discovery of Noah's fire-setting? Or…what other choices did they have? Would Caleb help Noah run away? What if Noah set another fire?

It didn't occur to Ben to wonder about Noah's motivations or even to be shocked by his actions. He accepted reality with the lack of perspective that makes children far more pragmatic than adults usually realize. But Ben also had a well-developed sense of justice, and while he didn't want anything bad to happen to his friend, unlike Caleb, he was quite clear that this was something that shouldn't be concealed.

Despite his hurry, Ben's caution took him on a rather circuitous route along the rocky bluffs of the lake shore. The wind had come up and even though the sun still shone brightly, it was cold here. The path wound back away from the lake in among a grove of cedar trees that offered shelter from the breezes, while the sun streamed through the branches, making little islands of light. Ben's feet crunched the needles on the path as he sang his new song softly to himself.

"Lalalalala," he sang under his breath. "Laladahla."

Ben felt the eyes on him and stopped. His song stopped, too, mid-syllable, and his breath came faster. The small hairs on his arms stood on end. Someone was there.

His body tensed for the fight he knew was about to come, but he heard no steps.

Slowly Ben turned his head and looked back at the small rock ledge behind him. His eyes met the eyes he had known were there, but they were not Caleb's.

They were the golden eyes of a gray wolf standing not twenty feet away. It was a large animal with the glossy fur of good health and vitality. Jim's warning not to come alone to the woods had been forgotten and now returned to him in force. He felt fear rising into panic.

Ben remembered what his father had told him about not making eye contact with strange dogs, but he couldn't look away. The wolf did look just like a big dog, but Ben had no illusions: this was a wild creature. The wolf stood unmoving on the ledge, as if it, too, were seeing an animal it didn't recognize.

Afterward, Ben could not have explained why he did what he did next. It was an impulse that came into his head with an insistency he did not question.

Ben began to sing.

"Lalalalala," he sang. Then louder, "Laladahla."

"I dream of journeys far away," he sang, his voice rising.

"I dream of leaves that fly.

I dream of coming home someday,

Someday, my love, to you.

Lalalalala. Laladah, dahla, dahla.
Of coming home to you."

The wolf and the boy kept their eyes on one another.

"I dream of mountains far away," sang Ben, beginning another verse.

"I dream of birds that fly.
I dream of coming home, someday,
Someday, my love, to you.
Lalalalala. Laladah, dahla, dahla.
Of coming home to you."

Ben's voice died away as he watched the yellow eyes that glinted from the rocky ledge.

The wolf shook itself, its thick mane rippling in the sunlight.

"Lalalalala," sang Ben, now more afraid than before. "Laladahla."

The wolf seemed to be studying him as if it were curious, and now Ben felt an emotion he had never known—half fear, half wonder—as he kept singing.

"I dream of sailing on the sea.
I dream of summer skies.
I dream of coming home, someday,
Someday, my love, to you.
Lalalalala. Laladah, dahla, dahla.
Of coming home, to you.
I dream that we are shining trees,
I hear the breezes sigh,
I dream of coming home someday,
Someday, my love, to you."

Lalalalala Laladah dahla dahla.

Of coming home to you."

The wolf turned and looked back, and then it moved away, deeper into the woods. It turned its head again to gaze at him as Ben sang, louder and with joy.

"Lalalalala Laladah dahla dahla."

His voice echoed against the rocks and floated out over the waves.

From deep in the woods another voice rose and fell in the wind. Ben listened, frozen.

Then he ran to the nearest tree, grabbed a low branch, and hauled himself up as high as he could go.

As the business of the festival carried on in the wake of the great disaster, Elisabeth was left to deal with some very angry patrons. No one had been seriously hurt, but this did not stop several of them from making threats to sue. Elisabeth did her best to calm them with her kind consolation, tea, homemade pie, and ultimately a case of champagne. Afterward, although everyone seemed restored to good humor, she wasn't entirely sure that they wouldn't be consulting their attorneys as soon as they returned home.

Finding Roger on the porch, she expressed her concerns to him somewhat coldly. She couldn't help feeling that this was entirely his fault, and she told him so.

Roger listened to her attentively, but without expression.

"No worries," he said.

"What do you mean 'no worries?' We could be sued. We could lose everything." Elisabeth was really angry. "How could we have no worries?"

"Simple," said Roger complacently. "We have Goat Insurance."

She looked at him, stunned. "Goat Insurance? There's no such thing as Goat Insurance."

"We have a goat on the premises. He's got insurance. Didn't I tell you? I looked into it when we started the goat yoga, and it seemed like a good idea. All the studios have it. At least," he added, with a scientist's devotion to accuracy, "All the studios with goat yoga."

Chapter 58 ❈

Ben sat in the tree for a long time. He tried to listen for sounds that the wolf was still nearby, but he could barely hear anything above his own breathing and the pounding of his heart.

And then he heard the calling of a familiar voice, and he raised his own voice to be heard.

"Dad! I'm here! I'm over here!"

Pali soon appeared around the curve of the trail and Ben looked down at him from above.

"Dad! There's a wolf! I saw the wolf! Did you hear it?"

Pali had respect for Ben's judgement and did not doubt.

"You saw it here?"

"It was there." Ben pointed at the ridge.

"How long ago?"

"I don't know. I lost track."

"You'd better come down."

"But Dad…"

"We'll be okay."

Ben scrambled down from the tree, and Pali clasped him in a bear hug, then held him away so he could see his son's face.

"Are you all right?"

Ben nodded. Pali decided that this was not the time to

investigate why Ben had ignored all the warnings to stay out of the woods.

"But, Dad, I have to tell you something. It's really important."

Pali was a calm man with a great deal of patience, but he wasn't keen on lingering in the woods with a wolf nearby.

"You'd better tell me then. But walk and talk, Ben. Walk and talk."

And as they headed back toward the park, Ben poured out his tale in a rush of words.

As soon as he could make sense of the jumbled story, Pali had his cell phone out. He placed calls, first to the police and then to Jim. He allowed Ben to tell Jim what he knew, and he listened again to the details of Ben's story.

When they hung up, Pali put his hand on his son's shoulder. "Come on, Ben, let's keep moving."

Ben had to half-run to keep up. "They won't shoot the wolf, will they?"

"I doubt they'll even find him today. But the worst they'd do is shoot him with a tranquilizer gun."

"Where are we going now? What are we going to do?"

"Well, first we're going to take you home, and then I'm going to help with the search for those boys."

Ben pestered to be allowed to come the whole trip home.

Chapter 59

P ali was going to drop Ben off at the house but remembered a pair of field glasses he thought could be useful and came inside to get them.

"Dad, please let me come. Please. I can help."

Pali was firm. "No. I need to focus on Noah and Caleb. I don't want to be worrying about you."

"But Dad—"

"You heard me. I said no."

Ben was about to ask again when he saw his father's face and stopped.

He waited until Pali left the room before kicking the kitchen table leg in frustration.

Something caught his eye and he looked up, startled. There were Noah and Caleb standing at the patio door, exhausted, tired, and dirty.

Without thinking, Ben let them in. Noah looked scared, but Caleb had an expression Ben couldn't decipher. A change seemed to have come over him. His swaggering and threats had dropped away.

"I didn't know what to do," he said. "My dad's gone, and my mom's over at the hotel not answering her phone."

Caleb looked at Ben, and his voice quavered a little.

"You've got to help."

Ben nodded nervously. He heard his dad's footsteps on the stairs and figured it was a fifty-fifty chance he'd holler goodbye and go out the front door, and then he would be left alone with Caleb and Noah. Ben wanted to smack himself on the head. What had he been thinking?

The next moment Pali came into the kitchen.

He didn't miss a beat.

"Well, hello, boys. It's Caleb, isn't it? And Noah?"

They nodded, and Ben could tell that Caleb was considering making a run for it.

But Pali looked Caleb in the eye and spoke with frank kindness to him. "I was just going out to look for you. How about you both sit down and tell me what's going on?" Pali seemed perfectly at ease. "Ben, get us all a glass of water." He looked at Noah. "You thirsty, Noah?"

Noah nodded.

To Ben's surprise, Caleb and Noah sat at the kitchen table, and gulped down their water. Pali calmly poured more for them from the big pitcher on the table.

"You guys want to tell me what's been happening?"

They were silent, looking from Pali to Ben, and Caleb's face began to shift back to the sullen look that was his usual expression. The silence grew, and Ben was remembering Noah's sudden escape at the cemetery. But Ben's experience with animals had taught him how to send out signals of calm that were soothing to frightened creatures.

"How about I start?" he asked gently, keeping his voice quiet and his body still.

"How about I tell you a story I heard just this summer? I think maybe Noah's been feeding his bad wolf. Maybe that's the whole problem."

Pali looked with intelligent curiosity at his son. "Tell us what you mean," he said quietly.

Ben took a deep breath and began to tell the story.

As the Festival moved on, Fiona and Oliver walked back to their cars, happily relieved of responsibility.

They stood together in the warmth of the Indian summer and breathed the lake air. Down the driveway and across the road was the hotel dock, and Fiona could see some of the guests sitting on the edge, their feet dangling. It looked so inviting.

Oliver followed her glance, and seemed to be considering something. At last he spoke.

"Time for a cocktail?"

Fiona looked at him in disbelief, but not because it was before noon. "Do you mean—together?"

Oliver looked her up and down as if it were she who was being surprising. "Well, of course." He sniffed. "We can go to my house. I have been experimenting with daiquiris. Most refreshing."

She contained her astonishment. Oliver had never shown the slightest interest in any kind of social interaction with her. On the contrary, he had announced his policy to avoid it.

"What about not confusing colleagues and friends?" she asked, quoting him to himself.

He shrugged, not in the least discomfited. "A man should learn to sail in all winds."

"Ah," said Fiona, nodding as she considered this. "Well, in that case." She gave him an impish smile. "I thought you'd never ask."

The police came, and Emily, and Jim, too. Emily wept and hugged her sons as they looked uncomfortable, and after some confusion and conversation, they all left again, taking Noah and Caleb with them. Jim stayed behind to make sure Ben was okay.

"You've had one heck of day," he said, "but all's well now. I think we'll all sleep a little easier."

"What about the wolf?" asked Ben.

Jim looked at them for a moment, slightly uncomfortable.

"Well, looks like in my worries about full disclosure, I pulled the trigger a little too soon."

"What do you mean?" asked Ben with an intensity that Jim thought was odd.

"There's no wolf. If there had been, we'd have found him. The team did DNA testing on the scat we found, and it was ordinary coyote. So, no need for alarm."

"But—" said Ben.

Jim gave Ben a rueful glance "I made a mistake, Ben." His eyes crinkled in a funny little smile. "Hope you're not too disappointed."

Ben looked at Jim, and then at his father.

Pali's face was a mask of good manners. "You've had a long day, too. We should let you get back."

The two men shook hands, and Jim turned to Ben.

"You're a good kid, Ben."

"But…" began Ben again. He stopped when he saw his father's face.

Chapter 60

R oger felt a sense of satisfaction that the festival was over. It had been far more disruptive to the hotel's routine than he would have liked, and Fiona's reassurances had not convinced him that Robert had not been traumatized by his appearance at the event.

Roger firmly believed that Bartholomew Salazar had created what he called "a threatening atmosphere" for the animal, and that some time out of the public eye would be in Robert's best interest.

"I'll pay Ben for the days off," he told Fiona, and they agreed that Robert should have a quiet week's sojourn in the peace of Fiona's barn. With these arrangements made, Roger headed back to the mainland to tend to matters at Ground Zero for a few days, leaving a serenely contented Elisabeth to oversee the post-festival cleanup.

Joshua was already standing at the door of the shop looking out when Roger pulled up in the pre-dawn hours and parked illegally in front of a driveway. He got out and stood staring at the parking lot.

There were tents of every color and shape arrayed before him, their coolers, grills, bicycles, lawn chairs, and clothes lines jauntily set up alongside. The smell of essential oils wafted now and then across the pavement, along with the faint lingering scent of charcoal and grilled tofu.

Roger picked his way through the narrow passages between the tents and their equipage and came to stand next to Joshua. Together, they gave a long look at the tent city before them.

"I've started up the LaVazza," said Joshua, referring to the newest of their coffee machines, which had only recently arrived from Italy.

"Good," said Roger.

"It has a nice quality about it. Very easy to use. And the coffee is excellent."

Roger nodded approvingly.

They stood together in silence, looking out over the collection of tents. No one stirred within, and all was silent.

"Got time before class. Want to try some?" asked Joshua after a while. "Should be ready."

"Sure," said Roger.

"Sometimes, you have to bend with the wind," remarked Joshua, holding the door for Roger.

Roger stopped for a moment to look back at the encampment, then together they went inside.

Emily Martin made a call to Nika, asking whether she could bring the boys over that evening "for a little chat." Nika agreed, but Ben was horrified.

"Please, Mom. Don't make me do this."

Nika exchanged glances with Pali. "Ben, I think they want to apologize. It's important to let them—"

"But, Mom. Caleb hates me, and Noah probably does now, too."

Nika looked sympathetically at her son. "You don't have to spend all evening with them. Just be polite."

B en had an anxious day in anticipation of a visit from the Martins. He spent the afternoon at Fiona's barn and found the work a distraction. Everything was in perfect order by the time he was ready to leave, and Ben felt better.

As always, Fiona offered him a snack, and they sat on her back porch chatting while he drank lemonade and ate cookies.

"How's Robert today?" she asked conversationally.

"He's good. He's eating well and has lots of energy." Ben looked seriously at Fiona as he spoke. "I think he's recovered from all the crazy stuff over the weekend."

"What about you?" asked Fiona lightly. "Have you recovered?"

Ben looked embarrassed, and Fiona regretted having said anything.

Ben took a bite of cookie. "There's a lot of good and bad in people," he said after a moment. "And, I guess that goats are just the same."

Fiona didn't smile. She was impressed once again by the maturity of Ben's thinking. "I think you're probably right."

Ben stood up, brushing the crumbs off his jeans.

"I have to go. Want me to take this stuff into the kitchen?"

"That's okay," said Fiona. "I'll take care of it."

She smiled at him, and he looked embarrassed again.

"Thanks for everything, Ben. You're a big help around here."

"That's okay. Thanks for the cookies, Ms. Campbell."

Fiona waved at him and watched as Ben took off for home on his bicycle. She didn't know that he was thinking about her smile.

Fiona wondered to herself that Ben had such an intricate nature. Even though he had a boy's innocence, he seemed so complex. She tried to remember whether she had had such thoughts at his age. She remembered a feeling for injustice; loving animals; and deep, painful longings for love and beauty. She remembered a dawning interest in the intellect, and a craving to learn.

But she doubted she had carried Ben's sense of mortality—of the tenuous nature of existence. It resonated from him, not as tragedy, but as joy. He belonged to the world and it was his. Was this, she wondered, the consequence of being so much in nature? Of seeing dying animals and dead ones, killing one another, feeding on one another? Was this even, perhaps, the result of the hunting culture she so deplored? That rather than the thoughtless casual killing she had always imagined, it built, instead, a sense that life was tragic, hard, ephemeral, and worthy of respect. Maybe hunting was an attempt to belong and mingle in the cycle of nature rather than to pose somewhere above it: removed, sterile, and alone.

Fiona thought of the hunters she knew—a mix of men, some thoughtful, some not. And then she thought of Pete. The question was always there, lingering in the background. She had to know. She had to ask. It was all a question of the right moment. He had arrived unexpectedly late last night. Now that he was back for a few days, she had another opportunity.

When she brought the plate and glasses in, she went upstairs. She could tell that Pete had gone for a run. He had left his wallet and watch on the dresser with his passport. And there was something else she had never seen before. She picked it up and turned it over in her fingers, gazing at it with dawning understanding. She felt, all at once, the tumblers fall into place.

The Martins arrived after dinner, and it was just as awkward as Ben had known it would be.

Caleb and Noah sat on the couch on either side of their mother, while Ben and his parents arranged themselves in chairs around the room.

Emily began with a little speech. "After all your help the other day, we wanted to come to say 'thank you.'" She looked at each of her boys in turn. "Didn't we, boys?"

Neither of them answered. Caleb's face was neutral, but he took a short, shallow breath that revealed his annoyance. Noah put a finger in his mouth.

Nika saw that this wouldn't go well.

"Why don't you boys go grab a brownie from the kitchen and go outside?"

Silently, all with approximately the same long-suffering expression, the boys trooped out, following Ben.

Emily waited until she heard them go outside before she spoke.

"We're getting help for Noah. I just want you to know." She bit her lip, and Nika saw how deeply hurt and embarrassed she was. She felt a flash of sympathy. "I'm sure that's the right thing," she said comfortingly. "You'll get to the bottom of it. He'll be all right in the end."

Outside, Ben, Caleb, and Noah, waited in various poses of bored boyhood. Ben was holding onto a column of the porch with one arm, leaning out over the edge. Noah squatted on the grass looking for bugs, and Caleb sat on the steps, chewing on a cuticle.

"Hey!" said Noah suddenly. "I found a toad." He looked up, his eyes shining.

"Come see!"

Caleb and Ben glanced at one another, and in that moment, a look of understanding passed between them. For the first time, Ben saw a genuine smile cross Caleb's face, a smile of affectionate amusement at his little brother. "Let's see," he said, rising from his step.

The three boys bent over the toad, and Ben showed Noah how to be gentle when stroking the toad's soft round tummy.

Emily appeared at the kitchen door. "Come on, boys. Time to go."

Noah and Caleb didn't waste time heading out. Ben hung

back and returned to his column swinging while Pali escorted their guests to their car.

As she was getting into her vehicle, Emily paused and turned back to Pali.

"I understand congratulations are in order. You're going to be featured in *The New Yorker*, I hear."

Pali nodded. His wonder at the prospect was still so profound, he could barely speak of it.

"Just think," said Emily, her voice returning to its usual bright timbre. "If I hadn't started the Literary Festival, none of this would have happened. Just think if I hadn't come here."

Pali smiled his slow, warm smile.

"Just think," he said.

He watched, still smiling, as they drove away and then turned briskly to his son, who had wandered around to the front of the house.

"Come on, Ben. There's still some light. Let's go hit some balls."

Fiona was waiting for Pete in the kitchen when he came down from his shower.

"Ready for a drink?" he asked, opening a bottle of wine.

"Yes, please."

He handed her a glass and poured one for himself.

"Have you ever gone hunting?" she asked, without preamble.

"I've gone along on hunts, but I've never shot." He leaned

with his back against the kitchen counter as he spoke.

"Why not?"

"I don't see the point in it. I have no objection to eating meat—or in this case, birds—in principle, but I do object to killing things for fun."

"Did your...companions... eat what they killed?"

"Perhaps. Or perhaps the birds were given to someone who would eat them. I don't really know." He looked directly at her.

"Have you?"

"Gone hunting?" Fiona was surprised. "No. Can't imagine it. Although, as you say—and as you know—I'm obviously not opposed to eating meat." A sudden memory popped into her head. "I went fishing once, when I was a little girl, with a friend's father. I caught a fish, but I was so upset about it, I made him throw it back."

She thought for a moment. "I do eat fish, though. There are people who say that if you eat meat—or fish—you should, at least once, have the experience of killing what you eat."

"That seems a bit medieval, but I see the point."

Fiona looked at him and took a deep breath. "I have," she said, "a small earnest question."

Pete looked at her quizzically and was silent for a few seconds.

"There's something you've been working up to for quite a long time."

"Yes." She was looking directly into his eyes.

He nodded slowly, not in answer to her question, but in acknowledgement of some unfinished business. "Let's have this conversation."

He took her by the hand and led her into the living room.

"Sit down," he said as he seated himself and gave her his full attention.

She sat, gazing at him, aware that something important hung in the balance.

"Do you think holding a gun in your hand makes you more respectful of life?"

Pete looked at her as if he were trying to make out something in the distance.

"More respectful?"

Fiona just looked at him, deeply uncomfortable.

"Do you mean," he asked, "Does holding a gun in your hand make you a better or worse person than you already were?"

She shrugged slightly, her eyes on his.

He gazed back at her, his changing thoughts moving across his face.

"The morality is in the man, not in the machine. Surely you know that?"

"Yes, yes, but does the experience…does knowing you can kill make you think more about life?"

"It damn well makes you think more about dying. Sorry. I don't mean to be glib. But only someone who's already inclined to think about those kinds of things will recognize the moral questions. After all, any fool can pick up a gun, and the world is full of fools."

He was studying her as if scanning for her thoughts.

"I don't think I'm asking about morality," she said. "At

least not just morality. I'm asking about a sense of…fragility… you know—here one moment and gone the next. Does that intensify, do you think?"

Pete seemed to relax, his eyes still on her face. "That depends. I've seen men retreat into themselves after they've shot someone, changed forever. Usually they get through it—but not always. Some never come out of it. Then there are the handful who seem to grow into the power of it, or who perceive themselves as weak and the guns as compensation for what they lack. They're the dangerous ones."

Fiona was silent, listening. Now that she had started the conversation, she needed to let him speak.

"So…" he went on "…maybe having a gun in your hand makes you more of what you already are, but you could say that about almost anything. What you do always brings out more of whatever part of you it uses. I suppose, though, to get back to your original question, that seeing death makes you more aware of the tenuousness of living."

"Do men need to kill?"

He didn't hesitate. "Some men do."

His expression shifted, and he seemed now to revert to his usual manner. There was affection in his voice when he asked, "What is it you actually need to know?"

Fiona knew that he knew. She took a deep breath and reached into her pocket. She drew out what she had found on the dresser and opened her palm so he could see it. It was a small gold pin with an insignia crowned by a winged eagle.

"I found this."

Their eyes met, and Fiona saw the steel in him. It had

always been there, but usually tempered with the glint of humor he always seemed to be just barely suppressing. Now that glint was missing.

"It's a trident," he said calmly.

"I know what it is. And I know what it means. You're a Navy SEAL."

"I've retired from the service."

"Have you?"

Now, he did smile.

"If you're asking me something that I haven't told you, then you know I won't discuss it."

"There was nothing you could have told me? It might have given me some comfort."

"I doubt that. In fact, certainly the reverse." He sounded regretful, adding, "I've been looking for the right moment."

She looked at him with new understanding. "Now might be good."

He studied her face, and she saw clearly that the deep seriousness of his nature was kept camouflaged by his playful demeanor.

"Well, now you know."

She looked back at him, studying his face. "But it's still not everything, is it?"

He held her gaze steadily, but his answer was a kiss.

Chapter 61

I t was a humid fall evening, and as the sun set, a soft mist rose from the ground and magnified beams of shifting orange sunlight. Ben and Pali had been shagging balls in the field near the house, but the light and the mist now made it impossible. They were walking back home through the wet grass when something made them both stop.

There, standing on a low hill, just beside the woods, they saw what they both thought at first was a shadow. As they looked, straining their eyes to see, a shape emerged from the rising mists.

"Dad?" whispered Ben.

Ben looked at Pali, and their eyes locked. Pali's head came up, his shoulders straightened, and he gave the slightest nod of his head. They both stood perfectly still to keep from startling the creature before them.

It was a gray wolf with golden eyes. He was very large with a mature male's ruff and a magnificent tail. He stood, head high, on full alert, watching them with a sultry wariness.

Ben saw his father's eyes move as if searching for something in the air around them. His gaze settled back on his son's face, and like the sun gradually revealing itself, he smiled his slow, warm smile.

Ben wanted to speak, to ask questions, but something stopped him. Instead, he looked into his father's eyes and then back at the wolf that seemed half real creature, half golden mist. They stood together in silence, in the glow of the setting sun, and let the awe absorb them into its presence like the mist that surrounded them, settling on their skin and hair, filling their eyes and lungs.

The wolf shook its head and seemed to respond to something, and then it lifted its head to the sky, and after a moment that seemed suspended in time, it began to sing. Its voice started with a low rumble and rose to a rolling howl that Ben could feel in his chest. He felt the hair on his arms and neck rise, but he didn't know how to describe what he felt. He did not feel fear. He felt communion.

The wolf howled on, its voice seeming to spin into the mist as if it were both sound and color, surrounding them as it rose slowly to the sky until at last, with one final crescendo, the wolf put down its head and was silent. It looked at them, its golden eyes tinged with green, and Ben felt that he was staring into another soul.

They watched as the wolf seemed to merge into the mists and fade back into the shadows.

They stood still and waited for a very long time, but it did not reappear.

Chapter 62

After so many meetings underground, the book club decided it was time to change things up. It was always crowded wherever they went, and they usually had to take turns sitting down, and besides, Emily Martin was too busy to notice.

"Let's meet for dinner at the hotel. We can schedule it during one of her meetings."

They all knew who "her" was.

One evening soon afterward they gathered in the open for the first time since their encounter with Emily at Nelsen's. They had been reading Hemingway, and the conversation had turned from literature to Cuba to food.

"I'm a fan of hot foods. Nothing around here ever really seems to measure up."

"That's because you think taco night at the church basement is hot food."

"When I was stationed in Albuquerque, I really fell in love with green chiles. Nothing has ever seemed as good."

"That's interesting. I was talking to my cousin in California, and he was saying that you build an immunity to hot foods, and that's what makes you seek hotter and hotter things. You just aren't affected by it anymore.

"I got a ten that says you can't finish a Bloody Roger."

"Not worth it for ten."

"Twenty, then."

"Nope. Last time I tried one, my mouth burned for an hour. And that was without swallowing."

"I'll do it," said Oliver.

They all looked at him with surprise. He had been so quiet that no one had quite realized he was there. Not long ago, they would have gleefully encouraged him, but he was a book club regular—a founding member, even—and no one wanted to humiliate him. Poor bastard didn't know what he was in for. Immediately they began backpedaling.

"That's okay, man. You don't have to."

"It's pretty hot, you know."

Only Eddie was quiet, as he watched the scene play out in front of him. Years of bartending had built a professional distance that came naturally to him in crowds.

But Oliver was adamant. He waved over the waitress. "I'll have a Bloody Ro—Mary, please."

She looked at him with dismay. "Are you sure? I mean…"

"I'm sure," said Oliver. He tapped his finger on the table. "Put it right there, please."

Reluctantly, she brought him the beautiful glass. With all its embellishments, it looked like something out of a magazine.

Oliver lifted the glass. "Who dreamed that beauty passes like a dream?" he murmured.

"Hey," said Jake. "That's Yeats!"

Oliver smiled and drank his Bloody Roger with one long swallow. Finishing, he patted his mouth with his napkin and sighed.

Everyone was silent, waiting.

Oliver looked at them with feigned innocence. "What?"

The laughter erupted around the table as, one by one, they each took twenty dollars from their wallets and handed it over to Oliver.

He smiled modestly, and then, with a grace no one anticipated, he turned his winnings to buying a round—although no one ordered a Bloody Roger.

The evening ended with much backslapping and banter.

"Didn't think you had it in you," commented Jake on the way out.

Oliver smiled his mysterious little smile. He had a passion for habaneros.

It was a short walk home across the field, and Ben was silent for a long while. "Dad," he said at last, "Remember what you said about angels?" His voice was hushed.

"Which part?"

"The part about them being scary. What was it that you said?"

"I think I said, 'angels are majestic creatures of God.' Is that what you mean?"

Ben nodded slowly to himself, turning an idea over and over in his mind like a wave-tumbled rock in his hand. "Maybe that's what we all are."

"Angels?" Pali glanced smilingly at his son, filled with affection for him at this childish idea.

Ben's face was solemn. "No," he said. "Majestic creatures of God."

Chapter 63 ❖

On the night of the town meeting, Pete watched as Fiona rushed around the house looking for things. First her sandals, then her keys, then her phone. They had all been precisely where they belonged, but her state of mind had made her hasty and distracted, and she had to look three times before she found them.

"Would you like me to drive tonight?" he asked. "You seem a bit...inattentive."

She looked at him regretfully. "I'm not sure I want you to come."

"Why not?"

She took a deep breath, thinking about her answer, and decided to be candid. "I will be humiliated."

Pete frowned and put his hands on her shoulders. "You can't be humiliated. What is it that Eleanor Roosevelt supposedly said? Not without your permission?"

She gave him a weak smile. "It will be an ordeal."

"All the more reason I should come. And afterward," he touched his forehead lightly to hers, "I will console you—with scotch, good conversation, or...other things."

Her smile was real this time. "May I have all three?"

"I think we can work something out."

"I would like you to drive," she said, handing him the keys. When they arrived, the town hall was packed with people. All three television stations from Green Bay were there. Their satellite trucks were positioned along the road, engines running to generate power for transmission. Their cameras were aligned across the back of the room, focused on the long table at the front.

It was big news to have the head of a town—even one as small as the Town of Washington—acquiring property for her own enrichment. Reporters from other major news outlets around the state had come to attend as well, and they mingled with the crowd in search of quotes for their stories. There were so many people that there weren't enough chairs, and Islanders leaned against the walls and against the tables that held the ubiquitous cookies and coffee urns. The crowd overflowed into the hall. The room was unairconditioned, and the autumn heat mingled with so many bodies was stifling.

A well-dressed silver-haired man in a dark suit sat alone in the back of the room. He seemed absorbed in reading some documents and only looked up when asked to make room for those looking for seats in his row.

"Who is that guy?" asked Jake of no one in particular. People shrugged and carried on with their conversations. No one knew, and no one particularly cared.

Before the meeting could even begin, people were lined up along the center aisle in front of the new microphone, waiting for a chance to speak. A cynic might have been forgiven for wondering whether it was because they held strong views or merely wanted to see themselves on camera.

Fiona was a basket of nerves, but having learned the techniques of the legendary Lars Olufsen, she waited until the last possible minute to arrive at her place at the table in front of the room. Oliver trailed along behind her, carrying his laptop for notetaking.

Looking out at the sea of hostile faces, Fiona wondered what percentage of the Island population was here. As her eyes roamed the room, she saw the man in the dark suit and felt immediate misgivings. He could be a reporter, but he looked too well-dressed for that. All kinds of dire scenarios crossed her mind, including the State Department of Justice having come to launch an investigation, all ready to be captured on camera. At this point in her tenure, nothing would surprise her. With difficulty, she turned her attention to the business at hand.

It was the Catholics' turn to lead the opening prayer, and the tiny balding priest had a rich, carrying voice that belied his stature. When he was finished, the crowd stood dutifully for the Pledge of Allegiance, and Fiona gaveled the meeting open.

Before she could speak, Fiona could see Stella elbowing her way past the line of people waiting to speak. She pushed her way past the polite Island crowd. "Let me through!"

Stella stood before the microphone facing Fiona.

"I am here to speak on behalf of the Committee of the Concerned."

There were some murmurings, and Fiona shot a glance at Emily Martin. She saw Emily's head turn in a swift reflex to look at Stella, eyes wide with surprise. It was clear that she had not known this was coming, but she made no attempt to stop Stella from speaking. A fleeting mental checkmark flew through Fiona's mind. She had not counted on Emily for integrity.

Stella took her time before speaking. She looked inordinately pleased with herself, settling her shoulders and lifting her chin as she stood before the microphone. Her speech, written for her by her felonious nephew, Dean Hilliard, had been practiced for days before a mirror. After last year's humiliation, including Dean's arrest and the confiscation of her vintage car, Stella could feel the hammer of justice poised to strike its blow. It was to be, she knew, the high point of her life. The cameras were rolling.

Her voice rang out.

"This community has seen enough of the lies, manipulations, and outright malfeasance of this Chairman. Her term has been one scandal after another, and now, I think, we have every right to wonder whether she is just a liar and a cheat, who has put herself in office for her own benefit."

There were exclamations in response to this, but it was impossible to tell whether they were in protest or agreement.

Stella's voice carried over the voices in the hall.

"Despite her lies to the contrary, no sensible person could believe that she didn't know that a trust held in her name was buying up property. The legal term is *cui bono*—who benefits—and we can all see—no matter what she says—exactly who these purchases benefit: your Chairman, Fiona Campbell."

The room erupted in response to this speech, and it seemed possible there could be a riot. Stella's face held a malefic satisfaction as the cameras zoomed in. She had more to say, but she was content to allow the emotions of the room to build.

"Madam Chairman!" The man in the dark suit stood up, addressing Fiona and the room full of angry people.

With great difficulty, and only with the help of shushing from the audience, Fiona gaveled the down the noise.

"Madam Chairman," he said again. "I understand that I may be out of order, but I believe I have some information that would be of interest to this assembly."

Silently, grimly, Fiona motioned for him to come up as she tried to prepare herself for the next ax to fall. She thought bitterly that it was, at last, time to sell and get off the Island, and the thought pierced her heart.

The gentleman approached the microphone at the front of the room, politely excusing himself to the people already standing there. Stella smiled her reptilian smile at him as he approached, and graciously stepped aside to make room for him at the microphone. She looked forward to hearing whatever he had to say.

He turned slightly to each side, to acknowledge the room. His formality identified him as an outsider, and his accent as a New Yorker.

Fiona's heart was pounding, but she, too, took refuge in formality. "Please state your name," she said.

"Dirk Richards, attorney for the Eldridge Trust."

The crowd burst into an excited buzzing, the cameras now zoomed in on him, and Fiona, her curiosity overcome by anxiety, reluctantly gaveled again for quiet. Out of the corner of her eye, she could see multiple reporters scribbling madly in their notebooks. "That's one way to identify who they are," she thought wryly.

She looked at the stranger standing at the microphone. "Go ahead, Mr. Richards."

Stella, her voice no longer amplified, yelled out. "This is a set up!" she cried shrilly. "He's her attorney. She can't run the meeting for her own benefit."

Fiona rapped her gavel sharply and with some pleasure.

"For the record, Mr. Richards is not my attorney. I did not know he was coming, and I don't know what he has to say. But, I think we should listen."

Fiona looked around the room as if searching for consensus, but this was an old Lars trick she had learned from close observation. This time, she had no intention of relinquishing control of the room.

"Yeah, let him talk!" shouted an elderly woman from the back. She was supported by general agreement from the crowd. There would be plenty of time for recrimination later.

Stella sat down, fuming.

Fiona smiled the political smile she hated so much.

"How do you do, Mr. Richards? Please go ahead."

"How do you do?" he responded. He had an engaging quality that seemed to captivate the room.

"I am here at the behest of my late client, Victor Eldridge. If you will all indulge me," he looked around politely at the crowd, "I would like to tell you a little story."

The room fell into a deep silence. Even the reporters stopped writing to listen.

"My client, as you may imagine, was a very wealthy man. He had no wife and no children. Only—" he smiled upon Fiona "—a niece of whom he was very fond. When he realized that he was dying, he had very little time—only a few weeks—but he wanted to do something for the one person in the world who had ever really loved him. She had never shown any interest in his business, or in his possessions, but he knew one thing about her. He knew she loved this Island."

By now, the crowd was enthralled and listening as if nothing existed except the voice of Dirk Richards.

"And so, secretly, he instructed me to begin the purchase of properties here, all with a specific purpose—to secure the rural character of the island and to provide economic support to its citizens who needed it. I am pleased to report that as of today, we have acquired more than 200 acres of shoreline properties, all contiguous along the western side. Although they are currently held in the name of the trust, they are to be transferred to a new entity—a land trust—and preserved in perpetuity for the enjoyment of the people of this place. There may be more purchases, but the bulk of the work, as directed by Mr. Eldridge, is complete."

There was a stunned silence. Even Stella was speechless.

The attorney looked around with a slightly apologetic expression.

"And that completes my statement. I thank you for your attention."

He walked back to his seat in the corner through the still silent room and sat down.

Out of the corner of her eye, Fiona saw Nancy make a movement to throw off her jacket. Then she rose. In the stillness of the room, she looked over at Fiona. She looked back at the New York attorney. She looked meaningfully and contemptuously at Stella. And standing all by herself, she began to clap.

For a few seconds, she clapped all alone. But then Jim stood. And Jake and Charlotte. And Oliver. And, with a wry, proud smile, Pete. And soon, in small bunches, sections of the crowd began to stand and clap, too. At last, everyone was standing, clapping, and cheering.

Fiona sat with her eyes closed against tears, stunned, while Stella, her face contorted with rage, shoved her way viciously back through the crowd and out the door, cameras following her as she went.

In the midst of the applause, Pete came over and pulled Fiona to her feet, and as the Islanders began to surround her with thanks and backslapping, he gave her a crushing hug.

She clung to him for a moment, still shaken, then pulled away to speak into his ear above the noise.

"Did you have something to do with this?"

"Well," he said, avoiding her gaze. "I may have mentioned that there was a meeting."

Jake made his way to Dirk Richards and leaned in to make himself heard above the noise.

"There's going to be a celebration at a local establishment. Care to join us for a little drink?"

"Why, yes." Dirk Richards looked around at the cheerful, open faces surrounding him. "I would enjoy that very much."

It was a boisterous, happy crowd at Nelsen's, and Eddie was kept busy mixing old-fashioneds. Jake and Charlotte, Pali and Nika, Oliver, and even Nancy—who rarely came out for a drink—all sat at the end of the bar with Fiona and Dirk Richards. Pete had been invited to play pool, and Fiona had laughingly sent him off. She was not in need of consolation.

When he reached a lull in his work, Eddie leaned across the bar.

"We like to look for the *deus ex machina* in our local events, Mr. Richards, and I think, this time, you get the prize."

Dirk Richards looked both confused and gratified.

"Well, er, that's, er, that's very kind. It's a first, I must say." He looked at the faces of the people who surrounded him. "But, really, I suppose, if you want to put it that way, the real *deus ex machina* here is Victor Eldridge, and from beyond the grave, you might even say."

His eyes twinkled. Against all expectations, he was enjoying himself. There was something appealing about these people and this place. "And call me Dirk."

He held up his drink.

"To Victor," he said.

"To Victor!" they all echoed. Fiona thought of the toasts they had shared that long-ago summer in Paris. "To Victor," she whispered.

Dirk Richards looked around and saw Nancy standing nearby. "I'm feeling a bit over-dressed. "Would anyone mind if I took off my tie?"

"Of course, not," said Nancy.

"Go right ahead," said Oliver, who was still wearing his.

Dirk leaned in toward Nancy. "What's with all the money sticking to the ceiling?" he asked.

"Allow me to teach you a local game," said Jake, and he proceeded to remove a dollar bill and quarter from his pocket. "The proceeds all go to the baseball field."

Dirk Richards gave Nancy a dazzling smile. "I'll bet you know all the rules. Any tips?" he asked.

That night, when they got home, Pali came up to Ben's room to say goodnight. Ben had been reading and was already under the covers, smelling of soap and toothpaste. Pali sat on the edge of the bed and noted the tan touched with sunburn on his son's face, the white blond hair on his arms. He was still a boy, but growing fast, and Pali saw that he would soon be too long for his mattress.

"Dad," said Ben in a low voice. "The other night. We both saw it, right? You saw it, too, didn't you, Dad?"

Pali nodded seriously, but he took a moment before speaking.

"Yes, Ben. I saw it, too."

Ben frowned, recalling the experience. "It was real, wasn't it?"

Pali thought for a bit before answering, remembering

with wonder his past experiences of presence and grace. This had not been merely a presence. It had been more like a benediction.

"I don't know."

They were silent together. Ben burrowed himself more deeply into his bed, and Pali pulled the covers up around him. Their yellow lab, Sugar, nestled in, too, arranging herself against Ben's legs.

Ben's voice rose from the depths of his blankets. "We won't ever forget that day, will we, Dad?"

"No, Ben, we never will." He leaned down to smooth his son's hair from his eyes and kissed his forehead.

"It was a day engraved on the soul of the universe."

Nelsen's was still packed with happy people. After he had won several rounds of pool, Pete came up behind Fiona at the bar, and lightly put a hand on her shoulder. She turned and looked up at him. Someone was leaving, and Jake moved over to make room. Pete slid onto the stool and signaled Eddie for another round. Fiona smiled fondly at him. "Spending your winnings?"

"We were playing for honor."

"That's an unusual concept these days."

"Doesn't seem to be, really. Not here."

Pete seemed distracted, and Fiona studied his face, trying to gauge his mood.

"What are you thinking about?"

He looked at her. "Doesn't it show?"

"It kind of does, actually. But only the general activity, not the specific topic."

He nodded but said nothing for a moment.

The bar was particularly noisy. Along with the islanders, there was a big group of tourists celebrating a birthday, and they had been drinking for some time. Pete leaned in to speak in Fiona's ear, putting his arm around her to get as close as possible. He smelled of soap, and shaving cream, and leather, with a little bit of whiskey as a top note.

"I'm not leaving the Island again without you."

Fiona froze, then started to pull away to reply, but he held her tight, his lips next to her ear.

"So, here's my question: Are we staying, or leaving?"

This time she did pull away. "That's your question?"

He was laughing at her. "Well, it's one of them. I have a list."

Fiona simply looked at him, bemused. She had been pondering this same question for some time.

"Does it have to be either-or?"

"Well, I could stay, and you could leave."

Fiona sighed and looked at him out of the corner of her eye.

He pulled her back and whispered in her ear again.

Fiona leaned her head back against his arm and smiled at him. "Byron? Really?"

"It seemed appropriate. For once."

"Yes," said Fiona happily. "I suppose it did." She added,

almost as an afterthought, "And…of course."

Pete brought his hand triumphantly down on the bar, making Jake jump. "Eddie!" he called.

Eddie looked up. He had never seen Pete so effusive.

"Drinks for everybody!"

Eddie looked from Pete's face to Fiona's and broke out in a broad grin.

"You got it."

Soon, there was crush of people reaching in to congratulate them.

Chapter 64

Fiona dreamed that she and Uncle Victor were floating on big inflatable chairs in the lake. Their chairs were anchored, so the waves merely rocked them without pushing them in to shore. There was no one else in sight, and the sun was low, the heavy summer air warm and sweet, and a soft breeze occasionally blowing the scent of the cedar trees out to them from the beach. Their conversation was desultory, but not without meaning. It felt, rather, of profound consequence.

Fiona felt a sense of deep peace, as they floated there in the soft waves, that they were of one mind, joined in this tranquility, this moment of beauty that even in her dream seemed something apart from reality and, instead, a momentary glimpse of the eternal.

Sometime after the morning yoga practice, when the Lutheran Men's Prayer Group had departed to their respective employments, a young man in a blond ponytail entered the shop. He took a place at the counter somewhat diffidently and ordered an herbal tea. This, only a short time ago, would have been a heresy that would have drawn the ire of Roger, but now tea was a regular—if not routine—part of the menu.

Terry and Mike nodded politely and went on with their conversation.

As he waited, the newcomer watched the yoga campers packing up their gear. Joshua brought him his tea. "Anything else?" he asked, in beatific tones. The young man looked familiar in a way he couldn't quite place.

The ponytailed one looked up at Joshua, his face awash in a combination of youthful sorrow and righteousness.

"I thought you said there was no camping here, but I come back this morning and find this." He gestured toward the activity in the parking lot. "Dude. That's not cool."

After the kitchen and bar had closed for the night, Elisabeth and Roger sat together in a pair of rocking chairs set off by themselves on the long sloping lawn of the hotel. The contented murmurings and laughter of a few lingering guests still floated down from the porch, and from around the back came the distant bustle of the kitchen crew cleaning up.

Amid the soft rush of the waves, the crickets, and frogs, and katydids sang boldly in the darkness. The cooling fall night had slowed their songs, forming the timeless sounds of the night.

Rocco lay on the grass nearby, not sleeping, but watching. This was his life's work. The grass was dewy and cool, and the air was filled with smells. He had worked hard and eaten well, and it felt good to be lying near his people. Rocco sighed deeply and rested his head on his paws, eyes open, watching.

His big ears twitched from time to time, sometimes to listen, sometimes to flick away an insect.

The nighthawks were singing with their distinctive call as they swooped overhead.

"We called them 'eepers' when we were children." Elisabeth's voice seemed to drift like the birds.

"That is how they sound," agreed Roger.

"Roger," began Elisabeth tentatively.

She paused so long that he turned to look at her.

"I think it's time for you to adjust your recipe for Bloody Marys."

Roger tilted his head, and in the darkness, he reminded Elisabeth of Rocco: intelligent, alert, and waiting for direction.

"Have you tried one?" she asked.

"I don't like tomato juice," said Roger.

Elisabeth was silent for a moment, absorbing this information.

Before she could speak, Roger perked up suddenly, alert to a new idea. "Maybe nobody does. Maybe that's why nobody ever finishes them." He stared off into the darkness.

"Why didn't I think of that?" He shook his head at himself and turned to look at his wife. "Do you think we should take them off the menu?"

Elisabeth had not been prepared for such a simple solution to this problem that had been plaguing her for months.

"I think that might be best."

"But what about the Sprinters?" he asked earnestly. "Won't they be disappointed?"

Elisabeth took a breath to speak, stopped, and then tried again. "I think they might find other forms of amusement." She had a sudden idea. "How about this?" she asked, sitting up straighter in her enthusiasm and leaning toward him. "How about we have a new, special selection? We can call it our 'Extreme Cocktail Menu.' Slogan: For the adventurous traveler; try it at your own risk."

Roger, who had a deep appreciation for inspired thinking, nodded as he considered this, then looked at her with admiration. "What would I do without you?"

He reached out to take her hand as Elisabeth smiled happily into the darkness. Rocco stirred and stretched out more comfortably on the cool grass as the eepers circled overhead, feeding voraciously on mosquitoes while, still further above them all, the stars swirled on in their eternal hum.

It was late when Roger and Elisabeth crossed the quiet lawn arm in arm and went inside to bed, Rocco padding contentedly behind them.

Late one afternoon at the ferry dock, while a run of paying passengers disembarked, a gathering of people in their most festive attire waited at an adjacent dock to board the ferry for a chartered trip. They were already prepared to be happy, but their happiness was warmed and mellowed by the champagne that was being passed.

At the specified time, the ferry pulled away from the Island dock, the engines churning the water of Detroit Harbor while the guests stood at the railings on the top deck. A spontaneous cheer arose as they departed, and champagne glasses were raised in a toast.

One car only stood poised to be the first off, while behind it was a long table covered with a deep blue cloth with places set and vases of pink, white, and yellow flowers. White lights were strung across the deck. There were many ice buckets filled with bottles of cold champagne still waiting to be opened and another long table piled with food artfully arranged on tiered trays and platters.

The bride stood laughing on the top deck, her ice blue silk dress blowing in the wind, her hair around her face. Captain Palsson, having given the helm over to the Mate, came up the stairs and stood with his back to the pilot house ready to officiate. The groom stood beside him.

No one noticed when Pali felt the weight of a hand on his shoulder and smiled to himself.

The seasons were shifting. It had been a cloudy day with a bland, milky light, but now, in the early evening, the sun broke through in yellow-orange beams through deep blue clouds. All along the horizon was a narrow, gleaming band of light that colored everything with a rosy glow. Towering cumulous clouds meant storms were moving away to the south, but to the north, the sky was clear and blue. The wind was slow and steady and the lake was calm.

As the ferry left the harbor, the groom caught his bride's eye and, with his mischievous smile, held out his hand to her. To the sound of the waves, amid the brilliant light of an autumn sky, she came to him, not tremulous but confident and joyful. As she passed by along the length of the boat, her friends reached out to touch her hands, her arms, her dress, her flowers, blessing the bride and groom with love and good wishes.

The little ferry circumnavigated the Island while Fiona and Pete, standing in a circle of friends, looked at each other, clasped their hands together, and repeated ancient words. Then, they slowly turned to face the life ahead.

A joyous party crossed Death's Door together many times that night, and when the ferry at last reached the mainland dock, the gangplank was let down for the bridal car's getaway. They sped off as the car was pelted with rice, petals, old shoes, and not a few champagne corks.

"So," said Pete, his eyes on the road. "Really? Byron? You had to quote Byron?"

Fiona laughed. "It could have been Longfellow."

"I'll let it pass, then. Where to?"

"Surprise me," said Fiona. "But let's make the most of it."

Pete grinned. "Oh, I think we will."

He reached for her hand in the dark and held it for a long moment. "And then, home to the Island."

As the car escaped along the twisting road down the peninsula, the gangplank was lifted, and the ferry pivoted and headed back across the Door with the steady persistence of a good and loyal dog. Amid the sound of voices, laughter, and music, it carried its passengers—who were filled with that particular rapture that comes from champagne—back home to their Island.

A freighter's lights blinked at the horizon as it headed northeast toward the straits of Mackinac. The wind was coming up, and the moon rose full and red, surrounded by a few bright stars. The Island lay dark against the last deep light of the night sky. Although his muse was invisible in the moonlight, the Captain's hand guided the little boat to the safety and mystery of the Island, confident that their path was sheltered and that they were not alone.

The End

❖ Acknowledgments

Writing a novel draws upon every experience the writer has ever had, everything ever read, every story ever heard. Sometimes attribution is difficult. The story of the two wolves is not mine. It is an Indian story found in many places. I am indebted to unnamed others for their records of it, and for leaving their imprints on my mind and in this book.

My gratitude to Maggie Howell of the Wolf Conservation Center in New York for answering my wolf questions, and to my persnickety and always correct copy editor and friend, Alicia Manning. Any errors—and missing Oxford commas— that remain are my own. I would be remiss if I didn't also point out that Alicia deserves credit for something even more fundamental. When she uttered the phrase "I have a small earnest question" at a meeting, I knew instantly that it would be the title of my next book.

My thanks, too, to my Island hosts Susan and George Ulm for their warmth and generosity; to my publisher, Eric Kampmann, my patient and enthusiastic editor, Megan Trank; to Michael Short and to Mark Karis for this beautiful edition; and to Lita Robinson for proof reading.

Finally, and my love and gratitude to my husband, Charlie, for his insight, his encouragement, his support, and his patience.

And now a word about Moses. Many of my readers, when they met my big, gentle, intimidating German Shepherd, assumed that the character of Rocco was based on him. Instead, the reverse is true: Moses was based on Rocco. After writing about such an amazing dog, I felt I had to have one of my own. He was the dog of a lifetime, a canine soulmate. We trusted one another, understood one another, and protected one another. We sang and splashed together. But our time together was very short. I am grieved to say that at the end, when he died suddenly of a ruptured tumor on his heart, I was not there to hold him in my arms.

Not everyone will understand the sacred bond that is possible for a human being to have with a dog, but I trust my readers will. I wrote much of this book—and most of the others—with him lying under my desk or at my feet, and in ways I did not foresee, this is a memorial to him. I will miss him forever.

J. F. RIORDAN